BLINDSIGHT

Book 1 of the Psychic Agent Series

BY SARAH RAPLEE

WINDTREE PRESS
HILLSBORO OREGON

Windtree Press
Hillsboro, Oregon
http:windtreepress.com
email: WindtreePress@windtreepress.com

Publisher's Note: This is a work of fiction. Names, characters, places, and incidents are a product of the author's imagination. Locales and public names are sometimes used for atmospheric purposes. Any resemblance to actual people, living or dead, or to businesses, companies, events, institutions, or locales is completely coincidental.

Book Layout ©2013 BookDesignTemplates.com
Cover Design by Karen Duvall, Duvall Design
http://duvalldesign.wordpress.com/book-cover-design/

BLINDSIGHT by Sarah Raplee -- 1st ed.
ISBN 978-1-9449734-6-9

Reviews

Read Romance Junkies 4-Heart Review online at
http://romancejunkies.com/reviews/blindsight/

*"If you are looking for a heartwarming, captivating
paranormal romance that will keep you turning the
pages, BLINDSIGHT is the book for you. A perfect 10!"*
~ Author Diana McCollum

Dedication

This book is dedicated to the following people who
inspired and informed this book:
Blind Professional Hikers Trevor Thomas and his
Guide Dog, Tenille
Staff, Clients and Canines at Guide Dogs for the Blind
in Boring, Oregon
My husband, Chuck, a Natural Born Dowser
Gifted Psychic Laurie McQuary
and
The Heroic Federal Bureau of Investigation Agents
who protect and defend us all

1

MENDOZA DIDN'T REALIZE he was *un muerto que anda*—a dead man walking.

The psychic FBI Special Agent undercover as Hector Guerrero, highly-skilled bodyguard, knew better.

Sitting at a white-linen-covered table reserved for off-duty employees attending drug lord Marcus Mendoza's wedding reception, Hector forced his fists to unclench.

The agent's psychic Talent had enabled him to infiltrate the Mexican drug lord's criminal organization with relative ease. Sadly, killing Mendoza would prevent the FBI from hunting down the rest of those responsible for the Cartel's seemingly-unending list of horrific crimes.

For that reason Hector was willing to wait to exact his personal revenge.

Gunshots popped outside the mansion.

Hector's hand was halfway to his empty armpit holster before he remembered all weapons had been checked at Security. A woman screamed. Mariachi music trailed off on a discordant note. Pulse pounding, he slid off his chair into a crouch, ready to flip the table onto its side for cover.

A glance through the open French doors revealed a couple of teenaged boys talking to a uniformed guard standing under a string of white paper lanterns. One of the boys pointed into the shadows on the far side of the brick patio. The guard nodded and slung his rifle over his shoulder before striding to the open doorway.

He spoke to a big blond guy Hector recognized as the bride's brother. Blondie nodded and motioned the guard away. Waving and smiling at the crowd, the big American climbed the steps onto the musician's dais. He took a mic from one of the blue-clad mariachis and tapped it a couple times.

"Todos buenos," he said in broken Spanish. "Just kids with firecrackers. Fourth of July is only two weeks away."

Murmuring voices mixed with scattered applause. Blondie waved again and left the stage.

Hector slid back onto his seat. He rolled his shoulders to relax tense muscles.

At this point in the investigation the FBI was biding

Acknowledgements

This book could never have been written without
the help and support of my husband, my family
and my sisters-in-writing,
Diana McCollum and Judith Ashley.
We made this journey together!

My writing tribes gave me the guidance, hugs and
encouragement that kept me going as well as a
big dose of tough love when needed: They include
the following people:

The folks at Windtree Press
especially Maggie Lynch

The Rose City Romance Writers Chapter of
Romance Writers of America

My fellow Genre-istas at
Romancing the Genres Blog

Sisters in Crime

The Bend Writers Lunch Bunch

My Beta Readers Louise Pelzl, Diana McCollum
and Chuck McDermed

its time. And none of the Cartel's competitors was foolish enough to attack this fortified wilderness compound on the drug lord's wedding night. Mendoza's army of men toting rifles and wearing body armor guarded the grounds. In addition, an unknown number of psychic Talents, either willing minions or unwilling slaves, bolstered the compound's defenses with their abilities.

It was concern for those psychics enslaved by the Cartel that had aligned Hector's personal goals with his boss's objectives.

Dr. Jim Grayson, Senior Special Agent in Charge of Global Exceptional Resources, didn't like Hector's personal vendetta against the Cartel. But the Bureau didn't employ another psychic agent with Hector's rare Level 10 Dowser Talent.

Rumor had it the Special Agent could find anything, or anyone, anywhere. Combined with his Mexican-American heritage and fluency in Spanish, he was the most suitable choice. The only choice, really. The Bureau aimed to locate and destroy the Cartel's secret facilities in North America—and to rescue the Cartel's psychic slaves.

Having no better option, Doc had bent the rules to include Hector on the risky mission. The agent's assignment had begun in the Sonoran Desert south of the Mexican border, but had eventually led him to this fortified compound one volcano east of Mount Saint Helens in Washington's Cascade Mountains.

Which was why, despite his personal feelings, Hector found himself attending Mendoza's June wedding to the daughter of an American arms dealer.

His gaze slid past the bridal couple moving toward the cake table to focus on a tall, powerfully-built man who held himself apart. Hector's jaw tightened. Gregory Killingsworth, Mendoza's security chief, continuously scanned the crowd with ice-blue eyes that missed nothing. No doubt he scanned for uninvited Talents with his Hound ability that sensed and tracked unshielded psychic energy.

Luckily, Hector's shields were flawless. Anything less would be a death sentence.

Killingsworth locked gazes with him for a moment. Hector dipped his chin to acknowledge his Cartel boss and then pretended to study someone on the far side of the dance floor. He kept his expression neutral while hatred as focused and lethal as a laser surged through his veins.

Killingsworth was another monster the agent had slated for a reckoning.

Applause erupted around Hector and cameras flashed. The newlyweds had cut the cake. The agent forced himself to join in as though he really *was* one of Mendoza's off-duty bodyguards.

A hard-edged young waitress in a tight black skirt and white shirt appeared in a swirl of perfume strong enough to make his eyes water. She shoved a tray of fluted glasses under his nose. "Champagne, Hector?"

Flashing a smile that felt more stiff than charming, he snagged a glass from her tray and winked. She raised an eyebrow, snapped her gum and sidled away with a half-smile on her lips.

Hector swirled the pale pink liquid in his long-stemmed glass and watched bubbles race around the rim in an endless circle. The tang of alcohol teased his nostrils.

Glancing around to make sure no one was watching, he poured his champagne into his neighbor's empty glass. He couldn't take a chance on dulling his thought processes.

Being Hector was like wearing an ill-fitting-but-familiar old suit that pinched in a couple of places, but not so badly he couldn't ignore the discomfort most of the time. He had to be at the top of his game, one-hundred per cent in character to survive long enough to bring down the Mendoza Cartel.

The murmur of the crowd muted. Casting a glance over his shoulder, Hector spotted Killingsworth staring through the open French doors beside the musician's dais like a lion spotting a threat—or prey. The back of the agent's neck prickled.

Turning in his seat for a better look, he made out a shadowy female figure wearing a long gown. Why was Killingsworth so interested in her?

A swirl of iridescent fabric the color of sagebrush in springtime accompanied a dainty, green-slippered foot into the soft circle of light spilling from the ballroom.

Conversation near the doorway hushed. Every male in the room homed in on the woman who left the shadows, a woman like no other the agent had encountered in the underworld of the Cartel.

Coppery curls spilled over the curve of one shoulder in a long, loose ponytail. In the warm glow of the chandeliers, rhinestones shimmered in her burnished hair and winked from the frames of her mysterious dark glasses. Her demure, floor-length gown failed to conceal her curves or the sweet, girl-next-door sexiness she exuded.

For the first time in nearly four years, desire unfolded in the agent's belly.

In the world of the Cartel, women survived and sometimes thrived using a combination of cold cunning and artifice. They grew cynical and hard, or worn-down and resigned. Yet everything about this young woman sang the siren song of wholesome, soul-deep beauty. Even the crowded ballroom's air smelled fresher with her in the room.

She hesitated, brushing back an errant curl with a small hand covered in sage-green lace. Beneath the twinkle of her dark glasses her wide mouth curved into a smile full of promise.

One of the blue-suited mariachis descended the dais steps and spoke softly to her. She nodded. Tucking one of her hands into the crook of his arm he led her to the little stage. He murmured something into her ear and she smiled. They ascended the three steps and crossed to the middle of the small, raised stage. The mariachi guided her gloved hand to a microphone stand.

Hector's heart bucked like a wild burro. *¡Mierda!* The woman was blind.

He tightened his grip on the empty glass in his hand. Mendoza's Hound preyed on the vulnerable as well as the Talented. He liked his women the way he liked his torture victims: tied up and helpless to fight back.

A month ago, Hector had been tasked with driving a battered young woman home to Seattle after her night with Killingsworth. The memory of the girl's bruised body and empty eyes haunted him. The agent was tired of pretending to be a hired gun and sick of watching bloodsuckers drain the life out of their victims.

Musicians struck the opening chords of a popular ballad. The wedding singer's pink lips parted. Iridescent green fabric stretched across the ripe mounds of her breasts. Her breathy soprano was sweet and true as his mother's agave syrup. She sang of the wordless communication between lovers and the importance of faith in a future together. Her ivory skin glowed with emotion. She almost made him believe in happy endings.

As the last chords of the song faded Hector joined the other guests in heaving a collective, melancholy sigh.

Deafening applause broke out.

The wedding singer took a step back and made a graceful curtsy worthy of a debutante. Hector forced himself to look away. She was old enough to know better than to believe in fairytales.

So was he. What was the matter with him?

Scanning the room, he noted Killingsworth had moved to Mendoza's table. The drug lord leaned toward Killingsworth and gestured toward the wedding singer. He said something Hector couldn't make out and raised his brows. Killingsworth's gaze found the woman. Baring his teeth in a wolfish smile, he nodded.

Hector's hands fisted. Something was going on below the surface he couldn't quite put his finger on— something to do with the woman. She was important to both Mendoza and Killingsworth.

The only interests the two men shared were Mendoza's security and the Mendoza Cartel's psychic slaves. A blind woman wasn't much of a threat. He leaned back in his chair and shoved his hands into his pockets. Being sightless didn't preclude her being a Talent, in which case she was an unknown.

When she reached for the mic again Hector focused on assessing the effect she had on the rest of her audience as opposed to the effect she had on him. She re-worked her magic on the crowd with a song about everlasting love. Everyone seemed mesmerized by her voice. The eyes of the jaded criminals around him widened like those of children hearing reindeer hoof steps on the roof on Christmas Eve.

His pulse quickened. The wedding singer was Talented.

He'd have to use his dowser Talent to search for psychics in the mansion to confirm his guess. He'd bet a month's salary the woman was here tonight because Mendoza's Hound had targeted her for kidnapping.

He could follow when they transported her to the prison camp the Bureau had been unable to locate for so long. They'd finally have a chance to rescue the psychics enslaved there and to cut off one of the Cartel's sources of power. He might learn exactly what had happened to Lori and the baby—exactly *who* had murdered them.

It wasn't his responsibility to keep Killingsworth from brutalizing the woman.

¿De veras? his mother whispered sternly in his head, giving voice to his conscience. *Truly? I taught you better than that, mi hijo.* His gut knotted. Mom had a habit of popping into his thoughts whenever he faced an inconvenient truth. Her telepathic Talent only worked with her children.

Lucky us.

He watched Killingsworth scan the crowd. The man's gaze settled momentarily on the beautiful redhead and his icy eyes darkened. Resisting a strong urge to punch someone, Hector rose and headed toward the patio.

Outside, the pungent odor of marijuana rode the

chill breeze wafting across the patio. Two teenaged boys slouched on a wooden bench under a string of colored paper lanterns, sharing a joint. They watched a couple make out behind a potted palm.

Hector slipped down the gravel path around the corner of the mansion and into the shadows.

Once he was certain he was unobserved, he removed his bowtie and shoved it into his jacket pocket. Then he unbuttoned his top shirt buttons and pulled out his St. Jude's Medal. While his Talent didn't require the use of a focus object, using the tool made things easier. The metal disk warmed his fingertips.

He inhaled and exhaled deeply several times, concentrating on the feel of air flowing in through his nose and out through his lips. Easily slipping into a meditative state, he focused his Talent on his talisman and silently posed his question. *Who inside the mansion at my back is Talented?*

Impressions flashed through Hector's mind. The first was a blurred image he recognized as his partner, Drew Grayson. No surprise, as last week Drew had told him he would be undercover onsite during the wedding.

Killingsworth was next. Then the wedding singer— he'd been right about her being a Talent. The image of an older black male who reminded him of Preacher from the cult television classic *Firefly* appeared, followed by an attractive woman who bore a familial resemblance to the older man. Hector didn't recognize them. Were they psychic prisoners forced to help guard the compound?

He took a cleansing breath. Just before he opened his eyes, a glimpse of Marcus Mendoza's despised features registered on the backs of his eyelids.

¡Mierda! His eyes snapped open.

The Bureau had no idea the drug lord was Talented. Despite the cool June evening, he began to sweat. He automatically tucked his talisman into his shirt and re-did the buttons while he pondered the implications of Mendoza having a psychic ability. The fact the man had been able to keep his Talent hidden for years meant it was key to the drug lord's power, or to his downfall. Maybe both

Hector needed to inform Doc Grayson ASAP. Doc would assign FBI scientists to analyze all their data on Mendoza. They'd ferret out what his Talent might be. The squints loved a new challenge.

Hector fished his bowtie out of his jacket pocket and fastened it in place. He needed to focus on his mission. Discovering the Talented wedding singer was the break he'd been waiting for. Tracking her when Killingsworth took her to the hidden prison camp might finally give the Bureau a location for SWAT to attempt to rescue the prisoners.

All he had to do was let another innocent woman be kidnapped by a fucking monster.

So the end justifies the means, mi hijo? Creo que no. Do the right thing.

Bile rose in his throat. When it came to ethics, Mom was always right. She'd kept him from the Dark Side more than once.

He returned to the ballroom where the wedding singer continued to mesmerize her audience with a beautiful rendition of *Amor Eterno*. She enchanted *him*, and he was in on her secret. What was the full extent of her abilities?

At the end of her soulful performance the mariachi led her to an empty seat at one of the long tables lining the ballroom walls. Hector wondered how much Spanish she spoke or understood. She didn't look Hispanic.

His thoughts were interrupted by Killingsworth moving toward the unsuspecting woman like a snake stalking a helpless blind songbird.

Hector surged to his feet and snagged two glasses of champagne from a passing waiter's tray. Not allowing himself to think about the possible consequences of his actions, he forced his body to relax, assumed a bored expression and strode around the edge of the dance floor. He pretended to be oblivious to Killingsworth behind him. The hound wouldn't risk disrupting Mendoza's celebration by making a scene.

The pretty wedding singer must have heard him approach because she turned her face toward him. Her rhinestones flashed. What color were her eyes behind those bejeweled glasses?

"Hello," the agent said. Where was smooth-talking Hector when he needed him?

She lifted one graceful auburn brow. "Have we met?"

"I'm Hector Guerrero, your biggest fan." Like she hadn't heard that line before. Something about her put Hector off his game. Was it the glasses? Or her disturbingly-familiar scent, a blend of vanilla and something he couldn't quite put his finger on?

He cleared his throat. "I come bearing champagne. You sing like an angel, Miss—?" Shit, could he sound any cheesier? He set a glass on the table in front of her.

She turned her head toward the barely audible sound. Her nostrils dilated. Her full lips curved into a shy smile. "Smith. Melisenda Smith."

A Hispanic given name and an Anglo surname. Interesting.

"Melisenda suits you." He pulled out the cushioned folding chair next to hers and sat down. "A beautiful name for a beautiful woman."

She slid a lace-gloved hand across the tablecloth, found her glass and took a tiny sip of champagne.

A cautious woman. When he got her somewhere private, her restraint would make it easier to convince her Killingsworth was a sexual predator. He didn't want to frighten her by revealing he knew about her secret Talent.

Telling her he was an FBI agent while he was

undercover would be foolhardy. If Mendoza found out, he'd be a dead man. After she agreed to leave, he'd contact Doc Grayson and explain the situation. Doc might be pissed at him, but he'd protect Melisenda.

The musicians launched into a slow number. Melisenda swayed like a delicate flower in a gentle breeze. The thought of her frightened, confused, locked in a safe house among strangers for who-knew-how-long did not set well with Hector.

His shoulders twitched. It was better than letting Killingsworth have her.

He dredged up what he hoped was his charm. "Dance with me, Melisenda Smith."

Smiling, she shook her head. "I've been on my feet for an hour."

So much for charm.

He heaved a sigh. "Good point. A toast then, to beauty and music, the language of the soul." He raised his glass to hers and watched her take another cautious sip.

She set her drink down and tipped her head to one side as if she could see straight through him from behind her dark lenses. "Are you a friend of the bride or the groom?"

Hector blinked. "Uh, I'm here for the groom. I'm one of his bodyguards, currently off-duty."

He scanned the room for Killingsworth and spotted him moving toward the bar. Biding his time. Sweat beaded Hector's upper lip. How long before

Killingsworth ran out of patience?

"So you're here out of loyalty, Hector?" Melisenda said.

The question caught him off guard. A bitter laugh escaped him. "I'm here because I want to keep my job." He shifted in his chair, angling his body toward her. "What about you?"

Color blossomed in her cheeks. She picked up her champagne and held the fluted glass between them. "I need to keep food on the table."

He narrowed his eyes. Her body language told him there was more to it, but he didn't want to spook her. He changed the subject to a humorous description of a mismatched couple on the dance floor.

When the lively music ended, the trumpet player teased the first liquid notes of the old Beatles' ballad, *Yesterday*, from his instrument. The rest of the musicians joined in the second refrain. More richly-dressed couples rose from their tables and headed for the dance floor.

Melisenda's smile turned wistful. Was her resolve wavering? "I bet you dance like you sing—beautifully," he said.

She moistened her lower lip with the tip of her tongue. "Dancing's against the rules."

He leaned closer and lowered his voice. "Whose rules?"

Worrying her lower lip, she tucked a stray curl behind her ear. Her rhinestones flickered. "My rules, from the Wedding Singer Rule Book."

Hector smiled at her little white lie. "There's no such thing."

"There *is* a rule book. I wrote it myself. Two-ninety-nine at all major ebook stores." She was even pretty when she frowned.

He shook the thought out of his head. He had to get her onto the dance floor so they could slip outside where he'd deliver his warning. He couldn't let Killingsworth kidnap another woman on his watch. Doc would have to understand.

As he slid his chair back, the rubber-tipped legs stuttered across the polished floor. Melisenda flinched.

¡Mierda! The last thing he needed was to frighten her. "Please, I haven't danced with anyone in a long time."

She raised her chin and her rhinestones sparked. "Forgive me if I don't believe you."

A muscle twitched in his jaw. They were running out of time. Intending to overwhelm her resistance with action, he grabbed her lace-gloved hand. An electric buzz bolted through his hand and up his arm. He hesitated.

Her fingers tightened. The overwhelming sense that she yearned to trust him dragged out a piece of the truth he'd never intended to share. "I haven't danced since my fiancée died. Maybe I can, with you."

Heat rose in the agent's face. What the hell had come over him? Why would he reveal something related to his real past, not Hector's imaginary one?

Melisenda's face paled. She wrenched her hand away.

"You couldn't have known," he said in what he hoped was a soothing tone. He glanced around. No one seemed to have overheard him.

What had just happened?

He'd once met a Touch Telepath that could transmit thoughts and sensory details through skin-to-skin contact. This was different, as if he'd been overwhelmed by her emotional energy.

"I know what it's like to lose someone you love," she said softly. "I'm so sorry for your loss."

His throat tightened. It had been years since he'd last heard those words. He reminded himself he knew next to nothing about her. He'd be a fool to let her get under his skin. His goal was to get her out of Mendoza's compound to safety without blowing his cover. Doc employed expert squints to sort out the complexities of Talent.

Taking care not to let his fingertips brush her skin, he lifted a long curl off her shoulder and pretended he'd felt nothing. "Your hair is like burnished copper. So beautiful."

The silky strands slid between his fingers. The way she trembled tugged at a place in his core he'd thought long dead. *¡No manches¡* This was not the time for his libido to resurrect itself. He had to focus on getting her out of here. Afterward, she'd be Doc's problem.

Itching for action, he caught her hand again and pulled her to her feet. The buzz of her energy climbed his arm and his blood hummed in response. Her lips parted but she did not resist. He led her onto the dance floor.

Placing his hand at the small of her back, he felt her breath catch. With a soft sigh she relaxed against his chest and followed his lead as if they'd danced together a thousand times. As if they belonged together. He yearned to forget the ugly world that threatened them both and relax into the moment with Melisenda.

The hair on his nape lifted. Her Talent messed with his emotions. He bolstered his personal psychic shield to block her energy. Losing his focus could get them both killed.

A couple danced through the French doors onto the patio. He would lead Melisenda outside so he could get her alone and convince her she was in danger.

She leaned back and smiled up at him. "Are you always so persistent?"

"Yes," he said, calculating the distance to the doors.

"And do you always get what you want?" Her rhinestones sparkled. His gaze settled on her lush lips. *If only.*

He forced conviction into his voice. "Of course."

Out of the corner of his eye, he caught movement from where Killingsworth leaned against the bar and watched them. Hector tensed.

"What about you, Melisenda? Do you always get what you want?" he said. He watched Killingsworth's second-in-command approach his boss. He said something to Killingsworth, who scowled and replied.

Tensing, Hector dropped his gaze to Melisenda's face. Her cheeks were flushed below her dark glasses.

"No," she said. Tiny beams of light speared from her rhinestones as she shook her head back and forth. She smiled and licked he lips. "But I intend to get what I want tonight."

Only half listening, Hector glanced toward the bar. Killingsworth followed his man toward the bride and groom's table. Mendoza must have issued a summons.

This was his chance to slip outside unnoticed with the girl. Continuing to banter on autopilot with her, he danced her over to the French doors and outside.

2

NIGHT AIR PERFUMED WITH jasmine cooled Hector's face. After a moment the music ended. Relaxing his hold on Melisenda, he hooked her arm through his and scanned the area. The teens were gone, but several couples milled about on the patio.

Where could they go for privacy?

Melisenda squeezed his arm and leaned into him. The soft swell of her breast pressing against his biceps stirred his pulse. She tilted her head and the rhinestones in her glasses caught the lantern light.

"I adore the rose garden in back of the mansion." Her tone turned wistful. "Did you know each type of rose has a unique scent?"

The unlit rose garden was an ideal location for a private conversation. "I'll take you there," Hector said.

"You can educate me."

He led Melisenda onto the white gravel path he'd taken earlier. They crunched around the corner of the mansion and the pale ribbon ahead faded into shadow. His footsteps slowed.

"What's wrong?" Melisenda said.

"It's dark as hell." *Sonovabitch!* Had he offended her?

She laughed and tugged on his arm. "Can't you smell the roses? Just follow your nose."

Her scent filled the air. Vanilla and—something that reminded him of home. He shook his head in frustration and let her lead him through the darkness, her familiar territory.

He had to find her a ride home. "How did you get to this gig?"

"I rode with the mariachis from Portland. Mr. Mendoza hired a limo. I'll leave with them in the morning."

Judging by the way the mariachis treated Melisenda, they'd agree to leave tonight if she faked an illness. The tricky part would be hiding their departure from Killingsworth until after the fact.

The honeyed scent of roses reached him. He recognized the outline of the stone gazebo silhouetted against the starry sky. Mendoza's staff used the small open-air building for a preferred hook-up spot.

Melisenda let go of him and climbed the stone steps as if she'd done it many times before.

"We can have some privacy in here," she said, and disappeared inside.

In spite of the desire heating his blood, Hector tasted bitter disappointment. If she meant what he thought she meant, she wasn't as innocent as she appeared. He followed her inside, his pulse spiking into the danger zone. Could Killingsworth have recruited her? Had he misread the situation totally, been disarmed by her blindness?

He followed her into a deep, smoky shadow between two square openings that let in the glow of the stars. Her wholesome perfume mixed with the seductive scent of roses. Disappointment morphed into anger. And lust. Definitely lust, damn her.

He grabbed her upper arms and yanked her against his body, then crowded her back into the rough stone wall, hating that he wanted her, wanting her anyway.

Her hands flattened against his ribcage and she squeaked like a mouse cornered by a cat.

"Isn't this why you brought me here?" he rasped.

She shook her head violently. "Not like this. Please, not like this."

Was that a sob? He touched her damp cheek. *"¡Perdón!"* Stepping back, he raised his hands palm-out. What the hell was going on with her?

"No!" She grabbed the lapels of his jacket. "I mean, I want…like this."

Rising on tiptoes, she pressed her lips to his as tentatively as a sixteen-year-old virgin. Soft and sweet like he'd first imagined, they heated to a slow simmer.

He gave up trying to figure her out and acted on pure instinct, gentling his lips, waiting, relinquishing control. His hands dropped to rest on her hips.

She opened to him and his tongue delved into her mouth, tasting sweet champagne and hot cinnamon.

With a little moan she slid her hands up to his shoulders. A blast of aching loneliness and searing desire erupted from her. Uncontrolled emotional energy crashed through his psychic shields like an exploding volcano, vaporizing his personal psychic defenses. He was ten years old again, flat on his back after falling from the top of the jungle gym, hurting in every cell of his body but unable to speak or move or even breathe.

Except he remained vertical, anchored to Melisenda by arms that had turned to stone.

The fact that her first kiss in two years ended in disaster didn't surprise Melisenda Sepulveda. Sadly, every man she'd ever kissed had passed out.

What threatened to shock Meli's curly hair straight was the way cocky-sexy Hector had transformed into dangerous-sex-demon Hector, who had about-faced into steal-your-heart-tender Hector like a crazy romance novel hero from hell—and when her "freak side" took over he'd remained stolid and upright while she couldn't dredge up the strength to break away from his heat.

Guilt weighed heavily on her shoulders. When she'd realized by his obvious distraction that their dance was only another pity dance arranged by one of the bride's relatives, she should have brushed him off. Instead she got mad.

She told herself he was the perfect person on whom to test her freak side. After all, he was a minion from the Dark Side. If she lost control and blasted him with a kiss, she wouldn't feel one bit guilty.

Steely hands flexed on her hips with bruising force. He remained rooted in the stone floor of the gazebo like the evergreens were rooted in the volcanic soil of the mountains.

She worried her lower lip. Was he conscious? Or was he out on his feet, like a horse? Her freak side should have felled him like a Taser. What was wrong with him?

Wrong? Or right?

Meli banished the dangerous thought. "Hector? Are you okay?"

Before the accident stole her sight, she could have searched his eyes for a glimmer of awareness. Although at midnight, in the back garden of this mountain hideaway, his eyes would probably be lost in shadow.

Like his soul?

Hector drew a ragged breath. His champagne-and-cake-coated exhalation caressed her upturned face, derailing her thoughts. Tendrils of what he'd called her burnished copper hair tickled her cheeks. The man had the silver tongue of a poet—or a con man—and the well-honed body of a well-trained bodyguard.

A shiver shook her. A drug lord's bodyguard.

Over the mariachi music dancing in the distance, she heard him make an effort to speak. "Uh-yoo-duh-muh..."

Her pulse did a drumroll. She had to get away from him. But how? Releasing her grip on his wide shoulders, Meli repositioned her hands on his linebacker chest just inches from her nose. Summoning all her strength, she gave him an experimental shove.

She might as well have tried to move a boulder. "Let me go," she said firmly in case he could hear her. When nothing happened, she said it louder in Spanish. "¡Déjame ir!"

His hands flexed, pulling her hips more firmly against his sculpted body. Her breath hitched. She could feel his erection through their clothes.

Maybe I should kiss him again.

She shook her head at the wayward thought. Breaking the rules had gotten her into this mess. *Only one glass of champagne. No dancing. Do not kiss a wedding guest, no matter how tempting or aggravating he may be.* She'd broken them all.

A muscle spasm rippled beneath her palms. Hector groaned. His breath heaved in and out and his fingers pinched her hips again. She pressed her lips together to keep from crying out. The last thing she wanted was to draw an audience.

With a final shudder, the spasm passed. Hector's hands fell from her body.

A sigh escaped her lips. She stepped back.

"Shun-uh-uh-mick!" he said with force.

She jumped and the sole of her slipper slid on the cobbled flooring. She half-fell against a rough wall. The *zzit* of tearing fabric made her cringe. Bruises and scrapes would heal. No way could she afford a replacement gown.

Not important right now. Focus, Meli!

"No te preocupes," she said loudly, in case he was coming around. "Don't worry. You had a seizure. I'll get help."

She started back toward the exit, fingertips skimming the wall for guidance. Her lace gloves snagged on sandpapery stones. She added *new gloves* to her mental list of things she needed that she couldn't afford.

Behind her, breathing like a marathoner crossing the finish line, Hector ground out one slurred, but eloquent, word.

"Shonovabitch."

Meli froze. He was definitely awake. He sounded punch drunk. If she hurried—

"¡Ayúdame!" Pain roughened his breath. "Help me!"

She pressed her lips together. She should leave,

but...the man was in pain, pain she'd unintentionally inflicted.

Well, sort of unintentionally. She'd known she might lose control of her emotional energy and knock him out, but she'd never expected him to remain conscious and suffering. The opportunity to test herself had been too good to pass up.

Meli's throat tightened. She'd believed her kisses were an all-or-nothing proposition. Either she'd control her freak side, or she'd knock the guy out. But Hector had withstood the effects of her psychic sucker punch well enough to remain conscious and hurting.

Trying to help him would only put her at risk. She didn't owe the bodyguard anything. She lifted her chin and moved on toward the exit.

Her footsteps tapped out an uneven rhythm as she felt her way along the wall. She gritted her teeth in frustration.

Normally she depended on Freddy, her big golden retriever/yellow lab cross, for guidance. They were a good team. She trusted him with her safety on a daily basis. Plus Freddy was her only family.

But Mendoza's bride had insisted she do without her Guide. Then she'd left her cane in her bag at the reception.

Hector's voice took on a soft, desperate note. "Please."

Her face burned. She couldn't abandon him without an explanation. Heaving a sigh, she turned.

"I don't know how to help you. If I did, I would. I'm sure you'll feel better soon." She hoped so. In the past, she'd never done anyone permanent damage.

"Who do you work for?" he said, sounding much less befuddled.

She frowned. "I'm self-employed." Surely he wasn't addled enough to believe he could sue her employer or get her fired?

"Who sent you?" The faint rustle of fabric betrayed movement.

Meli's heart climbed into her throat. It was time to get out of this godforsaken gazebo. She spun around and hurried the last few steps to the exit.

The shuffle of footsteps behind her shot her pulse into overdrive. She stifled the self-defeating urge to run and carefully descended the three steps.

If she could make her way around the mansion to the wedding reception, she doubted the bodyguard would pursue her through the crowd. The drug lord would notice, and Hector would have to admit the blind wedding singer had kicked his butt—with a kiss, no less. That was something no sane minion would tell Marcus Mendoza.

At least, she hoped not.

The crunch of gravel told her she was on the path. A loud thud sounded in the gazebo behind her.

"*¡Chinga a tu madre!*" Hector swore in vulgar Spanish.

She flinched.

He'd tasted like a good time, all cake and champagne and fireworks. At least, until she'd lost control and blasted him. She quickened her pace.

When would she ever learn? Breaking the rules led to nothing but trouble.

Thank God she'd taken care to count steps because she was in unfamiliar surroundings. Fifteen would take her to the curve where the path turned at the back corner of the mansion.

The music grew louder when she rounded the turn, but not loud enough to disguise heavy footsteps pounding toward her down the gravel walk. Pulse racing, Meli stepped aside to let the runners pass. She pressed her back against the cool stucco wall of the mansion and prayed they wouldn't find Hector before she'd made her escape.

Two sets of footsteps thudded past, but the third halted near where she stood in what she hoped was the shadows. She swallowed, hating how vulnerable she felt without Freddy.

Someone heavy chunked up the gazebo steps. "We got him," a man called out in a voice she didn't recognize.

Her heart skipped a beat.

The deepest male voice she'd ever heard rumbled a few feet away from her. "I didn't think you were stupid enough to betray the Cartel, Hector." Fury sizzled in the man's tone like water droplets in a hot frying pan.

The hair stood up on the backs of Meli's arms.

She'd needed Gregory Killingsworth's approval to perform at the wedding. Mendoza's security chief's masculine *basso profundo* had fascinated her during the required pre-hire interview. Now the menace in his tone turned her insides to water.

What had she gotten herself into?

With the thugs inside the gazebo and Killingsworth's attention focused on Hector, this was her chance to get away. Inching along the wall toward the music, she tried to ignore the persistent prick of her conscience. Whatever Killingsworth wanted with Hector couldn't be good, and her kiss had left the bodyguard exposed. But she could do nothing to help him. She had to leave while Killingsworth was preoccupied.

Killingsworth's footsteps crunched toward Meli. "You've been consorting with a traitor, Miss Smith."

Terror threatened to immobilize her. She powered through the fear and shook her head. "I just met the man, Mr. Killingsworth. I'd hardly call one dance and a garden walk to cool off *consorting*. Whatever business you have with Hector has nothing to do with me."

She forced herself to step onto the path and stroll away from him, when she wanted to run like a rabbit.

Gravel crunched and a large hand caught her elbow in an iron grip. "On the contrary, my dear. Our business has everything to do with you."

"Let me go!" She tried to jerk away, but he hauled her back against his body and pinned her arms. Where Hector's scent was earthy and woodsy, Killingsworth's held the sting of menthol. How could she ever have found this *pendejo* attractive?

Hector's hoarse yell carried an unspoken threat. "She's nobody, Killingsworth. Let her go."

Her heart stumbled. He was trying to help her get away.

Amusement colored Killingsworth's reply. "I don't think so, Hector. She's one of us, a Talent. And you know I have a weakness for redheads. She might prove…enjoyable. In addition to useful."

He tugged one of her long curls. Gooseflesh puckered her skin. She forced herself not to shrink away from his touch. Her intuition told her fear was this man's drug of choice.

To distract herself, she dredged up some righteous indignation. *You have no idea who you're dealing with, you pervert. I've taken self-defense classes.*

The loud *thunk* of a fist on flesh sounded in the vicinity of the gazebo. Her heart hitched. A heavy thud followed.

Killingsworth swore and tightened his hold on her.

"Run!" Hector's raw cry bolstered her courage.

She stomped on Killingsworth's instep, shifted her hips and twisted to knee him in the groin. Air whooshed out of his lungs and his grip slackened. She found his belt with her hands and kneed him again. He gagged and folded to the ground with a satisfying clunk.

"Hector?" she called, needing to orient on his voice.

"Run, dammit!" His shout ended on a cough. The sickening sound of fists pummeling flesh caught at her heart. He'd invited a beating so she could escape. Alone.

Should have thought that one through, Hector Protector—blind woman, fortified compound, who-knows-how-much surrounding wilderness. Not a good plan, but a noble gesture.

Inspiration hit her like the boom of a bass drum. She could turn the tables, give Hector a chance to beat down their assailants one at a time. They'd escape together.

Killingsworth groaned and scuffled in the gravel behind her.

Meli turned back and threw herself on top of him before he could rise. Air whooshed out of his lungs a second time and the fight left him momentarily. Screaming to get his men's attention, she drew back her arm and slapped him. The crack of flesh-against-flesh hurt worse than the sting that spread through her palm and fingers.

Had he even felt the blow?

Hearing one of his minions shout, she fisted her hands and punched at his head as hard as she could. With a dull thud, her left-sided blow found his cheek. The force of contact jarred her, but she ignored the agony in her knuckles and straight-armed him with the heel of her right hand in what she hoped was the middle of his face. Flesh flattened and bones crunched. Vaguely aware of footsteps pounding down the gravel path from the gazebo, she cradled her injured left fingers against her chest and tried to breathe through the pain.

Rough hands pulled her off Killingsworth. She kicked and stomped and yelled like a wild woman, hoping to keep Killingsworth and one minion occupied while Hector dispatched the other.

"*¡Hemos capturado a Héctor!*" someone shouted from the gazebo.

Her abductor jerked her wrists together behind her back and pinned them with one hand. He fisted her the hair with the other. Meli's heart plummeted. She sagged against the man holding her. Her plan had failed. Killingsworth had Hector. He had them both.

Gravel scattered as Killingsworth clambered to his feet. He huffed like an angry bull preparing to charge.

Her mouth went dry. She forced herself to count her breaths, to think of anything except the coming blow from a fist the size of a soccer ball.

For the first time in her adult life, Meli saw stars.

3

A WARM, WET TONGUE LICKED Meli's cheek in a rhythm as persistent and annoying as a dripping tap. She moaned in protest and covered her face with her arm. Her knuckles throbbed. "Go 'way."

Blowing in on a blast of dog-food breath, Freddy's deep, firm *woof* woke her up. She straightened her glasses. Her jaw ached and her head throbbed. Her bottom lip had swollen to the size of Freddy's food dish and she was pretty sure the coppery taste in her mouth was blood. What had happened to her?

Memory kicked in and her heart dropped into the pit of her stomach. What if Killingsworth's minions had hurt Freddy? He was all she had left.

Meli pushed herself up on one arm and then had to wait for her brain to stop sloshing around inside her skull. After a couple of seconds, she steadied. Her searching hand found Freddy's long, silky fur, part of his golden retriever heritage from his sire. "Are you okay, boy?"

His big, warm tongue licked the back of her hand in reassurance. The knot of worry in her chest relaxed minutely. Freddy was her only family, the only one who cared whether she lived or died. If she lost him, Meli didn't think she could go on.

What would be the point?

With shaky fingers, she inspected every inch of the big lab mix. He exhibited his usual patience. Finding no injuries, she hugged his baby-powder-scented neck and blinked back tears. If anything happened to Freddy, she would never forgive herself.

Her Guide whined and Meli let go of his collar. The bedsprings creaked from their weight shifting. She flopped onto her back and explored the covers by touch. The puffy spread was crisscrossed by evenly-spaced lines of stitching like the ones on the quilted comforter in their assigned room.

She stilled. Flaring her nostrils, she caught a spicy whiff of Singing Tiger tea. She'd left a half-empty cup on her nightstand this morning. Hope blossomed in her chest.

Exploring the surface of the queen-sized bed by touch, she encountered her canvas backpack. *Yes!*

She discovered someone had unzipped the compartments of her pack and left her belongings in a jumble inside. Her stomach growled the way it always did after she'd lost control of her freak side. She dug out a water bottle and pain reliever capsules. After washing down the pills, she wolfed down an energy bar. Then she took inventory.

The bad guys had removed her cell phone. No surprise there. Also her nail file and scissors. Dang, these guys were more cautious than Homeland Security Agents.

Setting the bag aside, she scooted to the edge of the bed and rose to her feet. Every beat of her heart pulsed in her aching head. When her blood pressure equalized and the pain receded she made halting progress toward the door. Her hands flattened against polished wood. Bingo. She located the cold, smooth handle and pushed the lever downward, but the door wouldn't budge.

Meli swallowed her disappointment. Of course the door was locked from the outside. She'd assaulted a drug lord's lieutenant. Sniffling, she returned to lie down on the bed beside her Guide.

Freddy's tags tinkled as he raised his head.

"I'm sorry, big guy." She rolled over to face him and scratched behind his ears. How could she have been so reckless? A warm tear slid down the side of her nose and plopped onto the quilt. She should never have kissed the sexy bodyguard, never have danced with him, never have agreed to sing at Marcus Mendoza's wedding in the first place, no matter how much they needed the money.

Exuding concern, Freddy snuggled closer.

Meli rubbed her cheek on his soft fur and inhaled his dog-and-baby-powder scent. "This is all my fault. I plowed through the rules."

Freddy huffed his agreement and licked her tears anyway. Her heart ached. She could have lost him. What would she do without him?

She sat up and stroked his big, square lab head. "What was I thinking? I suspected Marcus Mendoza was a criminal. Why else would he spend ten-thousand dollars for a wedding gig in the middle of nowhere?"

The mariachis had filled her in on the drug lord's reputation during the long drive from Portland. She'd walked on eggshells ever since—until she'd met Hector.

Her Guide's tail thumped in agreement. Rule number one was *don't accept gigs from criminals.*

She'd put their lives in danger by accepting an offer she knew was too good to be true. She'd had it all figured out. Singing at Mendoza's wedding reception would give them the rest of the money they needed. She'd get trained for a stay-at-home job as a voice coach. Freddy could retire, she'd partner with a new Guide and she'd be able to keep Freddy with her in his golden years.

Meli snorted. And they'd live happily ever after. *Right.*

Freddy gave her hand a gentle nudge with his nose,

seeming to urge her on. She drew a shaky breath. "I broke rule number two, *no dancing*. I thought *one little dance can't hurt*. That was the champagne talking."

She heaved a sigh and stroked Freddy's back. "We came up with the rules to keep ourselves out of trouble, didn't we, Freddy? Nothing good ever comes of breaking them."

Her Guide's tail swished against the bedclothes. She caught another comforting whiff of baby powder.

When Hector had pulled her into his arms for the slow dance, her skin had simmered with what she'd thought was the heat of their mutual attraction. How could she have been so naive?

As if he could read Meli's thoughts, Freddy sighed.

Her throat tightened. She gave the comforter a half-hearted punch with her fist. She wasn't sure what she'd expected from Hector's kiss. But when she protested after he pushed her against the wall, he immediately relinquished control. His surprisingly tender embrace had snared her with sweetness. But their deepening kiss evoked the feelings she kept bottled up inside. Dangerous feelings. The resulting blast of sexual heat and loneliness was way beyond her ability to control.

Meli swallowed. She'd been wrong about losing control with Hector. She felt guilty as hell.

"Why would Hector try to protect me from Killingsworth? And why did *el pendejo* tell me his business with Hector had everything to do with me?

None of it makes sense."

A deep doggy snore rumbled the silence. The corners of her sore mouth tipped up. In his old age, her Guide was prone to doze off without warning.

She stripped off her torn gloves and pondered Hector's possible reasons for trying to help her in the garden even though she'd blasted him. Bringing the gloves to her nose, she inhaled a mixture of dog and baby powder and Hector's heady cedar scent.

Her spirits lifted. Maybe the bodyguard would help her again. She'd bet Freddy's last liver treat Hector knew what Killingsworth wanted with her, and why the scumbag had referred to the three of them as Talents.

She and Freddy didn't have much choice. The odds were huge they couldn't get through the wilderness without help—or even out of Mendoza's compound. They had to rescue Hector.

But how?

Hector awoke slumped in a hard chair with his chin on his chest. When he tried to move, his wrists and ankles felt like they'd been gnawed by sharp-toothed rodents. He squinted at serrated plastic bands binding his bloody wrists to metal armrests.

His gut tightened. *¡Mierda! I lost the fight.*

His jaw ached and his head pounded like sin. The last thing he remembered clearly was Killingsworth's goons beating him down after he'd tried to distract them so the wedding singer could escape. They must have worked him over pretty good.

The woman had screamed and then—had he dreamed the needle jab in his arm? Or had he been drugged? He frowned. How long had he been unconscious?

Hector scanned what he could see of the small, windowless room. The harsh scent of bleach permeated the air. A concrete block wall as gray as purgatory was broken only by a closed steel door. Harsh light from the single naked bulb revealed a tool-laden workbench set against the wall to his left.

Recognition kicked his pulse up a notch. Mendoza's basement torture chamber. Nothing like bleach to disguise the odor of blood.

His heart stumbled. Whose blood? What had happened to pretty the wedding singer?

His first thought while recovering from her kiss had been that Killingsworth suspected he was a cop and had used the woman to test him. He shook his head and then winced when pain speared his skull. *He* had initiated contact with *her*, not the other way around.

Yet everything about her kiss had screamed naive innocence. Her psychic blast had left Hector with an impression of aching loneliness and passionate desire, not a coldly calculated attack by a trained Talent. He'd bet money she was a wild Talent the Cartel had targeted for kidnapping.

She was crazy-powerful, or she'd never have been

able to break through his shields and immobilize a Level-10 Talent like himself, even briefly. No wonder Mendoza and Killingsworth wanted to control her.

Hector scowled. This predicament was his own damned fault. He had underestimated Melisenda as a potential threat, albeit an unintentional one. That's what happened when you let your guard down. You woke up tied to a chair in a torture chamber and watched three-and-a-half years of undercover work go down the drain.

The itch to move his stiff muscles had become unbearable. He flexed numb fingers to try to get the circulation going. The small movements didn't seem to do much good.

After a few minutes a single set of footsteps approached the door. A metallic clang stabbed through his head. The portal swung outward. A short guy with a hooked nose sauntered through the doorway. He recognized a thug named Jorge.

Hector and Jorge were not on the best of terms. The man was jealous of Hector's promotion into the ranks of Mendoza's personal body guards. Killingsworth treated Jorge with less respect than one of his pet dogs, but once in a while he threw the man a bone to bolster his loyalty.

The little man made a show of pulling out his Glock and aiming the weapon at the center of Hector's forehead. After a few seconds he shook his head and lowered the weapon. His humorless smile exposed crooked yellow teeth. "Soon you'll be begging for a bullet."

Jorge sidled over to the workbench and picked up one instrument of torture after another, seeming to search for something specific in the selection of burning, pinching, snipping and cutting tools. Each item clinked back onto the bench after a few seconds.

The agent swallowed his fear. Jorge didn't have the *huevos* to torture anyone. He only wanted to savor Hector's downfall.

Maybe there was a way for him to use the little worm to help him escape. He needed time to think, but torture would make it difficult to concentrate on an escape plan. On the other hand, if he goaded Jorge into pistol-whipping him, he could fake unconsciousness and win a reprieve.

Unless my head explodes.

A hacksaw clanked onto the pile of tools on the workbench. Jorge returned to prod Hector's chin with the hard tip of the gun barrel. The guy smelled like an ashtray.

"You know what we do to cops in the Cartel, Hector?"

The specter of the workbench raised the hair on the back of Hector's neck. Pistol-whipping was much less painful than the alternative. He glared but said nothing.

Anger glinted in Jorge's eyes. "You think you're too good to talk to me, cop?" He poked Hector's temple with the Glock.

Sharp pain shot through his skull, a sample of what was to come. He clenched his teeth. Sweat beaded his forehead.

Jorge laughed. "Not such a big man now, are you Hector?"

Curling his lip, Hector let his gaze fall briefly to the man's crotch. "Still bigger than you, Mini Me. Ask the ladies."

Growling, Jorge swung the pistol like a club.

Hector ducked sideways to avoid a direct blow. Agony exploded in his skull. He slumped against his bonds, only half-pretending to be knocked out. Forcing his thoughts to focus through a fog of pain, he welcomed the metallic smell of warm blood sluicing down the side of his head.

"¡Mierda!" Jorge hurried out.

Nothing like a scalp wound to impress the audience.

Hector gritted his teeth and watched a fast-spreading red stain mar the left side of his dirty white dress shirt. Killingsworth needed his victims to be strong enough to last long enough to produce worthwhile information. He might have bought himself time to puzzle a way out of this unholy mess.

There was no time to waste. He flexed his chest muscles to feel the warm gold disk of his St. Jude's medal move against his skin. Closing his eyes, he centered his attention on the talisman beneath his shirt. This situation called for the direct approach. The Agency's squints believed direct questions about how to accomplish something spurred Hector's Talent to scan the multi-verses that comprised his possible futures and tap into the one with the desired outcome. He experienced the desirable future vicariously through his possible future self.

It was as good an explanation as any. He didn't need to understand what he did on a rational level to do it well any more than an owl needed to understand how night vision worked to catch his dinner.

How will I escape from this room?

He first visualized himself standing in front of the closed steel door of the room. Next he moved his consciousness inside his vision-self to create the mental experience of being present in the future. He had to feel solid concrete beneath his wingtips, to look down at the door handle from a standing position. His muscles burned from moving after hours of forced immobility. He smelled bleach.

A rhythmic pulse in the air disintegrated his focus and shot his headache from *tolerable* to *agonizing*. With a groan, he forced his eyelids open.

A helicopter approached. Good news or bad?

After a moment, he remembered Mendoza had ferried the bride's arms-dealer father in on a helo for the wedding. This morning's after-wedding brunch must be almost over. The helo was back to pick him up.

With his head throbbing in time to the rhythm of the rotor, Hector couldn't do anything but wait for the aircraft to land. Besides, his attempt at dowsing had drained him. He needed to rest.

When the copter shut down a few minutes later, he repeated the visualization process. This time, he found the cold door handle with his left hand and pressed downward until the latch clanked. He cracked the door open and peered into the shadowy basement storage area. The only light came from a bulb at the foot of the stairs.

He pushed the door open wider and air stirred around him, carrying a familiar scent of vanilla and something he couldn't quite name. Small, strong shoulders supported his right arm. He turned his head to view his companion, but pain spiked white-hot.

His awareness returned to the present. His rapid breaths rasped the quiet, bleach-tainted air. The searing pain in his head faded.

An image of the pretty blind wedding singer who'd blown his cover formed on the backs of his eyelids. Long coppery curls, stubborn chin, rhinestone-studded sunglasses, dangerously-kissable mouth. She'd smelled of vanilla and…she'd been the person helping him in his vision!

Hector's eyelids snapped open. Unlikely as it seemed, she had to be the key to his escape. A wave of dizziness and nausea hit him. He retched. The dull ache in his ribs he'd been ignoring ever since he awakened exploded in his ribs.

¡Mierda! Jorge must have clipped him harder than

he'd thought. And one of his ribs was probably cracked from last night's beating.

When he could breathe normally again, he decided he'd better dowse for the woman while he had the strength. He conjured up her lovely face without much effort, but her name eluded him. He'd thought her name fit her because... Hell, he couldn't remember why.

With that high-octane kiss, Sparky would fit her. She'd probably hate the nickname the way he hated to be called Water Boy. Made him sound like a common water dowser...

Hector blinked. What did name calling have to do with anything? He needed to focus on remembering the wedding singer's *real* name. With people, names upped the odds of finding them.

He concentrated on remembering every detail. In his mind's eye she stood before him in her long-sleeved sage ball gown and matching lace gloves, rhinestones sparkling from the edges of her dark glasses, her lips curved into the smile that had found a chink in his emotional armor. His *simulacrum*, or vision-self, moved closer, inhaled her feminine, vanilla-ish scent, listened for the soft sounds of her breaths. He gritted his teeth and opened his dowsing senses.

Pain pounded Hector's brain like a devil with a drumstick. Knowing both their lives might depend on him finding—finding *Melisenda* gave him strength to push through the torment.

He flashed on her arrow-straight, pony-tailed figure descending a flight of utilitarian stairs—the stairs to this basement! She'd changed into jeans, a long-sleeved white t-shirt and white running shoes. He couldn't make out who was in front of her. Jorge grasped her right arm above the elbow. When she stumbled, he called her a whore in Spanish and gave her arm a vicious jerk.

Hector's gut knotted.

She lifted her chin. Her lips formed a thin line in her flushed face. The rhinestones in her dark glasses glinted like tiny knives.

He let go of the vision and the pain in his head receded. Not only was Melisenda alive and ambulatory, she appeared ready to do battle. If she could keep control of her Talent, she would be a formidable opponent.

Killingsworth had sensed both their energy signatures when she'd lost control during their kiss, but he hadn't experienced her Talent in action. He didn't know what he was up against.

At this moment the woman was the key. But dowsing for an escape route involved a strong dose of prophecy, and the probable future was as changeable as the weather. A shift had the potential to trap them in this hellhole.

Given the circumstances, all Hector could do was feign unconsciousness and hope Melisenda had a plan.

4

FOOTSTEPS APPROACHED DOWN the hallway. Slumping against his bonds, Hector half-closed his eyes and watched the door through his lashes.

Killingsworth entered with one of his half-dozen pet dogs on a brown leather leash. Hector believed the hound had a soft spot for canines because he felt an affinity for them. When her master halted, Bridget, his big German shepherd, automatically sat. Bridget cast an anxious glance at Hector. Just yesterday morning he'd thrown a ball for her. He liked dogs, and they liked him.

Apparently sensing Hector's injuries, the dog whined.

Killingsworth captured her gaze and stroked her

head. "No worries, my pet." Frowning, he turned to a young man of average height with medium-brown hair who stood in the doorway. "Take Bridget for a walk. Then kennel her."

The man accepted the leash. "Yes, sir."

A warm, fuzzy feeling washed over Hector. He recognized that voice. *Drew.*

He'd schooled himself not to react to his partner's presence. Drew's unique Talent was to be totally forgettable. He could go into a situation, interact, gather intelligence, and then leave with no one the wiser as to his true identity. After encountering him, details soon faded from a person's mind. Film and digital images blurred.

Only close relatives and people with long-term, repeated exposure to the Forgettable Man remembered him after they'd slept. And then only if they were highly motivated, like his parents.

Drew and Hector had worked together on this operation for over three years. Depending on someone to watch his back during an extended and potentially deadly operation had been highly motivating. Hector normally had what he called a *psychic feeler* out for his partner. A feeler involved dowsing within a specified area using a kind of mental feedback loop, like a song getting stuck as an earworm. This application of Hector's Talent was something he'd invented himself, a useful tool in his bag of tricks. He and Drew had become, to Hector's surprise, friends.

Drew left with Bridget in tow. Hector suppressed a grin. Things were looking up. Drew had his back.

"Miss Smith, please join us," Killingsworth said.

Jorge dragged Melisenda through the doorway by one arm. She held her bright head high. Aside from a red, swollen lower lip and a dark bruise covering one cheek, she appeared unharmed. The knot in Hector's gut loosened.

"Where's Hector?" she said, rhinestones flashing like tiny lasers searching for a target.

"Your boyfriend's over there," Jorge said, pointing.

Hector tried not to snort. She's blind, *imbecil*.

Frowning, she crossed her arms. "He's not my boyfriend. We only met last night. I don't even know the man." The set of her jaw said she didn't' want to know him, either.

Jorge laughed and shoved her toward Hector. Melisenda stumbled forward with a startled cry and sprawled on hands and knees on the concrete at his feet. Her head banged against Hector's shin.

Heat suffused his body. The bastard had shoved her for the hell of it. He closed his eyes to focus on his breath. He couldn't afford to lose control of his emotions.

"Idiot," Killingsworth said to Jorge. "I need them both in good condition for interrogation."

Hector missed Jorge's reply. With Killingsworth's attention elsewhere, Melisenda's bare fingers had slid up to encircle his ankle above his sagging sock. Warm energy percolated through his skin and up his leg like a healing balm. Within seconds the pain in his ribs and head noticeably eased. A different kind of heat settled in his groin.

She broke the contact and groped her way up his pant leg past his knee. With one hand on each thigh she pushed herself to her feet. He suppressed a groan having nothing to do with his injuries.

She found his wrist and fingered his bindings. A shadow flitted across her features. Gliding her warm palm up across his shoulder and neck, she feathered her fingers over his bruised and bloody face. Tingles of energy penetrated his skin. Once again, his pain eased. Her soothing vanilla-ish scent made him think of Mom.

He fought a grin. He had a hard-on in a torture chamber for a woman who reminded him of his mother. That was definitely a first.

I hope Mom never finds out.

Melisenda grabbed Hector's shoulders and shook him so hard his teeth rattled. "Wake up!"

The pain in his tender, battered ribs stole his breath. She let go and air escaped his lungs on a whistle. She lifted his chin and healing energy surged from her fingers through his head and neck to the pain in his chest. He squinted up at her. With her back to the audience, no one could see her face. Her lips moved but no sound came out. *I'm sorry. Trust me.*

What the hell was she up to?

"Are you sure he's not dead?" she asked over her shoulder.

"Definitely not," Killingsworth said, sounding amused.

"I said wake up, you selfish jerk!" She pulled back her hand to slap him. A last-second turn of his head absorbed most of the blow, but his ears still rang and his head pounded in protest. He dropped his chin to his chest, pretending to remain unconscious.

"How dare you pull me into your mess and then— then—?" She threw up her hands in apparent defeat.

The woman had bigger *huevos* than most men. She sounded as mad as one of Ma's wet hens, but she'd never convince Killingsworth she'd switched sides. Yet, they *would* escape. Nothing made sense—yet.

He heard her inhale deeply and watched her through his lashes. She turned and took a step toward Killingsworth.

"I apologize for my behavior last night, Mr. Killingsworth." She tucked a stray curl behind one ear, signaling sexual attraction.

An amateur move. Hector wanted to groan.

"My mind was muddled from too much champagne," she continued. "This morning the situation is clear to me."

Beside his boss, Jorge snorted.

"So I'm to believe you've had a change of heart?" Killingsworth said. He sounded like a parent who'd caught his child in a lie.

Apparently oblivious to Killingsworth's reaction, Melisenda hooked her thumbs in her rear pockets. "I'm a practical woman." She gave a small shrug. "And I like to be on the winning side."

Killingsworth's gaze dropped briefly to her breasts. "I see." He smirked. "I didn't realize the wedding singer business was so…competitive."

Hector's stomach burned. This was not going to end well.

"What can I do to prove I'm sincere?" She twisted the end of her ponytail around two fingers. "I'll do anything you want," she said in a breathy voice. "Anything."

Hector wanted to growl in frustration. She was Little Bo Peep baiting the Big Bad Wolf.

Killingsworth's pale eyes darkened. "You're more resourceful than I gave you credit for, Melisenda. It's time I learned your secrets."

"But, sir," Jorge said, *"El Señor Mendoza—"*

Killingsworth turned to cut him off with a raised hand. "The lady intrigues me. Hector won't be ready to be questioned for a while, thanks to your lack of judgment. Tell Blake we'll be in my quarters. I'm not to be disturbed."

"Si, Señor." Jorge shuffled out. The door clicked shut behind him, leaving them alone with the monster.

Bile rose in Hector's throat. There had to be a way he could—

Melisenda flashed him an unmistakable thumbs-up

sign behind her back as Killingsworth approached. Hector saw her shoulders tense like she was bracing herself for Killingsworth's next move. The hound's gaze rested on her face.

¡Mierda! Melisenda's plan wasn't to convince Killingsworth she'd switched her allegiance. Her goal was to seduce the man into a kiss. Then she'd blast him with her Talent.

Hector's heart lifted. Damned if she might not pull it off.

Silent as a serpent, Killingsworth grabbed her arm and shoved her glasses up into her hair. She gasped and shifted sideways but didn't fight him. Hector watched her profile. The monster lifted her chin. He stared into her sightless eyes.

After a few seconds she licked her lips. "Are you satisfied?"

"I will be soon," Killingsworth said, half-smiling.

Her hook was set.

The monster stroked her bruised cheek with the backs of his fingers. She stood her ground without flinching. "Beautiful, blind songbird with the jade-green eyes. Before long, I'll know everything about you."

He trailed his fingertips down the side of her neck. "How to pleasure you."

Her throat moved in a swallow.

"How to cause you pain." He gave the flesh of her injured cheek a vicious pinch.

She cried out.

The tie wraps bit into Hector's wrists and ankles. You'll pay for that, *hijo de puta*. That and every other mark on her body.

"No more games, Melisenda," Killingsworth said. "I know what you want, what you need. Wild Talent is a curse. I'll teach you to utilize the Talent you try to keep hidden, to bend it to your will—after you bend to mine."

The monster took her mouth like a beast savaging prey.

Melisenda's small sound of protest pierced Hector's heart. She arched her back. Her skin luminesced. And Killingsworth dropped like a dead man.

She staggered back, face as white as a ghost. Her breath fogged the air. She scrubbed her mouth on her long sleeve, leaving behind a smear of bright crimson.

Hector's pulse pounded. "Melisenda? Are you all right?"

She didn't appear to have heard him. She fumbled with her glasses and pulled them down onto the bridge of her nose. Light glimmered in her rhinestones like the last sparks in a campfire.

He'd never felt more helpless in his life. Had she over-used her Talent in the past twenty-four hours? "Melisenda!"

She balanced on one foot and slid the other forward. The toe of her white shoe found Killingsworth's inert body. Backing up, she took a long stride, threw out her arms for balance and kicked the unconscious man in the ribs like a soccer player kicking a winning goal.

"Bend *that* to your will, you freakin' psychopath."

Killingsworth coughed.

Hector grinned. It seemed that Melisenda and the Hound would both recover. Which was lucky because Mendoza's Hound was his best lead to the camps.

For now his goal was to get himself and Melisenda to safety alive. The last thing he needed was someone to take care of, but he couldn't leave her behind. She hadn't bolted last night when he'd given her the chance. She'd joined him in the fight. And she was the key to his escape.

He drew in a deep, wheezing breath and winced at the pain in his ribs. "Melisenda?"

She nodded.

"Workbench to your left. Get a knife. Cut me loose."

Turning without a word, she held trembling hands in front of her and crossed to the workbench. Her courage and self-possession were remarkable. He'd been an idiot to assume she was weak and helpless because she was blind.

Luckily, so had Killingsworth.

Her searching hand found the biggest pair of bolt cutters he'd ever seen laying on top of the workbench. Her fingers followed the handles down to blades fouled with hair and other residue. She stiffened and jerked her hands away.

"Back of the bench," he said. Pain from his bruised ribs clipped his words. "Knives on a magnetic rack.

Reaching across the workbench, she nicked a finger on a sharp point. "Ow!"

Note to self: give her more information about handling dangerous weapons. And find out how well she speaks Spanish.

Straightening, she slid the injured fingertip into her mouth and sucked, a move so innocently sexy his mind blanked for a couple of heart-pounding seconds. Then she got back to work.

Frowning, she fingered her way through the knives. She tucked a strand of bright copper hair behind an ear. He'd bet her red hair was God-given—not that he would ever find out.

Finally, she turned away from the bench. She moved toward Hector with a small, thin-bladed knife clutched in one white-knuckled fist. The dusting of freckles across her nose stood out clearly against her skin.

She was terrified, but she was a trooper. "How do you do that?" he said to distract her.

"Do what?"

"Home in on my location."

"It's quiet. I hear you breathing." Her knee pressed against his leg. The fingers of her free hand closed on his forearm and nervous energy buzzed through his thin shirt sleeve. "Hold still. I'll try not to slit your wrists."

He eyed the sharp, three-inch blade she'd chosen. "Thanks. You'll do fine." He certainly hoped so.

Laying the cold, smooth knife flat against the back of his hand, she wiggled the tip under the plastic band. The blade slid over torn skin. He gritted his teeth. A spark snapped between her fingers and his bloody wrist. He jolted.

"Sorry," she said. "Hold still." Twisting the blade, she sawed upward. The plastic parted like jello. She blew out a cinnamon-scented breath. "One down."

He raised his aching arm and circled his wrist to get the circulation going. "Thanks, Sparky."

She cut his other wrist free before squatting to sever the tie-wraps that bound his ankles. "Call me *Meli*."

Meli. Pretty and feminine, like the woman.

When she finished, he tried out the nickname. "Thank you, Meli."

She rose to her feet. "Can you stand?"

"Of course."

Her brows pulled together above her dark lenses. "Are you sure? I don't want you to faint."

"Men don't faint." He inhaled a labored breath. "We pass out."

"Same difference." She stepped aside.

He pushed himself to his feet and discovered they were asleep. His left knee buckled like a broken stilt. He would have fallen if Meli hadn't dropped the knife and pulled his arm across her shoulders to support some of his weight. Catching a whiff of her scent, he frowned. Vanilla and—

"Mr. Stability," she said. "My hero. Can you walk?"

He grunted in the affirmative. They didn't have much time. He pivoted toward the bench. "I need a weapon." With her help, he hobbled over. Blood returned to his feet with a vengeance, reminding him of the time he'd stepped barefoot on a prickly pear cactus.

Thankful for something other than Meli to lean on, he propped himself against the bench. He weighed their options in weaponry, then pocketed a folding knife with a six-inch carbon-steel blade. For Meli he chose a sharp steel pocketknife.

He turned to press the folded blade into her hand. "Don't lose this."

She shoved the little weapon into her pocket. "What about Killingsworth?"

His gaze skipped from the unconscious man to a clear container of white plastic tie-wraps he'd noticed on the workbench. He was going to enjoy this. "I'll tie him up. We'll lock him inside when we go."

Her relieved smile told him she'd been worried he might slit the bastard's throat in cold blood. The knowledge rankled, maybe because that was exactly what he wanted to do.

He grabbed a fistful of tie-wraps and got down on his knees, holding onto the bench leg for support. A couple of minutes later, Killingsworth's hands and feet were tightly bound and he'd been gagged with a dirty rag. Hector had taken grim satisfaction in hammering the man's cell phone to smithereens and stealing his keys.

He'd bought them time. Killingsworth's men believed the security chief had taken Meli to his quarters. They wouldn't dare to disturb the boss for an hour or two.

Meli helped him to his feet. His stomach growled. After using so much energy, they'd both need to refuel.

"I can walk on my own now," he said. "We need to get out of the compound."

Setting her stubborn chin, she shook her head. Her rhinestones flashed like warning lights. "First, we have to fetch Freddy. I can't leave without him."

His gut twisted. Meli's scent he couldn't identify?

Baby powder.

5

A FEW MINUTES LATER WHEN Hector unlocked Meli's room and opened the door, she shoved past him. "Freddy? Where are you, baby?"

One glance told him the infant was gone. He crossed the empty bedroom to check the bathroom.

"Where is he?" she said, her voice rising. She whirled in a wild circle, ponytail whipping around her neck.

"They've moved him, Meli." He snagged her arm to steady her. "I'm sorry."

The blood left her face. She shook her head violently. "I heard firecrackers. He hates firecrackers. He must be hiding."

The fact that there was no crib in the room registered. Not an infant then, a toddler.

She dropped to her hands and knees beside the bed, then lifted the bed skirt and patted the carpet. "C'mon, baby. It's okay, I'm here. Come on out."

Hector's heart twisted at the tremor in her voice. She was close to breaking down. He had to keep her calm and convince her to follow his lead. Otherwise they'd never make it out of Mendoza's compound. "Killingsworth won't hurt Freddy. He's moved him."

Meli sat back on her heels. She lifted her chin and seemed to see right through him from behind her dark lenses. "Moved him? In the helicopter? Why?"

Steeling his heart, he took her hand and pulled her to her feet. "Insurance. Freddy gives him leverage over you."

She grabbed his shirtfront with both hands and tried to shake him. "Promise me you'll find him!"

Pain that had little to do with his injuries lanced through him. "Okay, okay. Go easy on the bruised ribs."

She burst into tears.

Making shushing noises, he wrapped his arms around her and patted her back. What else could he do? "Don't cry, Meli. I'll find him. I promise."

For a moment, with Hector's strong arms around her, Meli felt safe. She rested her bruised cheek on his shirt and listened to the steady beat of his heart. Underneath the dried sweat and blood, he smelled like the charming rogue she'd danced with last night—only better.

He'd promised to find Freddy.

A warm drop of liquid plopped onto her shoulder. The metallic odor of fresh blood reminded her that before they looked for Freddy, Hector needed first aid. And they both needed something to eat.

"Look around," she said. "Where's my backpack?"

He pressed the bag into her hands. After rummaging inside the main compartment, she held out a bottle of pills. "Go wash up in the bathroom and take two these."

His breath hissed inward.

Meli cut him off before he could protest. "It's an over-the-counter pain reliever. Don't argue, just do it. You'll thank me later."

The bottle jerked out of her hand and his footsteps moved toward the bathroom. She followed him to the door. "Blood attracts bears. Take off your shirt and wash up. I'll find something for you to wear."

Water splashed in the sink. Hector didn't like being told what to do, but he wasn't stupid.

The only thing she owned that might fit him was her nightshirt—an extra-large Seattle Seahawks tee with long sleeves. She located the shirt in her small suitcase, snagged her backpack and waited outside the bathroom.

When the door opened, she handed Hector the shirt. Then she slipped past him to search for items they might need while trekking through the wilderness after they escaped the compound.

She stuffed a roll of toilet paper into her pack and tried to ignore the sounds of Hector dressing in the bedroom. The firmness of his chest and the corded muscles of his arms were hard to put out of her mind. And the gentle way he'd held her. She hadn't been held so intimately since—since—okay, she'd never been held so intimately by a man. Ever. Except for Papa when she was a little girl, which didn't count.

She sighed. What would it be like to explore his powerful male body with—?

"You ready?" Hector said from the doorway.

She nearly jumped out of her skin. Her cheeks burned. She pretended to search for something in her backpack. "Almost."

What was the matter with her? Freddy was missing. She had to focus on finding him and escaping from Mendoza's compound. They needed Hector, but she had to keep her guard up. The man was a dangerous distraction.

They'd need clean water to drink. After topping off the bottle in her pack, she located the trash can with her foot and pulled out three empty ones, which she rinsed out and filled from the tap.

Returning to the bedroom, she dug around in the nightstand drawer and pulled out her sealed plastic bag of goodies. When she offered a protein bar to Hector he snatched it from her hand. "Thanks. My stomach thinks my throat's been cut."

Meli was munching hers when she heard a soft pattern of taps on the door. She froze in mid-chew.

Barely making a sound, Hector moved to the door.

"It's Drew," a man's muffled voice said. The door opened with a soft whoosh.

"You took your sweet time. Bro," Hector said.

His friendly tone was reassuring. It hadn't occurred to Meli that Hector might have a friend in the compound.

The door clicked shut.

"I could have been here sooner and left you in your wingtips," the other man said. "Brought your running shoes. You're gonna need 'em."

Footsteps approached and Hector's warm hand settled on her lower back. "Drew's a friend. You can trust him."

Drew's subtle, spicy cologne reminded her of Papa's aftershave. Feeling reassured, she nodded.

"This is Melisenda Smith, the wedding singer," Hector added.

"I wish we were meeting under different circumstances," Drew said to her warmly.

"Me, too."

"What can you tell us?" Hector asked his friend.

"Only the wedding party and the immediate families were invited to stay for brunch. The other guests left.

Security is concentrated at the front of the mansion. Brunch is on the patio."

"We'll exit through a back door," Hector said.

"How long do you need to get out of the compound?" Drew asked him. "I'll take care of the guy watching the camera feeds."

Meli inhaled sharply. What did Hector's friend mean, *take care of the guy*?

"Twenty minutes," Hector replied.

"You look like hell," Drew said. "I'll give you twenty-five. You can buy me a beer later."

Hector laughed softly. "Thanks." His tone turned serious. "I have an urgent message for you to relay to Doc. Mendoza is Talented. I'm absolutely sure. Don't know what his psychic ability is, though."

A charged silence lasted a few seconds.

"Anything else?" Drew's tone was tense.

"Meli is a wild Talent, some kind of powerful expath. The Cartel wants her. I'm taking her with me."

Is that what they called her freak side? An expath Talent? Meli had a thousand questions but held her tongue. They had to escape from Mendoza's compound in the next half hour—and rescue Freddy. There would be time for questions later.

"Eight minutes to *go*," Drew said. "Godspeed." The door opened and then he was gone.

A few minutes later, Hector led the way down the stairs. He turned toward the back of the building. Soon they passed sounds of running water and clanking dishes.

A drop in air pressure informed Meli that Hector had eased the outside door open.

"Coast is clear," he whispered. He pulled her outside into the warmth of the sun and closed the door softly.

"Just try not to run me into anything." She tucked her hand inside his elbow. "It's like taking the lead in a dance."

"I'll be careful." His warm breath caressed her ear and her belly tightened. "Our eight minutes are up."

"Eight minutes?" She dredged up a blurry memory of Hector's partner's instructions. What was his name again?

"Not important. *¡Vámonos!*" Hector pulled her into a slow jog across the lawn.

She tried to give herself over to his guidance the way she did with Freddy, but it was hard to trust a stranger. She and her Guide were a team.

They slowed to a stumbling stop. Hector placed her palm against a rough stone wall. "The gazebo. Three steps up. Duck down inside so no one sees you through a window."

She found the first step with her foot and hurried up into the enclosure. Hector's soft footsteps followed. Those running shoes were a Godsend. Steadying herself against the wall with one hand, she hunkered down. With a low grunt, he crouched next to her. She worried her lower lip. Squatting had to be hell on his injured ribs.

He spoke into her ear. "We'll angle for the kennels. The dogs know me. I'll keep them quiet. We'll slip alongside the dog runs and then cross the last fifty yards to the rose arbor near the perimeter fence."

She forced herself to pay attention to his words despite the distraction of his nearness.

After settling her glasses on her nose, Meli nodded. "Let's do it!"

As they moved toward the kennel, Hector kept a psychic feeler out for a shift in the probable future. Sensing a shift would warn him of the need to dowse for another escape route.

By the time they reached the kennel building, Hector's ribs protested every quick, shallow inhalation. He sagged against a tan stucco wall and waited for the pounding in his head to subside.

Her hand squeezed his wrist and soothing energy seeped into the tense muscles of his forearm. "Are you okay?"

He squinted down at her frowning face. Her freckles reminded him of fairy dust. He matched his frown to hers. Waxing poetic over her was unwise.

"Peachy," he said, wheezing like a centenarian who'd lost his oxygen bottle. "Just need to catch my breath."

She lifted an eyebrow. "I forgot. You're a *macho man*."

The flow of energy from Meli climbed his arm and entered his chest. His painful respiration eased as if he'd been given a dose of morphine and an inhaler. He frowned at Meli's hand resting on his arm.

He'd taken a bullet to the chest from friendly fire during the debacle in the Sonoran Desert. Being shot by the good guys was always a risk when you were deep undercover. A Bureau Healer had numbed his pain enough for him to manage without medical intervention until he'd convinced Mendoza he was one of the lucky few to escape capture.

Meli channeled her energy like a healer to relieve his pain and bolster his strength. She must have more control over her Talent than she believed. He'd never heard of a healer who packed a psychic punch like Meli's, though. Doc would be intrigued by her for sure. The boss would probably try to recruit her. Properly trained, she'd be a major asset.

"You sound better," she said.

He *was* better. "Let's go."

He led her to the rear corner of the small building. A breeze cooled the back of his neck. He stole a peek through the cyclone fence to see which animals were in residence.

Bridget ran over to lick his hand through the wire fence. He scratched behind her ear with one finger and scanned the other four runs. The next two were empty.

Killingsworth's old deaf pug lay asleep in a sunbeam in the third. In the far run, a yellow lab mix lifted his big, square head. Hector jerked back behind the wall. His ribs throbbed.

Did Killingsworth have a new pet? The K-9s were Belgian shepherds.

His feeler hadn't signaled a shift. Did that mean the dog wasn't a threat, and they should ignore it? Or would the animal's barking give them away?

Water boy, my ass.

People had no idea how difficult it was to use his Talent effectively. Dowsing was not a point-and-click ability. Accuracy often depended on unpredictable variables he might not even know existed.

The Lab barked once. He must have caught their scent.

Meli drew a sharp breath, dropped his arm and bolted past.

What the hell had gotten into her?

She dragged the fingertips of one hand along the chain-link mesh of the kennel run. The steel wire whispered. Tail wagging, the mutt yipped again.

Hector clenched his jaw and loped after her. He'd never killed a dog in his life and he didn't want to start now, but she might have left him no choice. If the mutt didn't shut up, someone would investigate.

This was why he liked to work alone. If anyone's mistake forced him to the Dark Side or got him killed, he wanted it to be *his*.

Meli halted on the far side of the enclosure and extended one hand, palm out, toward the agitated dog like a cop stopping traffic. The big animal quickly sat down and shut up.

Grinning like she'd won the lottery, she dropped her hand. The dog stared at her with adoring eyes.

I'll be damned.

When Hector reached her, she threw her arms around him. Joyful energy as golden and nourishing as Mama's fresh tortillas flowed from her body into his. Holding her soft curves close and letting his eyelids fall seemed like the most natural thing in the world to do. His thoughts spun in neutral and he was at one with the Universe.

After what felt like a long night's rest she loosened her hold on him and tilted her head back. "You did it, Hector Protector! You found Freddy."

Freddy? Blinking in the light of her dazzling smile, he dragged his gaze from her lovely face to the big dog's furry one and back. "*Chica*, that's only a dog."

Her smile disappeared. "Saying *Freddy's only a dog* is like saying *Ben Franklin was just an old bald guy*," she said. "We're partners. Together, we can do virtually anything. Freddy's a dog genius."

Hector slanted a second look at the big Lab. Calm brown eyes that shone with intelligence gazed back at him from a face gone white with age. "What about the baby powder?"

"Baby powder?" She tilted her head to the side like she was trying to understand what was behind the question. "His deodorant spray smells like baby powder. The scent puts strangers at ease around him."

His heart leapt. There was no kidnapped child!

He planted a kiss in the middle of her forehead. A spark stung his lips as he pulled away. He couldn't stop grinning. "He's a goddamned miracle, Sparky. Let's spring Freddy and get out of this hellhole."

Freddy was fine. Meli was so grateful to Hector for finding her Guide that she didn't care if he called her Sparky. By the time she'd checked Freddy over from nose to tail, her face ached from smiling.

She wiped dog slobber off her chin with her shirtsleeve. "He's okay," she said, "thanks to you. You're my hero."

Meli heard Freddy's tail swish the air.

Hector helped her to her feet. "Will he stay beside us?"

She straightened. "Absolutely. Do you see his harness and leash anywhere? He'll be more effective if we have our gear." That was the understatement of the year.

Soft footsteps indicated he was moving. Metal clinked. "Got 'em. Let's go."

"But I need to put his gear on. "

"No time. Wait until we're outside the compound. I'll take care of you."

Not wanting to argue, Meli brought Freddy to heel.

"Follow me back around the kennel," Hector said."

She followed the sound of his footsteps. Freddy stuck to her like glue.

In one of the kennel runs a dog whined. Hector murmured something and the animal grew quiet.

A large hand on her shoulder stopped her, then dropped to enfold her hand. A quick spurt of energy fired down her arm and out through that point of contact. His fingers tightened.

"It's an open thirty-yard sprint to the rose arbor," he said softly. "You and the pooch can wait there out of sight."

"Wait for what?"

"I'll be engineering our escape. When I'm ready for you, I'll whistle."

A wisp of warm energy tried to sneak down her arm to his hand. She pulled the energy thread back and sighed. She couldn't seem to keep her energy to herself around him. The constant effort to control her freak side—her Talent—was wearing her down.

"Ready?" Hector said.

She nodded.

"Now run like hell!"

Meli clung to his hand and ran. The energy she'd shared with him must have done him some good because she could barely keep up. Was he aware of what she'd done?

He pulled her to a stop and Freddy leaned against her leg. The sweet, elegant perfume of roses surrounded them. He stood so close she felt his breath on her face. Was he listening for sounds of pursuit? All she heard were the sounds of their breathing and the musical call of a faraway bird.

He grabbed her shoulders. "Sit!" he hissed, and pushed her down so she collapsed onto her butt on the grass.

Thorns pricked her back through her thin cotton shirt. She scowled. Who did he think he was, pushing her around?

"Cut it out!"

Hector dropped to the grass. She crossed her legs, tailor-fashioned, and patted the grass beside her. Freddy lay down.

"Give me your belt," Hector said. "I need to cobble together a line."

Did he have to be so bossy? "A line? Why?"

He hesitated. "We have to descend a twenty-five-foot cliff to the river."

He was afraid she'd freak out! Because she was blind? Or because she was a woman?

Meli tamped down her indignation. He didn't really know her. She kept her voice level. "If it makes you feel any better, I've done some rock climbing."

"Great!" he said with so little enthusiasm she knew he didn't believe a blind woman could climb down a cliff. Her fingers fisted around Freddy's collar.

"Our belts, Fred's leash and parts from his harness, tied together, should give us a strong, twelve-foot line," Hector said.

If they were lucky, but no guarantees.

"We'll drop off the line into the river and float a little way downstream. The hound will have trouble tracking us through moving water."

"What hound?"

He hesitated a little too long. "You know, tracking dogs."

Meli shivered. Those dogs would be trained attack dogs.

Apparently sensing her mood, Freddy whined.

She didn't mind giving up her belt, but she was reluctant to sacrifice Freddy's gear. Without his equipment, communication between Meli and her Guide would be crippled while making their way through the wilderness. On the other hand, if they couldn't get down the cliff, nothing else would matter.

She reached for her buckle.

Metal chinked as Hector undid his. He kept his voice low. "Creeks flow into the river downstream. We'll work our way up one under the cover of trees."

She worked the braided leather of her belt free of her last belt loop. "Won't someone see us in the river?"

Leather whispered through belt loops, Hector removing his belt. "This section of the river is too full of boulders and snags for boats to navigate. There's nothing but walk-in wilderness on the other side."

He took her belt from her outstretched hand. Snaps popped as he removed the stiff handle from Freddy's harness. If his muttered curses were any indication, connecting the motley group of items to make a line was a difficult task.

"It's done," he finally said. "You two ready?"

"We're ready."

"I'm going to crawl over to anchor the line to a fence post at the edge of the cliff. Mendoza didn't run the fence along the cliff top because it would have spoiled his view of the river."

Meli held tightly to Freddy's collar and listened to Hector scuffle away. Pebbles pinged down the cliff like warning shots. She forced herself to continue breathing. *Please, God, don't let him fall.*

The next thirty seconds or so were punctuated by furtive noises she couldn't readily identify. She hugged Freddy and worried her lower lip. Dirt and stones skittered down the crag again. She held her breath.

A low whistle, Hector's signal, came from the cliff's edge. Exhaling, she let go of Freddy's collar and scuttled toward the sound. His tags tinkled behind her. The rush of the river grew louder in front.

A strong hand grabbed her upper arm. "Whoa," Hector said in an urgent whisper. "There's a cliff, remember?"

"I'm at least three feet back." With an effort, she suppressed her irritation. "Thanks anyway."

He released her arm. "You'll go down first, the dog second, I'm last."

She'd have to let go and drop the last few feet into the water. Hector would lower Freddy—

Her heart slammed her ribs. Freddy didn't have hands. She grabbed a fistful of Hector's tee shirt. "How do we get Freddy down?"

Strong fingers pried hers loose from the cloth. "I told you; you go down first—"

"But *how* will you get him down?"

"Don't worry about it; I'll figure something out."

Her stomach dropped. He didn't have a plan to get Freddy down the cliff! If she descended first, he could leave her Guide behind.

She crossed her arms over her chest. "Freddy goes down first."

"Have it your way," Hector said, his voice flat. He grunted and Freddy let out a surprised yip. Claws scrabbled the ground, sending a small landslide of soil and pebbles pinging down the cliff face.

The splash that followed surged her forward, heart a-quiver. "Freddy!"

6

AN ARM LIKE AN IRON bar clamped around her waist and a calloused hand covered her mouth. "He's fine," Hector said, his breath coming fast and hot in her ear. "Swims like a champ."

White-hot energy blossomed in her chest. It took everything she had not to blast him with her rage. Instead, she singed his palm that covered her mouth.

He jerked his hand away. *"¡Mierda!"*

Meli shook with fury. "You arrogant ass! Freddy's old. You could have given him a heart attack. I should push you after him."

He snorted. "If you'd gone down without arguing, you could have helped him."

Her hands balled into fists. In spite of the way she'd handled things in the torture chamber, he didn't trust her to blow her own nose. She fought to keep her voice low. "I'm not an idiot, and I'm not your little slave."

She listened to his heavy breathing slow. When he spoke, his voice was devoid of emotion. "We don't have time to argue."

Pressing her lips together, she nodded. He was right. What mattered now was making sure Freddy was okay.

Pulling off her glasses, she stuffed them into her bra for safekeeping. "Hand me the knit gloves from the side pocket of my pack."

A moment later Hector pressed the gloves into her hand. She pulled them on, thankful for the little protection they afforded.

"Here's the line," he said, and handed her the makeshift leather rope.

"There's no safe way to do this. The line is too short to run around a tree for extra support. The knots in the line won't slide without injuring you if we try for a proper belay."

Meli frowned. He'd risk serious rope burns in this scenario, but she didn't see any way around it.

"Find a toehold and lean outward so you can walk down the face. When we reach the end of the line, I'll whistle. Take a deep breath, push away from the cliff face with your legs and release the line."

His fingers unexpectedly slipped a strand of hair behind her ear. "Can you swim?"

"Of course." Inhaling the scents of soap and man-sweat, she struggled to hold onto her anger.

"Let the current take you downstream," he said. "I'll be right behind you. There's a fallen tree jutting out from the near bank about a hundred yards down. Fred's made it up onto the log. Angle toward shore and you can't miss it."

For a second she couldn't move. Freddy hadn't been swept away. He was waiting for her.

Keeping the rope taut across her shoulders, she backed toward the edge of the cliff.

"You're there," Hector said.

She braced one foot in a toehold against the cliff face, leaned back and braced the other. The pull in her arms and shoulders reminded her she hadn't climbed the practice wall at her gym in a few weeks. Slowly, Hector fed her the rope while supporting her weight. She forced herself to take her time on the descent.

When his low whistle reached her from above, she knew she'd arrived at the end of the line. She gave an answering whistle. The rush of frigid water below promised freedom. Bending her legs, she inhaled deeply and shoved with all her might before letting go of the line.

A second of free fall and then the liquid ice that was the river scalded her skin. The impact when she struck bottom forced a burst of air from her lungs. She shoved against the rocky bed and shot to the surface.

Sucking in a welcome lungful of life-giving air, she

fought to keep her head above water. The river spun her on her way downstream like an ice cube in a storm drain.

After a few dizzying seconds she stopped fighting the current and began to swim with it instead. If she drifted too far out, she'd be swept past the log where Freddy waited. She angled left toward the bank.

A second later her body slammed into an immovable object. She tried to grab onto the obstacle but her hands slipped on the smooth, curved surface. The current tried to suck her underneath. She threw an arm as high as she could and grabbed a woody stub. Chest heaving, she clung to the log like a bedraggled limpet until her toes found purchase on the river bottom.

Freddy barked once somewhere to her left.

When she'd caught her breath she felt her way sideways with care, moving into shallower water toward her Guide. Icy cold nipped her legs like the dogs of winter and the current fought her every step.

Freddy's tags jingled over the rush of the water. The log shook beneath her hands before his warm, familiar tongue bathed her freezing face in dog slobber. Meli rubbed Freddy's soggy ears. Who knew wet dog could smell so good? "I'm sorry, baby. After what he did to you, it would serve Hector right if he fell off the cliff."

Freddy whined.

Where was the pendejo?

Her heart skipped a beat. He might be arrogant, but

Hector was courageous and he kept his promises. They needed his help to find their way through the wilderness. Like it or not, the three of them were in this together. They were a team. Hector liked to be in charge, but he would learn.

A man-sized splash upstream had her straining to hear anything to indicate Hector had surfaced. Seconds passed without a splash, without a whisper, without a curse.

Her heart thudded in the hollow of her chest. "Hector?"

Freddy's damp fur brushed her arm. The unhappy *whuffling* noises he made under his breath grew fainter as he moved away from the bank.

Had he spotted Hector? Meli lunged back through the icy water. She struggled to keep her footing in the strong current.

Like all guides, Freddy had been trained in *intelligent disobedience*. Faced with a novel situation, he would take the lead and use his own judgment to decide on a course of action. It wasn't in Freddy's nature to stand by while a man drowned, not even a man he didn't much like.

She pulled herself along the log and called out over the rushing water. "Hector?"

Freddy barked his hurry-up bark. She surged forward. Her heart lifted. "Hector!"

Why didn't the man answer? Freddy barked again.

Memories of her struggle to find and save her

parents after the car crash came flooding back. Newly blind, she'd done everything she could, but it hadn't been enough. "Hector!"

Her teeth chattered. Water lapped her chin. Any further out and she'd be in over her head. "H-Hector!"

Nothing. Fingers of cold squeezed her heart. Tears mixed with river water on her cheeks.

Freddy yipped and ran past her toward the bank, his nails clicking and scratching. A jarring impact shook the log. She nearly lost her grip.

Hector's hoarse-but-still-cocky voice called to her. "Miss me, Sparky?"

Her heart turned over. Her muscles turned to mush. She laid her forehead against the wet wood and sobbed. Hector was alive. She and Freddy weren't alone in the wilderness.

Sloshing sounds moved toward her. A strong arm encircled her waist. "What is it? Are you hurt?"

Hating that she couldn't stop crying, she shook her head. He put her arms around his neck and carried her toward shore. With a grunt, he lifted her and set her on the ledge.

"Why d-didn't you answer m-me?" she said.

"You and Fred were making enough noise for all of us."

He'd heard her cries, but hadn't bothered to answer. Just as he hadn't bothered to explain about getting Freddy down the cliff. If she wasn't so cold her teeth clattered like a nutcracker on meth, she'd have slapped him. Instead she scooted back until she bumped into her backpack. She hugged her knees to her chest and tried to quell the anger that burned in her belly.

An unmistakable *slosh* indicated Hector had hoisted himself out of the river. Freddy shook himself and showered them both with water.

"Sonofabitch," Hector said.

"Ya th-think?" Her tone dripped acid but the chattering of her teeth kind of ruined the effect.

Freddy squished over and sat down beside her. She held him close to try to share the heat smoldering inside her. Something poked her left breast. Remembering the glasses she'd stowed in her bra, she pulled them out and settled them firmly on the bridge of her nose. Wearing them made her feel less like a half-drowned porcupine.

A big hand clasped one of hers. "You're even colder than me," Hector said, apparent concern lacing his voice.

Meli steeled herself and singed his fingers. Swearing, he jerked his hand away.

"I'm f-fine," she lied. "Don't touch me!"

Freddy whined.

For a moment, Hector said nothing. He cleared his throat. "Drew's right. I'm a lousy partner."

Drew? Meli frowned. Hector's FBI partner had already faded in her memory, like a number looked up in a phone book and dialed once. "That's an excuse, not an apology," she told Hector. "Does the fact we risked our lives by jumping back into the river to save your sorry ass mean anything to you?"

He took her hand in both of his this time. "Thank you for having my back. I'm sorry for scaring you and Fred. I promise I'll do better."

Meli jerked her hand away. When they touched, she was likely to forgive him anything. She had to maintain her objectivity or they'd never be an effective team.

"I said *don't touch me.* It's dangerous. Freddy's the only one who's safe around me when I'm furious."

A minute later she heard the sound of fabric ripping. She and Freddy both jolted. What the heck was Hector doing? "You said you didn't want to make noise."

After another rip, he answered. "I'm working on my partner skills. I'm going to tether us together so we don't get separated."

Meli blinked. He was ripping up his clothes to keep her safe. *Technically, they're my clothes*, she reminded herself sternly. *And he's putting me on a leash.*

He caught her left arm and tied a strip of damp cloth snugly around her wrist. "There'll be about two feet of play between us," he said.

The bracelet of damp cloth didn't feel like a leash. It felt like a lifeline. A lump the size of a base drum materialized in her throat.

A series of small tugs on her wrist indicated he'd anchored the other end of the fabric strip to his arm. He grabbed her hand and pulled her to her feet. He must have known she'd lied to him about touching her, but he didn't say anything. He simply helped her climb over the tree trunk and then led her along a rock ledge.

Soon the shelf ended and they entered freezing, shin-deep water. At least Freddy loved to swim. He'd inherited webbed feet from both sides of his family.

Hector stayed between her and the deeper water. Meli couldn't help smiling. *Hector Protector.*

Before long, her legs ached with cold and her feet in her waterlogged running shoes felt like chunks of firewood. *But I'm alive. Free. And I'm not alone.*

Their journey narrowed down to a haze of cold, wet misery.

Finally, the water sounds changed. Hector dragged her to a stop. "We've reached the mouth of Bear Grass Creek. There's a shallow cave here in the riverbank. You and Fred will wait there while I lay a false trail up the stream to mislead the trackers. This stream is an easy climb. They won't be hard to convince.

"The next creek joins the river in a small waterfall, making it appear to be a much steeper climb. In reality the slope eases after the first bit until the two slopes are more or less equal."

"Do we *have* to stay in the water?" Meli said, hating the whine in her voice.

"Water masks our trail. The Hound will have trouble following."

"The Hound? You mean the tracking dogs?"

His voice roughened. "Killingsworth. Some call him

Mendoza's Hound."

Remembering her last encounter with Killingsworth, Meli shuddered. "Why do they call him that?"

Hector hesitated. "Because he's good at tracking."

She had a feeling he wasn't telling her everything, but he wasn't treating her like a child, either. He'd answered her more truthfully than before.

They stumbled out of the river onto bumpy shingle. The lifeline tugged at her wrist.

"I have to turn you loose for a little while," Hector said.

All her instincts screamed for them to stay together. She worried her lower lip. Freddy whined and nosed her hand. She scratched behind his ears and told herself to "cowgirl up," as Mama used to say. "We'll be okay, boy." If only she felt as confident as she sounded.

Hector's end of the wet fabric line slapped against her jeans. "You'll be safe out of sight in the cave. High water has carved out a hollow in the bank under a big evergreen. The ceiling is too low for you to stand up, but you can sit on a boulder."

Meli shivered. If the bad guys showed up, she and Freddy would be trapped like cornered rabbits. "Are you sure it's safe?"

"Positive. Roots as big around as my arm hold up the roof. And guess what? It's dry inside."

Meli managed a smile. "Dry is definitely good."

Cool fingertips brushed her cheek. "I promise I'll

come back. Trust me."

She found herself nodding. Hector kept his promises.

"We'll need this again when I get back," he said. He wrapped the soggy strip of fabric around and around her forearm before tying it off.

His big hand engulfed hers and he pulled her a couple of yards across the gravel. "The cave entrance is directly in front of you. I'll hold the pack while you feel your way in and find a seat. The floor is covered in large gravel and mostly small boulders left behind during floods. There's a big flat one that would make a good seat."

The weight of her backpack lifted and she slipped out of the straps.

"Be careful; the footing is treacherous," he said. "Watch your head."

Meli clambered inside on her hands and feet like a monkey, feeling her way with care. Boulders the size of basketballs shifted under her weight. She whacked one hand on what turned out to be the side of a knee-high, relatively flat boulder.

Sucking on her scraped knuckles, she took a seat on the rough, dry stone. The odors of moist earth and river water mingled in the air. She imagined gnarled tree roots that looked like giant grapevines holding up the roof over her head.

Fred scrambled inside and joined her on her hard seat. There was just enough room for both of them.

She put an arm around his damp, furry body.

"Here's your pack," Hector said. The bag plopped down in front of her. "You'll be safe until I return."

Meli squeezed Fred tighter. *Safe* was a relative word at this point. "We'd feel safer with you."

"I have to hurry. You'd only slow me down."

She stiffened.

Hector's tone softened. "I'll be back before you know it, Meli."

She lifted her chin. "You'd better be or we'll go on without you."

7

MELI LISTENED TO THE sounds of Hector climbing uphill fade away until only the sound of rushing water surrounded their little hidey-hole. Goosebumps marched up her spine.

Freddy whined.

She swallowed her fear and forced a smile into her voice. Her Guide needed her. "Are you hungry, baby? Let's get you some breakfast."

Filling one of his collapsible bowls with a packet of kibble, she then moistened the dry food with water from one of her bottles.

The clean water she'd packed wouldn't last long. If they climbed high enough she'd be able to refill the bottles with snow, which was unlikely to be contaminated with bacteria that would make them sick.

But a bottle of snow would melt into a whole lot less water.

Sighing, she listened to Freddy enjoy his breakfast. When he'd finished she cleaned the dish with a wet wipe and stowed it in her pack.

Then she dug out her hairbrush to redo her ponytail. She felt like something a hurricane blew in. Appropriate, since change had stormed through her life over the last month. First Freddy's dismal prognosis, and then the scramble to find a way to keep him with her. Then she'd come up with a new life plan. She'd landed a gig that, along with her savings, would finance her change to a sedentary career giving voice lessons to aspiring singers. And then she'd kissed a man who hadn't passed out.

A mystery man. A drug lord's bodyguard. She shook her head. She had to keep reminding herself he was a criminal. Her instincts insisted he could be trusted. Especially when he touched her.

Catching a whiff of her armpit odor, she wrinkled her nose. What she wouldn't give for a long, hot bubble bath. Having done what she could with her damp hair, she returned the brush to her pack and pulled out Freddy's package of baby wipes. These would have to do in place of soap and deodorant.

A new worry niggled at her. An infection under these circumstances might turn deadly. Hector's bandage might not be enough to keep the germs out. She'd better change it out when they left the river for good. And she needed to find out if he'd been injured by the knots in their improvised line.

When she'd finished cleaning up, Meli stowed the used wipes in an empty pocket of her pack. They must pack out trash so as not to leave an obvious trail.

Next she opened the side pouch where she kept Fred's grooming tools. "A spa in a cave, Freddy. How many dogs can say they've had one?"

Freddy's soggy tail slapped the rocks like a flopping fish.

After partially drying him with his super-absorbent towel, she gave him a thorough brushing. The attention would calm his nerves. Her Guide loved to be groomed. He liked their routines. Poor Freddy's world had turned upside down in the last twelve hours along with hers.

When the task was complete, she stowed Freddy's stuff in her pack and tried not to worry. Surely Hector should have been back by now. When she tried to check the time, she learned the dunking in the river had ruined her Braille watch. She removed the useless timepiece and put it in the pack pocket where she'd stashed the used baby wipes.

Had Hector been captured? Maybe he'd fallen and injured himself. Or maybe he regretted his noble impulse to help them and had left them to fend for themselves.

As if he'd heard her thoughts, Freddy licked her hand with his big wet tongue and she heard his tail swish.

She smiled and stroked his head. "You're right. I don't really believe he would abandon us. Hector said he'd find you, and he did. He said he'd come back, and he will."

Freddy lowered his heavy head onto her lap. Meli scratched behind his ears. So far Hector had been a man of his word. But although he followed a code of honor, he was a drug lord's minion. She couldn't let him charm her into trusting him completely.

Her fingers stroked Freddy's short, thick fur. Strange that Hector was a fundamentally decent man. What had turned him to a life of crime?

She'd done things she wasn't proud of because of her love of Freddy. She'd broken lots of rules. Had Hector become a criminal out of love? Maybe he was born into the drug business and didn't want to betray his family. Maybe he'd fallen for the wrong woman.

She shook her head at her own foolishness. Rule Number Three was *mind your own business*.

Rumbling low in his chest, Freddy raised his head, jingling his tags. A helicopter's rotor pulsed the air before she heard it over the noisy river. Would someone spot Hector?

Hector waited under a Douglas fir for the helicopter to disappear over the tree-covered ridge north of the compound. At least he could catch his breath for a minute.

He'd pushed himself to the limit to get the job done quickly. The pinched look on Meli's face when he'd left had spurred him on as much as his need to get a head start on any pursuers. She wasn't sure he'd come back. Not surprising, given what she knew about him and the way he'd treated her at first.

Not being able to tell her the whole truth sucked. Psychic Agents were forbidden to share information about their secret FBI unit with the general public. Meli's practical streak kept her questions in check for now, but he had a feeling she would press him for answers at the first opportunity. Luckily, they would reach his emergency cache today. He'd call Doc with the satellite phone and they would be rescued before nightfall. Then she would be Doc's problem. Hell, Doc might even try to recruit her.

The thought of Meli intentionally putting herself in danger knotted his stomach.

When the sound of the helo's rotor faded, he worked his way down the last ten yards of the stream bank. Sweat trickling down his back added to the sting of his rope burns. The Seahawks tee shirt hadn't done much to protect him from the knots. Luckily the line had been too short to do much damage.

Killingsworth would send the K-9s after them any minute now. With luck, this false trail would delay them long enough for him to get Meli up Crook's Creek. So far his psychic feeler hadn't sensed a change in the probable future. They should make it to the cave where he'd hidden his survival gear ahead of the enemy. Ignoring his aching ribs, he grasped a huge gnarled tree root and swung down to the narrow beach in front of the cave.

Fred growled.

"Hector?" Meli's voice quavered.

Damn. He should have given her a heads-up.

Ducking his head, he peered into the dark hollow beneath the tree. Fred rose on stiff legs, hackles raised. Meli held a rock the size of a baseball in one fist. Her arm was cocked to throw. Did she really think she could hit someone?

Do not underestimate this young woman, his mother's voice chided in his head. *She is full of surprises.*

"Don't worry. It's only me," he said to Meli.

She dropped the stone. The jewels edging her dark glasses flashed. "It's about time!"

Fred growled.

Hector sighed. Would they ever forgive him for tossing Fred into the river? *I should have listened to Mom on that one.* She'd warned him not to lose his temper.

Meli laid a hand on the big dog's shoulder. "Give it a rest, Freddy. Hector tossed you off the cliff. Karma knocked Hector off the cliff. The scales are in balance."

Fred huffed, seeming unconvinced.

"We're a team," Meli said. Her tone brooked no argument.

Hector matched Fred's unfriendly stare and gave him the finger.

The dog's gaze flicked from Hector's eyes to his upturned middle finger and back.

He grinned. Made you look. Dog rules. I win.

With a long sigh, Fred drooped in apparent defeat.

"What took you so long?" Meli reached for her pack.

A glance at his waterproof Rolex confirmed he'd done the job quickly. "It's only been fifteen minutes."

"It seemed longer." She shrugged into the pack straps. "I heard a helicopter."

"They didn't spot me. I stayed under the trees."

"I owe you an apology," Meli said. "I forgot to ask you about rope burns from lowering me."

Hector swallowed. An apology? After the way he'd scared her? "Nothing serious. The line was short." He changed the subject. "We need to push hard to maintain our head start. Killingsworth's awake."

Meli froze like a rabbit who'd heard a twig snap. "How do you know that?"

¡Mierda! How in hell had he let that slip? He had dowsed for unconscious humans within a two-mile radius and come up empty-handed, but he couldn't tell her that. He was glad she couldn't read the expression on his face. "Wild guess."

Her brows arched high above her dark glasses. "Wild *guess*?"

"Your kiss didn't put me out of commission for long last night. Killingsworth ought to be awake by now."

She frowned. "With you, I foolishly held back."

He changed the subject. "The creek we'll follow uphill is a little further downriver. We have to stay in the water for a while longer. This should be the last time."

Ducking down, he reached into the cave and grasped her warm hand. Energy tingled up his arm and then subsided. "Watch your head."

She scrambled over the small boulders, holding his hand to steady herself. Once outside, she straightened and then stumbled. He caught her against his chest.

Her warm, soft curves molded to his body. His arms tightened around her. When she tipped her head back her rhinestones reflected the sunlight. His gaze settled on her parted lips.

Tired and battered as he was, he was tempted to forget common sense and risk another kiss. Instead, he set her back on her feet. "Miss me?"

Her rhinestones gleamed. "You wish!"

Relieved when she retreated into silence, he unwrapped the safety line from around her arm. She was a distraction he didn't need. His lack of focus around her might get them both killed.

Fred watched the re-tethering process like a magician's apprentice learning a new trick. The corner of Hector's mouth twitched. It was a good thing dogs didn't have thumbs.

When he'd finished tying the end of the tether to his own wrist, he tucked her hand into the crook of his arm. Energy prickled his skin through his sleeve. He ignored it. "Ready?"

She nodded. "Where are we going?"

"I hid an emergency cache of survival gear further up the mountain. Food, water filtration gear, a weapon and a satellite phone to call for help, among other things."

She cocked an eyebrow. "Expecting trouble, were you?"

"It's always good to be prepared."

They set off across the mouth of the creek. Fred stuck close to Meli. The bite of icy water made Hector hiss. He noticed Meli biting her lip, but she didn't complain

They continued along the edge of the river. At least the water was a few degrees warmer than the fresh snow melt in the creek. Keeping Meli and Fred between himself and the shingle, Hector set a fast pace. Movement would help keep them warm. Besides, Mendoza's helo might return at any time. They needed to get away from the river and into the cover of the forest.

A dozen minutes later, they reached Crook's Creek. The narrow, boulder-strewn stream tumbled down a steep, forested hillside. A long climb would bring them to the home stretch.

Meli stumbled. He caught her arm and righted her. Her freckles stood out against pale skin and her lips had lost their color. Exhaustion seemed to ooze from her pores.

"You okay?" he said. *Stupid question.*

Her smile was a shadow of its former self. "Wonderful. Thanks for asking."

She gestured at the water and grimaced. "How long until we can walk on dry land?"

"Soon." The sunlight dimmed. He glanced up at thunderheads building overhead and frowned. In these mountains, June electrical storms were rare. Lightning was particularly dangerous at high elevations.

On the other hand, rain was moving water that would help shield their psychic energy from Killingsworth and hide their scent trails from the K-9s. Lightning was another psychic energy barrier. So was the earth surrounding the cave where they would shelter until the storm blew over. The Saints were smiling on them today.

When the first rain shower began, they clambered out of the stream and made their way up the hillside under the spreading branches of towering ancient evergreens. Before long, Mendoza's helicopter flew past low over the river below. A surge of adrenaline gave them a second wind.

By the time they reached a spot where the slope was more gradual the rain had tapered off and the adrenaline had worn thin. They needed to rest and rehydrate. He called a halt and Meli slumped at the base of a Douglas fir at least a yard wide.

He dug in her pack for a water bottle, then pressed the container into her limp hand. "Drink."

Her rhinestones flickered in the gray light. "What about you?"

"Got my own."

She gulped half the water from her bottle and gave the rest to Fred. Exhaustion colored her every movement, but she dredged up the energy to comfort her Guide with an ear scratch.

Meli was a nurturer. The last thing she needed was to be an FBI agent. Once he explained how unsuitable her personality was, Doc would understand. He'd find her a safe haven.

Hector held onto that thought as they set out on the final stretch of their journey.

When Meli nearly broke her toe on a small boulder Hector should have helped her to avoid, she reminded herself he was tired and injured and running on fumes. When a big stick rolled beneath her foot, he jerked her arm to keep her upright and pain shot through her elbow.

Meli ground her teeth in frustration. She was tired and injured, too. She was tired of getting hurt. She was tired, period. "How long until sundown?"

"Not long," he said vaguely.

"We'd better make camp soon," she said. "The temperature will fall after dark." It was already growing cooler.

"I hid my emergency cache in a little cave. We're getting close. As soon as we get there, I'll call for help on my satellite phone. We won't have to spend the night on the mountain."

Meli's chest constricted. What was the matter with her? Being rescued was a good thing—hot baths, hot meals. Best of all, no more running for their lives from Mexican drug lords.

No more Hector Protector. She shook her head to dislodge the silly thought. She and Freddy would be safe. They even had money in the bank. Mendoza had paid half her fee in advance.

Freddy woofed and trotted toward water whispering over stones to their right. Needing distance between herself and Hector, Meli let go of his arm and followed her Guide. "Let's fill the water bottles."

A big hand snagged her arm from behind. "We're practically to the cache. Hold on for a few minutes until after I make the call. This water may be home to some nasty parasites. I have a filtration device in my cache."

A familiar ache filled Meli's soul. Hector couldn't wait to get rid of them. She jerked her arm from his grasp. "*You* hold on. Freddy's thirsty. He's been drinking stream water all along.

Ahead of her, Freddy began to lap water from the little stream.

"Fine." Hector released her.

Her cheeks grew warm. Why was she was acting bitchy?

To make amends, she decided to check his head wound. After all they'd been through, the improvised dressing must be filthy. She shrugged out of the pack and located Freddy's damp towel. Although the microfiber smelled of dog and baby powder, she felt no rough patches that would indicate caked dirt. Squatting by the stream, she soaked the towel in ice-cold water.

Freddy walked over and nosed her elbow. She wrung out the towel.

Clothes rustled as Hector moved toward them. "*Now* what are you up to?"

Her hands clenched the towel. He treated her like a child. If not for her, he'd still be strapped to a chair in Mendoza's basement. Holding in her anger, she wadded the wet cloth into a ball, raised her pitching arm and pegged him with the soggy missile.

He yelped. "What was that for?"

She shoved to her feet and offered him a smug smile. "I was going to clean the cut on your head for you, but do it yourself. Or not, if you want an infection."

His voice dropped into a dangerous register. "I don't need another mother. I can take care of myself."

Crossing her arms over her chest, she sneered. "Obviously not. *I* saved you from Mendoza's torture chamber. *I* fed you, I bandaged you, *I*—"

Thunder boomed directly overhead.

Meli shot mindlessly into Hector's arms. They encircled her as if she belonged in them. He smelled like river water and earth and man sweat and safety. She trembled against his chest and listened to the loud rumble roll away.

"You never cease to surprise me," he said, sounding bemused.

What the heck just happened? Five seconds ago she'd been ready to kick him for reasons she didn't understand. Now...

"Where'd you learn to aim like that?" Hector said.

She swallowed. "I was the star pitcher on our beep ball team at the School for the Blind. If I can hear it, I can hit it."

He released her but held onto her hand. "My cache is in a cave on the other side of the ridge, part of a lava cast forest. We'll be safe and dry inside."

Thankful he was willing to forgo their silly argument, she nodded. "I remember lava casts from when I was a kid. Papa took me to Mount Saint Helens."

"I won't make you walk that far," he said. "Two hundred yards, tops."

She smiled at his lame joke. "Point me in the right direction."

Thunder grumbled nearby like a wounded giant. She winced and Freddy whined. They both hated electrical storms. Hector tucked her hand in the crook of his arm. Her nerves steadied. They trudged up the slope to the top of the ridge and paused.

"We have to be even more careful now," Hector told her between labored breaths. "The downward slope is steep, uneven and treacherous. My cache is in a cave at the bottom."

The wind picked up as they descended. Strands of hair stung her face like tiny whips. At least her glasses protected her eyes. Freddy brushed past her legs. She and Hector half-slid down the hillside from giant tree to giant tree.

A crack of thunder had Meli clinging to Hector's arm with both hands. He shepherded them onward against the rising wind. At last the slope leveled off into a hard, relatively flat surface underfoot. Remnants of a lava flow?

Ahead of them, Freddy began to bark his head off. Hector halted, radiating tension. It took her a second to control her energetic response to her Guide's alarm. She called Freddy to her side, but he ignored her and continued to bark and snarl ferociously.

Hector urged her forward with his hand at her back. He yelled over the wind and Freddy's frantic barking. "C'mon. At this altitude we're sitting ducks for the lightning."

Meli dug in her heels. Something was wrong and Hector was trying to hide it from her. He was treating her like a child again.

"Tell me what's happening!" she yelled. "Storms scare Freddy. They don't make him mad."

"We can talk in the cave," Hector countered.

"No! Tell me now," Meli said, wincing at her own petulant tone.

He grabbed her arm. "Fred found my satellite phone. It's been compromised. Now move."

She went with him, trying to make sense of what he'd said. "Compromised? What's that supposed to mean?"

"Smashed. Pounded. Crushed."

If she hadn't already been covered in gooseflesh, the hair would have risen on the backs of her arms. "What do you mean, crushed?"

"A bear destroyed my cache."

8

MELI'S FINGERNAILS DUG into Hector's arm as though she pictured a hulking brute lumbering toward them with teeth as big as icicles and claws like grappling hooks. Her energy spurt lifted every hair on his body and raised his temperature a couple degrees.

He had to calm her down or the rain's disruptive force wouldn't be enough to hide her energy from Killingsworth. Patting her hand on his arm to get her attention, he shouted against the wind. "Take it easy. By the looks of things, it happened weeks ago. Fred's reacting to the bear's scent on what's left of my satellite phone."

Maybe the word *weeks* was an exaggeration, but the animal was long gone. To be safe, he'd dowse for the bear's exact location as soon as he had a moment to himself.

Drawing a shaky breath, she nodded. The wind whipped strands of coppery hair across her pale face. Her energy spurt pulled back.

Thunder rumbled. Fred whimpered. Hector glanced up at roiling gray clouds and caught an ice-cold raindrop in the eye. He cursed in Spanish and wiped his eye. Squinting downhill, he spied a shadow at the bottom of an ancient rockslide, the entrance to the cavity where he'd stashed his cache.

"I can see the cave from here." He pulled Meli forward.

Halfway down the hill he spotted a dark rectangular object about the size of a candy bar on the ground. One of his spare ammo magazines? Squinting against the wind, he veered slightly off-course to take a closer look. He hadn't stored his Glock and ammo in the bear-proof container—only scented items like food and first-aid supplies. He'd wanted the weapon readily available since there would be bad guys on his tail if he accessed his emergency cache.

Like now. Who knew bears were interested in things like guns and satellite phones? He bent over to scoop up the magazine and gasped when pain lanced his side.

Meli's grip on his arm tightened. "What is it?" Meli shouted over the wind. "What's the matter?"

"Forgot about my ribs." He schooled himself to ignore the pain. He had to keep Meli calm. "Found some ammo the beastie dropped." He shoved the magazine into his pocket.

"I hope he left your gun in one piece. Papa was a park ranger. He always said bears are curious. Curious and destructive."

A smattering of raindrops pelted them, saving him from having to reply. When they reached the scattered rubble surrounding the cave entrance, he halted. "I'm going to take a look inside before we hole up in here."

Meli nodded and called Fred, who was still fussing over the chewed-up satellite phone. Thunder rumbled closer. The dog shook himself and then slunk to her side.

Favoring his injured ribs, Hector squatted to peer into the small cavern. Stringy roots dangled in places from the low ceiling. He crawled inside and checked every corner in hopes of finding something the bear left behind. Disappointment soured his empty stomach.

At least the small cavern offered them shelter, however cramped. The roughly-rectangular space was twice as wide as it was deep. They'd have enough room to squeeze in side-by-side lying parallel to the front and back walls. A two-foot-diameter lava tube opening yawned darkly in the back left corner. He'd stashed his cache at the far end of the tube as a precaution before burying the outer entrance under a pile of rocks and debris.

He shook his head. He'd thought any bear would be too big to fit in the lava tube, so his survival gear would be safe. He doubted the bear would have left anything behind.

A crack of lightning sent the dog into the cave. He bounded over Hector's outstretched legs and stopped outside the lava tube. The wind howled like a wild creature. Fred growled.

Hector crawled back outside. "Cave's empty," he told Meli. "You'll have to crawl to get inside."

She grabbed Hector's shoulder to steady herself and dropped to her knees. His skin heated through his shirt. She was exhausted and no doubt having a hard time containing her energy. She shrugged out of her pack.

"Watch your head. The ceiling's low," he said.

She explored the opening with her hands, ducked her head and scooted inside.

He shoved the pack after her. His ribs protested. "I'll be back in a few minutes."

Her pale face appeared in the shadows. Her rhinestones glinted. "Where are you going?" He caught the edge of panic in her voice.

He hated to leave her alone during the storm but he had no other option. "I need rocks to camouflage the entrance. They'll keep out the weather, too. I'll only be a few minutes."

Lips pressed together in a thin line, she nodded and disappeared into the darkness. She'd be okay. He'd learned she was much tougher than she looked.

Ignoring his aching body and the cold wind, he

gathered stones and small boulders the bear had scattered and piled them on either side of the opening. By the time he was done rain fell in icy, wind-whipped sheets. Shirt plastered to his back, he dropped to all fours and backed inside.

A glance over his shoulder revealed a shadowy Fred and Meli on his left in front of the black circle of the lava tube opening. "You okay?"

"We're fine," she said. "What about you?"

"I'll live. It's only water." Really, really cold water.

From inside the cave, Hector pulled his improvised building materials over to block the entrance. He worked as quickly as his injured ribs allowed. He noticed a series of long, deep scratches gouged into the ancient lava flow around the cave entrance. Shaking rainwater out of his eyes, he peered more closely at the deep grooves. Claw marks. Luckily, Washington's few grizzlies lived far north on the Canadian border. He frowned at the size of the grooves. This black bear must be almost as big as a grizzly. The beastie's unusual size explained his long reach.

Hector got back to work. By the time he had run out of rocks his ribs hurt with every breath. He eased off tortured knees onto his ass and leaned against the side wall. Rain-laden wind gusted through the remaining six-inch gap in the wall.

He caught the spark of Meli's rhinestones in the shadows. "Maybe this will plug the opening." She crawled over and pressed quilted fabric into his hand. "I found this in the lava tube."

She must have explored while he worked—by touch. His fingers fisted in the blanket-like material. He'd expected her to have the good sense to leave that job for him. Carefully working the remnant of his sleeping bag into the gap at the top of the wall, he forced his voice into what he thought was a reasonable tone. "Next time let me do the exploring."

"Yes, Master," she drawled. "Forgive me, Master."

He gritted his teeth and continued to work. He didn't want another argument. But worrying about her taking unnecessary risks would drive him crazy. "You could have been bitten by something hiding back there."

When she didn't immediately respond, he allowed himself to hope she realized she'd put herself in unnecessary danger. He finished working the section of sleeping bag into the space at the top of the wall he'd built, leaving a small opening to serve as a ventilation hole.

Being careful not to kick his companions, he rolled off his bruised knees and angled his long frame so he could lean back against the cool, lumpy cave wall. Meli heaved a long-suffering sigh. He braced himself for her anger.

But when she spoke, she spoke gently, reasonably. "Freddy would have warned me, Hector. He wouldn't let me get near a wild animal."

The dog's tags jingled in response to the sound of

his name.

Dammit, she had a point. Fred was trained to protect her. Besides, any dog worth his biscuits would have chased wild critters away as soon as he got inside the cave. He plowed a hand through his wet, tangled hair. She was a smart woman. He had to trust her to think things through. "I hadn't thought of that."

After a moment, she said, "You'll learn."

He smiled in the near-dark. Thank God Meli was willing to end the argument and move on. Lori would have wanted to rehash things and drive him crazy over it.

Meli crawled over to sit beside him. Fred settled on her other side by the back wall. Despite Hector's fatigue, the warm press of Meli's shoulder and curve of her hip against him triggered a rush of awareness. In these close quarters he sensed her every movement as well as every spurt of her psychic energy. When thunder crashed, she jolted. Energy snapped through his shoulder and across his back like a fiery whip.

He and Fred both yelped.

She jerked. "Oh God, I'm so sorry!" She pulled her knees to her breasts to make herself small.

Needing to reassure her, he slipped his arm around her stiff, trembling shoulders. "Fred and I are fine. You're safe. Relax. Thunderstorms are rare in this area except for the occasional fall storm. Who knows how long it will be before we get another chance to rest?"

After a moment, she nodded her head and softened

against him.

His gut was telling him this storm was not entirely natural. He'd never heard of a Talent who could influence the weather, but that didn't mean one didn't exist. He wondered if Meli sensed the strange vibe that had been irritating his dowsing sense for the last hour. Asking her would set off a barrage of questions he was not prepared to answer. Explanations were Doc's job.

Thunder rolled through the rocks. She stiffened again.

He strategized aloud to distract her. "We have to get to a landline phone. Even if we had a cell phone, there's no signal up here."

"You can't fix the satellite phone?"

"No. We'll have to go east to Puma or west to the ranger station." He didn't remind her both the ranger station and the village were miles from their current location. Or that Killingsworth would guess they'd head for a landline. Hector's satellite phone had been their ace in the hole.

Light flickered through the small opening he'd left in the wall for ventilation. Thunder boomed and crashed like an airplane hitting the mountain. Meli cried out and energy rolled around within his torso like ball lightning. His lungs hesitated, but his heart pumped on, unperturbed. After a few seconds the force escaped down his arm draped across her shoulders and sparked from his fingers into the air.

Fred grumbled.

She tried to shrug off his arm. "Are you okay?"

He held onto her. "I'm fine."

The second time she zapped him hadn't hurt as much as the first. Either she was calmer, or the way he was holding her had mitigated the effects of her energy spurt.

"We'll head west," he said after thinking over their options. "The ranger station is closer than Puma."

She was quiet for so long he thought she had fallen asleep.

"Thank you for helping me and Freddy," she said out of the blue.

Fred lifted his head.

Hector squinted down at her in surprise. Her expression was lost in shadows. "Uh, you're welcome. Thank you for knocking out Killingsworth. I wouldn't have wished that job on a dog. No offense, Fred."

Fred laid his head on his paws with a grunt that could have meant anything.

Thunder peeled, sounding closer again. She flinched but only leaked a little energy.

A whiff of vanilla made him smile. "Have you ever heard of anyone getting struck by lightning in a cave?"

Sighing, she laid her head on his shoulder. "Point taken."

He couldn't see her face or hear much over the sounds of the storm, but the tension in her muscles gradually slipped away and her breathing grew slow and even.

The storm moved on. Thunder transmuted into low-pitched vibrations that buzzed through the earth and made his bones ache. Every bruise he'd suffered in the last twenty-four hours hurt anew. The hard ground leached the heat from his frame like a refrigerator.

Meli's knees fell sideways onto his legs. She stirred, clasped his shirt in one hand, and burrowed into his armpit. He tightened his hold on her and laid his cheek against her hair. For all her strength of character, she seemed so fragile and defenseless, so—

Warmth flowed through him from his cheek, their point of direct physical contact. Within seconds his entire face was no longer cold. His neck and shoulders were beginning to thaw.

Direct body-to-body contact must be able to break through Meli's shield when she slept. Normally a Talent's psychic shield protected them from spurting energy whenever they were unconscious. He hoped Killingsworth wouldn't sense skin-to-skin energy transfer.

Hector yawned as the warm energy flowed through him. His mind began to drift. *What would it be like to make love to a woman like Meli?*

Fred growled as if he could read Hector's thoughts.

"*Perdón*, Fred," he said softly. "Sorry."

The dog huffed and grumbled before dropping his head onto his paws.

Hector wet his lips with his tongue. Meli was beautiful and desirable, but she didn't have control over her potentially deadly abilities. He wasn't suicidal. She was completely off limits.

Fred started to snore like an old man.

Hector leaned his head back against the hard basalt wall and closed his eyes. His dangerous thoughts about Meli returned. He tried to distract himself by thinking about how to make the place more comfortable. The three of them would have to lie together again tonight to share body heat. He'd gather pine boughs for a mattress. Having Meli snuggled up against him would make up for a lot of discomfort.

The muted sounds of the tempest receded. A puff of rain-soaked breeze stirred the air and he scented wet dog, baby powder and vanilla. His lips twitched. The woman was full of contradictions. First, there was her virginal performance at the wedding, followed by a kiss so hot it almost fried his brain. She'd abandoned him in the gazebo, but later attacked Killingsworth and saved his ass in the torture chamber. She'd been ready to push him off the cliff after he'd tossed Fred into the river, but had panicked when she'd thought he had drowned.

Why did she share renewing energy with him whenever they touched? As far as she knew, he was a drug lord's bodyguard. Yet she tried to take care of him, whether he liked it or not. Lucky for him she trusted him when common sense said she shouldn't.

He pressed a secret kiss to the top of her head. His lips tingled. All day long, she'd been a trooper. Not that she hadn't argued with him a few times. Following orders wasn't one of her strong suits.

Not one of mine, either.

Closing his eyes, he bolstered his shields and indulged in dangerous piss-off-Fred fantasies about Meli until he drifted into a dream. A very *good* dream.

Sometime later, Meli snuggled closer to a warm, delicious male body. The muscled arm that encircled her felt like it could stave off an army. She didn't want to wake up from a dream this good, but the cold seeping into her bottom from a hard, ridged surface made sinking back into sleep difficult. Burrowing closer, she inhaled her dream man's woodsy, funky scent.

River water and sweat. She wrinkled her nose. Memory pushed her fully awake.

When she tried to sit up straight, Hector's arm tightened around her. "Coupla' more minutes…"

His exhausted mumble tugged at her conscience. A few more minutes on the cold stone floor wouldn't kill her. She wiggled into a less-cramped position and relaxed into his one-armed embrace with her head against his chest. His firm, well-muscled chest.

She sighed. If only he weren't a drug lord's minion. If only she weren't a powder keg waiting to be lit. If only her butt didn't ache from sitting too long on the floor of a *mierdoso* cave.

Freddy wriggled closer and warmed her like a furry heating pad. Soon he made soft whuffling noises deep in his throat that told her he was dreaming.

She drifted back to the soft edge of dreamland counting the steady beats of Hector's heart.

Freddy's whine snatched her back with a start. His whuffles resumed, telling her he was still asleep, but now she was fully awake.

They had things to do before nightfall. The temperature would drop to near freezing at this altitude. They needed a fire and enough wood to last the night.

Yawning, she reached up to pat Hector's jaw. Day-old stubble sandpapered the sensitive flesh of her palm. Awareness shot straight to her core. Her body tightened.

Quick as lightning, his hand clamped around her wrist like an iron bracelet two sizes too small. She gasped. "Hector! Wake up! It's me, Meli."

After a couple of ragged breaths, he released her. "Sorry. You startled me."

She rubbed her bruised wrist. "I'd say that makes us even."

Freddy nuzzled her elbow, so she leaned back against Hector and turned to scratch behind the dog's ears. The faint, fusty odor of his fur made her frown. "I think poor Freddy's still a little damp."

Her Guide let out an exaggerated moan and nudged her with his nose.

With a sigh, Hector dropped his arm from her shoulders and stroked Freddy's head. "I am truly sorry I had to toss you in the river, Fred," he said. "You're a trooper."

Hector's exhalations ruffled curls that had escaped her elastic band, making her scalp tingle. She swallowed. "I'd say you're forgiven."

The *slurp, slurp* of Freddy's tongue licking his hand confirmed her assessment. Hector chuckled. "No brownnosing, Fred."

Without the weight and warmth of Hector's arm on her shoulders, Meli shivered. She longed to reach over and pull him close, to feel safe again. Instead she hugged her Guide.

"Storm's over," Hector said. "Time to go out and locate my weapon."

"Good idea. I don't suppose you packed any bear spray?"

"Nope." A soggy plop on the ground outside turned up the volume on the sounds of bird calls and dripping trees. He must have shoved the piece of wet sleeping bag out. Stones bumped and rolled as he cleared the entrance.

What should be their next priority?

"We need a fire," she said. She considered the best way to gather standing deadwood, still attached to a tree or bush. Anything lying on the ground or in the open would be too wet to burn.

Hector grunted and a rock clunked to the ground.

"Sorry, I need to locate my gun before nightfall."

She stiffened. "I didn't say *you* had to build the fire. I'll do it while you see what you can salvage. I can strap sticks for kindling to Freddy with my bra."

Silence reigned for a moment. Why did the idea of a bra as a survival tool always give men pause?

He cleared his throat. "Someone may spot a fire. Besides, all the wood's wet. We might have to do without."

In other words, leave this job to the sighted guy— even if he's too exhausted to do it and also somewhat lacking in the area of woodland skills. Her hands fisted. When would he stop underestimating her? She pressed her lips together to avoid saying something she'd regret.

Freddy wriggled out of her grasp, tags clinking.

"Stay, Fred," Hector said.

The click of Freddy's nails on stone receded. She tried not to smile. He'd ignored Hector and exited the cave. Her Guide knew what he was doing. He didn't have to take orders from a stranger.

"I thought you said that dog was smart." Hector sounded exasperated. "I told him to stay."

She snickered. "He's smart enough to know you're not the boss of him. And to pee outside. He's old. He can't hold it like he used to."

Hector sighed. "Wait here while I search for my weapon. No point in you getting soaked again."

In other words, you'll only get in the way, Blind Girl.

Setting her jaw, she listened to him crawl outside. Then she followed him on her hands and knees. Standing up was a relief in spite of the fat drop of cold water that landed on her head.

"You're not the boss of me, either!" she called, unsure of his location. "I'm building a fire. If Freddy doesn't dry out soon, he'll catch pneumonia. And you're going to get wet searching the bushes for supplies. Besides, if you think I'm going to sleep in these damp clothes, you are out of your freakin' mind!"

Birds twittered. Water dripped. Freddy's tags jingled toward her.

"I didn't say you had to keep your clothes on," Hector said from behind her. He tweaked her ponytail.

She managed not to scream or jump out of her skin. Determined to ignore his teasing, she turned around. "What about Freddy?"

He snorted. "If he stays on your side of the cave, he can go commando, too."

She folded her arms across her breasts. "Asshole."

A blush warmed her face, just as he'd intended. She couldn't believe he'd reduced her to name calling. She waited for his next jab.

"Tell you what; I'll build you a fire—*after* I find my weapon—*if* I can still walk. Freddy gets the sweet spot closest to the fire." His voice dropped into a sexy drawl that raised goosebumps on the backs of her arms. "You and I have other options for staying warm."

"In your dreams." She'd been having similar dreams

only a few minutes ago. She licked her lips. The air grew heavy between them.

Freddy's frenzied barking jolted her. Strong hands grabbed her and shoved her toward the cave. "Get inside," Hector said, his voice low.

Not likely. She spun around and grabbed for Hector, hooking her fingers into the back of his waistband. She wasn't going to run and hide like a cornered rat while Hector and Freddy ran into possible danger. Although Freddy sounded more excited than scared.

"Dammit Meli," he growled. But he didn't remove her hands.

"I'm going with you. Hand me a rock."

He must have heard the determination in her words because he bent over with a grunt and then shoved a heavy, softball-sized chunk of smooth stone into her free hand. "Stay behind me. If I miss my shot, I'll duck so you can get one in. Don't throw until you feel me duck."

She hefted the stone to test its weight. It would do. "Duck fast!"

If the bear had returned, they might be able to scare it off. Black bears were often skittish. But damn, they were big. As a child, she'd watched a three-hundred-pound, six-foot tall bear break a huge tree branch to get to a food-laden backpack. A camper had tied the pack up at a height he'd mistakenly deemed safe. After that incident bears had haunted her nightmares for weeks.

With her in tow Hector moved toward Freddy, whose barks had deflated into occasional growls and embarrassed-sounding whines the way they did when he'd overreacted. She hung onto her primitive weapon, just in case. Freddy shuffled toward them.

It occurred to her Hector hadn't argued with her decision to back him up. As a vote of confidence, it wasn't much, but at least he'd sort of acknowledged her pitching skill.

Without warning, Hector halted. She plowed into his unyielding backside and lost her grip on the stone. To keep from falling she threw her arms around him. Awareness of her body plastered to the length of him ignited an unexpected wildfire of desire. She fought for control of her energy.

His rock clunked to the ground. He cleared his throat. "False alarm. Just a piece of canvas flapping in the wind."

Reluctant to let go of him, she worried her bottom lip. Had he sensed her reaction?

Freddy growled his disapproval and wedged his furry form between their legs.

"Freddy, no!" At her angry tone, his growl dissolved into an uncertain whine that twisted her heart into a knot. What was the matter with her?

She let go of Hector and crouched to give her Guide a reassuring hug. Tears stung her eyelids. She blinked them back. Freddy got upset when she cried.

"I'm sorry, Freddy. I'm so sorry." Her fingers found

his ears and she scratched his favorite spot behind them. "Who's a good boy? Who?" She scratched his other favorite spot on his back by his tail. "Freddy's my boy. Yes, you are."

Freddy's tail gave a tentative swish. He would forgive her, but she couldn't risk anyone coming between her and Freddy. Definitely not a drug lord's bodyguard with secrets.

"You and Fred wait by the cave while I search for my weapon." Was that frustration she heard in Hector's voice? Or something else? "Keep those rocks handy."

She nodded, thankful for some space. It was time to give herself a dose of tough love.

Hector looked back ten yards to where Meli slumped with her arms around a droopy Fred. She was beating herself up over snapping at Fred, and damned if Fred didn't look like he was blaming himself for what had happened.

The desire to go back and put his arms around her, to bolster her spirits, was strong. But he had a job to do, vows to fulfill. He couldn't let this woman distract him. He'd already put his mission on hold to get her to safety. He couldn't afford to let himself have feelings for her.

He circled a big evergreen. The sun peeked out from behind the cloud cover above the mountaintops to the west. Dusk would fall quickly in these mountains.

After doing a three-sixty scan of the area beyond the tree, he lowered himself onto a damp log. His ribs ached and he wasn't sure he'd have the strength to get back up after a dowsing session. But what choice did he have?

Cold moisture leached through his slacks. He pulled his St. Jude's Medal out of his tee-shirt, cupped the amulet in his hands and closed his eyes. Clearing his mind, he concentrated on his breath. When he'd relaxed enough to focus his energy through the golden disk, he closed his hands around the talisman and dowsed for bear.

By the time he'd located the only beastie within five miles, his head was pounding. The fact the brute was down near Mendoza's compound sent a zing of satisfaction through him. With luck, one of the bad guys would have a run-in with Brother Bear.

Hector pulled his energy back and mulled over his options for locating searchers. Although his shields should be strong enough to keep his location secret, he couldn't risk touching Killingsworth directly with his psychic energy. That eliminated dowsing for people. But the Hound would have sent for Mendoza's K-9 tracker teams to spearhead a ground search. He'd target the canines.

After locating Fred a few yards away and Killingsworth's pets inside Mendoza's compound, Hector counted six additional canines inside the five-mile radius he'd set for this dowsing session. He found two animals at two different spots along the far bank of the river. He'd bet they were trackers.

Of the four dogs on this side of the water, two remained at lower elevations near Crook's Creek. He located one near the road to Puma and the last a hundred yards from the ranger station to the west. Pulling back his energy, he decided to assume they were all trackers until he dowsed again after dark. Trackers would return to the compound to feed and rest their animals. Any canines remaining in the wilderness would most likely be wild.

His stomach growled. More dowsing before eating and resting might push him past the limits of his strength, but he felt naked without a loaded gun. He didn't relish the thought of facing either Killingsworth or the bear unarmed.

9

HECTOR INHALED DEEPLY a couple times to boost his blood oxygen level. He located his weapon and more ammo near the tree where Fred had gotten spooked. His bear safe full of food was lodged among some rocks in the nearby stream.

Heaving a weary sigh, he opened his eyes and tucked his Talisman into his shirtfront. His fingers shook. If he didn't eat something soon, he'd pass out. At least he didn't have to walk far. Maybe Meli had more granola bars squirrelled away. If not, a handful of Fred's kibble should get him to the stream and some real food.

A few minutes later, he'd eaten a couple handfuls of Meli's trail mix and drunk his last remaining half a bottle of water. His shakes began to subside. He licked

salt off his fingers. Luckily he'd put his Lifestraw®
water filter bottle in the bear safe.

Meli sat cross-legged on the ancient lava flow. Her
rhinestones glittered in the sunshine. Fred had
stretched out at her feet on the sun-warmed stone, his
longish golden leg feathers curling as they dried.

"Feeling better?" Meli said.

"Much, thanks. I'm prone to low blood sugar when I
overdo it on an empty stomach." It was the truth, more
or less. The only time his blood sugar plummeted was
when he had dowsed too much on an empty stomach

She tilted her head to the side. "Did you have any
luck in your search?"

"A credit card that's only slightly bent, a penlight
that works and a cooking pot I think I can repair. I'm
going to search down by the stream now."

She bent her knees and hugged them to her chest.
"We'll wait here for you. Maybe Freddy will dry out. I
don't want him to get a skin infection."

Her nose and cheeks were pink. "Better move back
into the shade. You're getting sunburned." He turned to
leave.

"Wait!"

"Now what?" he snapped. He winced. She didn't
deserve that. "Sorry. We're running out of daylight."

Her rhinestones sparked as she emptied her pack's
main compartment onto the ground. After zipping up,
she offered him the bag. "This will leave your hands
free."

His face heated. All she'd wanted was to help. "Thank you."

She handed him the bag with a smile that hinted she knew what he'd been thinking, but she didn't say a word. Lori would have reamed him a new asshole.

He hoisted the light pack onto one shoulder and headed toward the big evergreen in search of his gun and ammo. Having the pack would help a lot. When he glanced back, Meli had tilted her head to one side as if she were listening to his receding footsteps—or for the sound of approaching danger. One hand rested on Fred's back. The dog lifted his muzzle, scenting the breeze.

Shaking his head, Hector moved on. When they'd begun this journey, he'd been certain the two would be nothing but a burden. But they'd already surprised him more than once. Knowing they had his back felt good.

Remembering the way he'd snapped at Meli, he set his jaw. He wouldn't let that happen again. Meli and Fred deserved his respect. It was time he learned to work well with others.

After Hector returned with the gun and the scuffed and battered bear safe, he and Meli feasted on beef jerky and dried fruit. Then he climbed the slope to collect the driest green pine boughs he could find. They could use them to pad and insulate the floor of their shelter.

Exercise kept him warm despite the fact the temperature had dropped a good ten degrees in the half hour since the sun went behind the mountain. Aching in places he hadn't known he had places, he hooked the ends of an elastic cord around the green pine boughs he'd harvested.

Finding the tie-down and the hiking boots from his cache had been a true Godsend. His soggy running shoes could cause trench foot. He'd been ecstatic to exchange them for durable, breathable, waterproof, *dry* survival boots, even ones that had been clawed and gnawed by a bear.

He wished he had boots for Meli. And a pair of work gloves for himself. Suppressing a groan, he hoisted his load of evergreen branches onto his back. His scraped-up palms joined his ribs in protest as he made his way downhill. It was hard to find even footing in the rough, deeply-shadowed terrain. With each step, parts of him throbbed, ached or threatened to give out. And he was hungry again.

He grimaced. *And yet, she wants a fire.*

He paused to catch his breath. If he'd been alone, he might have done without. But to be fair, Meli and Fred were smaller and would become hypothermic quicker than a large, well-muscled man. Her request was not unreasonable. He'd have to gather standing deadwood after he delivered this load of pine boughs.

An owl hooted in the darkening forest. He resumed his downhill trudge. A line of bad poetry he'd written in college whispered through his head. *I made a maid yon leafy bed 'neath a faery tree, and there she let me pluck her flower and put a spell on me.*

He snorted. Best not to go there, even in his thoughts. Melisenda was many things, but a casual hookup would never be one of them. And anything more was out of the question. His subconscious mind was a reckless fool.

Halfway back to camp, a series of pops and snaps froze him in his tracks. A dog yipped.

Fred? Or one of Killingsworth's K-9s?

Carefully, he set the pine boughs on the ground so as not to make a sound. He pulled the Glock from his waistband at the small of his back. Not that he could hit a target in the semi-darkness.

A lungful of wood smoke sent him into a painful coughing fit. So much for stealth.

He dropped to the ground and crawled a few feet sideways, then wiped his streaming eyes on his sleeve. Lightning might have sparked a wildfire. He scrambled to his feet and tried to shout Meli's name, but what came out of his mouth sounded like a bullfrog with asthma.

Coughing up a lung, he returned his useless weapon to his waistband. He had to get to Meli. She'd never be able to outrun a forest fire she couldn't see.

Putting out a psychic feeler for a safe path through the woods, Hector alternated between a stumbling jog and a semi-controlled slide down the mountainside. He grazed a tree trunk that appeared out of nowhere and his ribs screamed, wrenched his ankle and pain shot up to his knee. He forced himself to go on.

Reaching the bottom of the slope in less than a minute, he flashed into the open, tripped over Fred and did an excruciatingly-painful belly flop onto unforgiving stone.

His lungs seized. His pulse pounded. Lights flickered in his peripheral vision. He blinked them away. Had he punctured a lung? Or only had the wind knocked out of him?

He forced himself to remain calm, told his chest muscles to relax. They didn't seem to be listening. Then small hands patted his back, warmed his neck. Energy crackled down his spine and rolled around in his chest. A straw-sized passage opened in his throat, allowing a sip of air to whistle into his lungs.

"Hector? Are you okay?" Meli shook his shoulders. Shards of pain speared his side like glass knives. His lungs stiffened and his head flopped like a puppet's. A warm, wet tongue licked his arm.

Meli's voice took on a strident note. "Hector! Can you hear me? Hector!" She shook him harder.

Fred whined and the shaking stopped.

Thank God! He needed a minute. His vision blurred. *And oxygen. Definitely oxygen.*

Meli struggled to push him over onto his back. He tumbled and cracked his head on unyielding stone. Sparks of light blossomed into stars and the pain in his head eclipsed the pain in his ribs. A reflexive gasp drew in a second sip of blessed air.

One small, strong hand on his forehead tipped his head back and the other tilted his chin up. The finger she used to sweep his mouth left a trail of salt on his tongue. She pinched his nostrils shut and lowered her face toward his.

A surge of adrenaline hit his bloodstream. Rescue breathing from Meli could easily kill him. He managed a torturous exhalation.

Her lips an inch from his, she froze, then released his nose. "Hector?"

He sucked in another whistling breath and forced it out.

Meli sat back on her heels. She yanked up his shirt and flattened her hands on his chest. Healing energy filled his lungs and spread outward. Pain receded and his vision cleared.

"Better?" she said, her voice shaking.

The straw in his throat had grown slightly larger. He managed a hoarse whisper. "Yeah."

Fred's square muzzle blocked his vision and the dog's tongue rasped his nose. After a couple more wheezing breaths, the vice around his lungs opened. He caught a whiff of wood smoke and remembered the fire.

The fire!

He swung his head to the left and then wished he'd moved more carefully. When things stopped spinning he focused on flames fluttering cheerfully inside a circle of rocks on the stone slab near the cave entrance.

I'll be damned. Somehow, she'd built a fire without his help. And she'd gathered a pile of deadwood to feed the flames.

The scent of savory meat and herbs made his stomach growl like a pack of coyotes. He grinned up at her. "What's for dinner?" he rasped.

Meli's fist connected with his shoulder in a punch that would leave one helluva bruise.

"What was that for?" He rubbed the spot with his knuckles.

Firelight lanced off the rhinestones in Meli's glasses. "Dinner? Are you crazy? You weren't breathing! I *know* you weren't breathing—"

She raised her fist to strike him again.

He captured her hand. "Got the wind knocked out of me. I'm okay." He paused for air. "I smelled smoke. Thought there was a wildfire. Ran and fell." He didn't mention the panic he'd experienced at the thought of her in danger.

The fight left her.

She tilted her head back as if gazing at the darkening blue of the sky. "I thought you were..." Biting her lower lip, she shook her head.

Hector's throat tightened. *Muerto.* She'd thought he was dead. Yet she hadn't hesitated, hadn't fallen apart—not until afterward. She'd jumped into the fray, the way she had when she'd thought he was drowning, and before that when Killingsworth's thugs beat him up in the gazebo.

Killingsworth. Hector's gut clenched. Meli's terror would have lit her energy like a homing beacon, something hard for the Hound to miss. Although the tons of stone and earth between them might have been enough to block his Talent.

She sniffed and wiped her nose on her shirtsleeve.

Hector swallowed. Mindful of the dark bruise where Killingsworth had hit and later pinched her, he reached up and cupped her damp cheek. He ignored the pulse of heat that climbed his arm. "Thank you for always having my back."

Heaving a wavering sigh, she nodded. "The stew's ready," she said. "Let's eat."

He struggled to sit up as she climbed to her feet. His ribs throbbed painfully but soon the intensity subsided into a dull ache. Meli's amateur energetic ministrations had worked wonders.

A couple minutes later Hector used a collapsible cup to dish stew into the two halves of his mess kit. He handed one to Meli, along with the only spoon. He'd eat with his knife.

They finished most of their meal in silence before he noticed Fred watching them intently. Drool darkened the stone in front of the dog. He set his not-quite-empty dish in front of Fred, who glanced at Meli for direction. "Tell Fred it's okay to eat the rest of my stew."

"But he's on a strict diet—" Apparently remembering they were running low on kibble, Meli relented. "Never mind. It's okay, Freddy. Eat."

The big dog gulped the stew and proceeded to lick the dish clean. Firelight glinted off the battered aluminum bowl Fred nudged toward Hector. The dog sat and stared at him with doggy eyebrows raised and a hopeful look in his eyes that tugged at Hector's heartstrings.

"Sorry, fella. *No mas.*"

"Not quite," Meli said. She set her dish and the cooled stewpot in front of Fred.

When Fred had finished licking them clean, Hector went to wash the dishes in the stream. He brought along the pack and empty water bottles to fill. Meli's four empty bottles would provide 'dirty' water for refilling his water filter bottle.

On returning he found Meli and Fred sitting by the fire. "I filled our empty bottles with water from the stream to refill the Lifestraw® whenever it goes dry."

She nodded. "I burned the dehydrated stew package and the used baby wipes. We need to put everything with a scent, like the baby wipes, into the bear-proof safe. You'll need to move the safe at least a hundred yards away from the cave. We can't take any chances with that bear."

He squelched the urge to tell her he knew all this. He needed to build up her confidence, not tear it down.

"Will do."

She transferred the package of wipes from the pack to the safe. "Where did you learn so much about wilderness survival?"

She stilled. Sadness flickered across her features. Fred lifted his head, watching her.

Hector winced. Had he offended her again? "I mean, you're a wedding singer." That didn't sound much better.

Her lips curved into a wistful smile. She pulled a small tube of toothpaste and a toothbrush out of the pack and dropped them into the bear safe. "You forget, my father was a park ranger. We did a lot of camping when I was young. After—After I lost my sight and my parents, I made it a point to learn what I needed to know to remain comfortable in nature. It was a matter of pride. Papa would have been so disappointed if I'd turned into a city girl."

The owl hooted in the distance. She tilted her head and waited until the sound faded. "Mama would never have let me give up the things I loved, either."

Her brows drew together above her flickering rhinestones. "I miss them so much. Uncle Deke made sure I finished my education, but he wasn't around much. He was in the army stationed overseas. He died a few years ago. Freddy's my only family now."

Her hand found Fred. She stroked the big dog, looking so forlorn Hector tried to console her.

"You know they would all be proud of you. Damned

proud."

She offered him an ashen smile. "I know."

Meli had dealt with loneliness and sorrow as great as his own, but it hadn't made her bitter. She hadn't given up, either. He reached for more sticks to feed the dying fire. The flames leapt higher.

Meli spoke softly. "Your fiancée really died, didn't she?"

"Yes." He turned the conversation back to Meli. "What happened to your family?"

A shadow crossed her face. "My parents—someone sideswiped us. Our car went off a mountain highway. I was the sole survivor at sixteen."

His heart stumbled. Orphaned at sixteen. He hadn't been much older when his dad died. He'd have been lost without the love and support of his mother and sisters. "I'm sorry."

Meli continued to stroke Fred. "The car ended up nose-down in the river. I managed to get out through a broken window, but the water swept me away. I couldn't get to my parents, couldn't help them. The current was too strong. A truck driver who'd witnessed the accident pulled me out of the river. He saved my life."

Hector went cold. Meli had almost died.

Firelight flickered across her somber features. "When I was swept away, my forehead bashed into a boulder. The force of the blow severed my optic nerve."

She lifted a shoulder and returned to sorting through her pack. "What can you do? Life goes on."

Meli had found a way to make peace with the tragic events in her life. Talking to her, his thoughts had touched on Lori's death without a shitload of grief and guilt weighing him down.

He frowned. *Anger, grief and guilt keep me going.* What would he do without them?

Meli had finished packing the bear-proof safe with anything that might attract a beastie. Hector welcomed the opportunity to have a few minutes of alone time. "I'll stash the safe in the woods a good distance from the cave."

When he returned he added some firewood to their pile and plunked down beside Meli. Welcome heat embraced him. He was bone tired. She must be, too, but she hadn't been idle. She'd gathered a little more firewood as well. She'd also arranged her wet, no-longer-white running shoes and socks on the stones of the fire ring to dry.

Fred rose from his spot on Meli's far side and trotted around to greet Hector. He scratched the dog behind his ears. "You dry yet, boy?"

Fred flopped down, stretched out with his belly toward the fire and sighed in contentment. "I agree, Fred," Hector said. "This feels like paradise."

Meli remained uncharacteristically quiet. Red nail polish gleamed on her dainty outstretched toes. "What about you?" he asked her. "Are you dry?"

She stirred and yawned. "I'm good. Gotta turn my shoes before they melt or catch fire."

"I'll do it," he said. "You might burn your fingers."

"Hector Protector." The corners of her mouth tilted up. "Thanks."

Afterward, she let him put an arm around her shoulders and softened against him like she had in the cave. Like she trusted he'd keep her safe.

God willing, he would.

10

HECTOR AWOKE WITH a start, disoriented by an unsettling dream. He blinked at glowing coals, the remains of their campfire.

Meli lifted her head from his shoulder and yawned.

He interlaced the fingers of one hand with hers and held on while he tried to remember the dream.

"We'd better turn in," she said.

"Give me a minute."

She nodded. Her rhinestones glimmered.

The dream had reeked of Talent. He didn't want to forget any details.

He'd sat at Mom's kitchen table in Albuquerque and watched Lori light four blue candles on a kid's superhero birthday cake. He pretended to be happy, but his heart ached for Meli. She belonged here, but she had lost her way.

Lori's twin sister, Leah, sat at the table. So did the Talented older man he'd sensed when he'd dowsed in Mendoza's garden last night. The squeals and laughter of children echoed from the living room. Fred trotted in from the dining room, tail wagging. Doc and Drew Grayson trailed behind the dog. Everyone greeted Drew and his father.

A heavy knock rattled the back door, and his spirit lightened. Had Meli found her way to the party after all? But when Leah opened the door, Killingsworth stood on the back deck with a huge grizzly bear on a leash.

At that point, Hector had jerked awake.

That the imagery was important, he had no doubt. ¡Jesús! Where was a Diviner when you needed to discern the hidden meanings of such a dream?

He untangled his fingers from Meli's. "I'm awake now. I'll get your shoes and socks."

He climbed stiffly to his feet and retrieved them for her. "I'll take you and Fred to go pee. Then you two can get settled inside the cave."

The old dog raised his head to gaze at Meli.

She pulled on one sock. "What about you?" she said and picked up the other.

"Before I turn in I'll move the coals closer to the entrance. I'm going to arrange some boulders to reflect heat into the cave."

"Good idea." She stifled a yawn.

After Meli put on her shoes, he took her and Fred behind the big evergreen and stood guard. Afterward he watched them crawl into the cave. Twigs snapped as they settled onto the pine boughs.

Hector gathered small boulders and laid them in a half-circle, leaving room for the hot coals. Then he chose two long sticks and bound them together with his wingtip shoelaces to form a giant pair of tongs. Pouring water over the wooden tips increased their fire resistance. Gingerly he moved the coals piece by piece to a spot inside the reflective stone wall.

He limped back to the smoking broken bits of the original fire, unzipped his fly and pissed on the embers. They hissed and steamed and stank of ammonia. When the smoke cleared, nothing sparked or glowed. Satisfied, he walked back to the cave.

The heat given off by the glowing coals warmed his skin. Taking great care, he worked his way inside their shelter and half-fell onto his back on the springy and slightly damp pine-bough mattress. A branch cracked and Meli cried out softly as she rolled toward him. She flattened her palms on his chest and his arm went around her. Desire for the soft, vanilla-and-pine-scented woman rippled through his battered body.

She gave an exaggerated yawn and rolled back slightly. "I've never been so glad to go to sleep in all my life."

He grinned. Subtle, she was not. "Me too," he lied. She managed to keep her energy to herself, which was encouraging. And a little disappointing.

After a couple of minutes her hand crept up to massage his shoulder. "I'm sorry I hit you. I'm normally not a violent person."

The corners of his mouth twitched. In twenty-four hours, she'd stunned him with a kiss, jumped into a fistfight with Mendoza's thugs to save his ass and knocked out Mendoza's Hound—also to save his ass. But the punch to his shoulder bothered her? "You didn't hurt me."

She dropped her hand to rest over his heart. "Good night, Hector."

He swallowed a groan. "Good night, Meli."

Staring into the darkness, he listened for her respiration to slow. What would happen to Meli when the cavalry came? Until the Bureau captured Killingsworth, she'd be in danger, safe house or no safe house. Doc would do everything in his power to protect her, but would it be enough?

Meli awakened to the pre-dawn chirping of birds. Freddy snored softly behind her. Cocooned on her side between the dog and Hector's chest, she was mostly warm. She wiggled to get away from a stick poking her stomach. Hector's big hands pulled her hips closer to him, then slid around to caress the bare skin of her lower back.

Her mouth went dry. That was no stick.

A frisson of pleasure vibrated her core. Her breath hitched. She struggled to control the surge of energy that erupted inside her. Hector's fingertips traced her lower spine down to the waistband of her hip-hugging jeans.

She needed every scrap of self-control to hold her energy in check. She didn't want him to stop. More than anything, she wanted to touch him the way he was touching her. Her breasts flattened against his chest as she slid a palm around his waist under his shirt and her fingers found the strong column of his spine.

His fingertips slid under her waistband to stroke the cleft at the base of her backbone.

Meli gasped, struggling to control the honey-sweet energy that surged inside her. Exquisite pleasure pulsed between her thighs, eliciting a low moan. Energy sparked between them where they touched one another.

Hector stilled. After a moment, he yawned. "You awake?"

Meli managed a feeble nod.

Removing those long, seductive fingers from inside her clothing, he patted her butt through her jeans. "I could lie and say I'm sorry, but I'm not. My only excuse is, the man-parts want what the man-parts want when the man's asleep."

He could do that in his sleep?

She didn't know whether to be offended or impressed. The man had skills.

He brushed a curl off her cheek and kissed the tip of her nose. "You're not ready for this yet, Meli."

Her cheeks heated. She withdrew her hand from beneath his shirt.

When he rolled onto his back, she fisted hands that wanted to grab his shirtfront and pull him back. She ached to kiss him, to explore his body, to feel his hands and mouth all over her. But he was right. If he could elicit this kind of response from her with a touch, making love to her would probably get him killed.

Shivering at the lick of cold air on her skin, she sat up and forced a perky smile. "Now what?"

He remained silent for so long her smile faded. She heard him swallow. What was he thinking?

"Now we get up and get moving," he finally said. "There's a hot meal and a soft bed waiting for us at the end of this trek. Hold onto that thought. For now, there are granola bars in the bear safe."

Freddy's tags jingled.

"C'mon, Fred," Hector said. "We'd better rustle up some breakfast."

Meli's stomach growled. His hands and knees shuffled as he crawled outside. Freddy padded after, nails clicking on stone like the ticking of a watch. She sighed and crawled after them.

After responding to nature's call in the pre-dawn darkness, Hector and Fred retrieved the bear safe. Meli waited on a low rock ledge. She had poured Fred's portion of kibble into his collapsible blue plastic dish. The dog gobbled up his breakfast while Hector accompanied Meli to the far side of the evergreen.

Back at camp, he opened the bear safe and pulled out two granola bars. Meli poured half a bottle of water into Fred's empty bowl. The dog began to lap it up, pausing when an owl hooted nearby. Hector took a seat next to Meli and handed her a sweet, nutty treat.

He sighed and unwrapped his bar. What he really craved was protein.

"I'd trade ten of these for a plate of *huevos rancheros*," Meli said, mirroring his thoughts.

"Or a steak." He grinned and took another bite, feeling better than he had any right to feel. His injuries were healing at an accelerated pace, thanks to Meli's healing energy. Killingsworth believed she was a liability when she was in fact an asset. Every miscalculation on the hound's part could be used to their advantage.

Finishing his meager breakfast, he noted the sky had turned pale pink behind the mountain to the east. The K9s and their handlers would be leaving the compound. He had to find a way to dowse without drawing Meli's attention.

Meli rummaged in the pack, pulled out Fred's grooming tools and began to groom the dog. She hummed a show tune softly in time with the steady rhythm of the brush. Fred stood patiently with his eyes half closed.

Hector's memory supplied the lyrics to Rogers and Hammerstein's *Oh, What a Beautiful Morning*. The waltz tempo of the song reminded him of their slow dance and how right she'd felt in his arms. Just over a day had passed since Mendoza's wedding, but it seemed like so much longer.

He shook his head and pulled out his talisman. He hated to lie to her, but he had no choice. "Nature calls."

Meli smiled and continued to work on Fred.

Hector stood and moved a few yards away. He couldn't leave them unguarded. Closing his eyes, he moved into a meditative state and focused on the warm disc in his grasp. He dowsed for firearms and dogs instead of people. Killingsworth might be able to sense his dowsing energy if the man was nearby.

A close grouping of three dogs and six firearms part way up the mountainside from the compound registered on his dowsing radar. His heart began to beat faster. If the dogs' handlers were armed, there were six men following. If unarmed, there were nine men in the hunting party.

Was the bear still around? The last thing he and Meli needed was to run straight into the beastie. He dowsed for and found the bear less than a quarter of a mile above their camp climbing downhill. The animal was headed straight for them. His heart banged his ribs.

A small object hit him in the back. His eyes shot open and he spun around. Meli's rhinestones flashed in the morning light above her flushed cheeks. "Lying to me is just *rude*," she said, tossing another pebble at him for emphasis.

He blinked. Apparently she'd known exactly where he'd stopped. Which meant she knew he's lied about going to pee behind the big evergreen.

Fred gave him a reproachful look from his seat next to the reloaded pack. The mats and dust were gone from the dog's now-shiny coat.

"Sorry. Time to go," he said, hoping to distract her. "Killingsworth and company are closing in about a half a mile away. The bear is even closer."

Meli fisted her hands on her hips. Her rhinestones sparked. "How can you possibly know that? Have you been communicating with Killingsworth? Is this all some kind of crazy, sick cat-and-mouse game?"

Mierda. Doc would have his hide for that slip. He blew out a sigh, whether of frustration or guilt, he wasn't sure. "I need you to trust me for now. I have a freak side like you, a psychic Talent that I'll explain to you later. That's how I located the bad guys and the bear. If we don't get going, you'll end up Killingsworth's slave and there'll be nothing left of me but bear shit."

Meli blanched. Even her rhinestones seemed to pale. "When we get to a safe place, you're going to answer every one of my questions." She hoisted her pack onto her shoulder. Fred climbed to his feet like an old man.

Hector shifted his weight to his other foot. What she asked could get him fired, but they had to get going. He'd weasel his way out of it later. "Okay. Let's go!"

She raised her eyebrows above her dark glasses and walked toward him. "You'll answer the questions truthfully. If we're in this for the long haul, trust has to go both ways."

Meli was right. Distrust between them could get them both killed. Besides, he'd never get her into a safe house without convincing her he was telling the truth. Forgetting for a moment she couldn't see him, he raised his right hand. "I do solemnly swear."

Nodding, she latched onto his arm. "What's the plan?"

"Just follow my lead," he said. No sense telling her he'd have to brainstorm on the fly.

For once she didn't argue.

Fred grumbled under his breath.

Hector set a course westward toward the ranger station, setting a brutal pace to stay ahead of the bear. What were his options to handle the beastie?

A head shot was out. The bear's thick skull would deflect the slug. If he could get him to stand up on his hind paws, maybe he could get in a heart shot. But he'd never hunted. Where was the beast's heart located? Mid-chest, like a man? How high? He'd probably just piss him off and pinpoint their position to Killingsworth.

He glanced at Meli's pinched face. She was counting on him to have a reasonable plan. How could he use the bear's natural instincts against him?

A hound belled, sounding too close for comfort. Ahead of them, Fred stopped and half-turned, sniffing the air. A deep growl rumbled in the dog's chest. Meli's grip on his arm tightened. "Freddy, quiet."

Hector smiled. Fred didn't like having strange canines and humans on his tail. Neither would Brother Bear. All he had to do was rile the bear and get him to turn on the search party. While Killingsworth and company fought the grizzly, he and Meli and Fred would climb above the ruckus and double back to the cave.

Killingsworth would never expect them to backtrack. The move was too risky. And if Hector could trick the bear into attacking the search party without firing his weapon, Killingsworth wouldn't know he'd manipulated the animal to create a diversion. A hound belled, nearer. He grinned. My bear trumps your three dogs, *pendejo*.

"New plan," he whispered into Meli's ear. "We have to push harder." A stray curl tugged his whiskers as he pulled away. She shivered. It humbled him that she trusted him with her life on his word alone.

The appearance of a twenty-foot-high stone bluff jutting out of the steep side of the mountain above them sent a thrill of triumph through him. He eyed the rocky, forested hillside surrounding the protrusion with satisfaction. It was as he'd remembered it, the perfect spot for an ambush.

He called a halt for a quick drink of water at the base of the cliff. Thankfully, the morning was cool. Afterward he caught Meli's hand and led her toward the slope. "You up for a climb?"

She raised a quizzical eyebrow. "Anything but a swim. I'd like to stay dry for a while."

"I need a minute to figure things out." He stopped and pulled out his St. Jude's medal.

She pressed her lips together and nodded. He closed his eyes and dowsed for the bear. His gut clenched. The beastie was only five hundred yards behind them. Killingsworth had closed the gap between his party and the bear as well. They were cutting it close.

He inhaled and exhaled deeply, opened his eyes and tucked the talisman back inside his shirt. "We'll climb to the top of this bluff. The bear is between us and Killingsworth's men." Remembering her reaction to the bear sign at his cache, he continued to speak softly as he led her uphill. "We'll be safe up there. He won't be able to see us or reach us."

She stumbled after him with Fred on her heels. "You do know bears can climb, don't you?"

He smiled. Meli sarcastic was much better than Meli subdued. "We'll be way out of reach. I'll peg the beastie with big rocks. The edge of the bluff is crumbling, so finding ammo shouldn't be a problem."

Meli shook her head but kept moving. "So you're going to fight a bear with rocks? Why should that worry me?"

"Not rocks. I'll hurl small boulders at him to make him mad. The breeze is blowing uphill, so he won't know how close we are—but he'll know he's being followed. Once he's riled, I'll throw stones down his back trail. He'll charge the sounds and run right into Killingsworth and his merry men. No fighting required on our part."

Meli shook her head. "You know this is a black bear, right? We're two hundred and fifty miles south of grizzly territory. He may just run the other way."

"Oh ye of little faith," he said. She might know bears, but his gut said this plan was going to work—and he trusted his instincts.

By the time they reached a height even with the bluff top, Hector's breaths were tortured gasps. His ribs creaked and his lungs wheezed. Meli didn't sound much better. They clambered onto the stony escarpment and sat for a moment to catch their breath.

A panting Fred showed up a few seconds later. He flopped onto his belly, sniffed the breeze and growled a wheezy warning.

Hector had Meli and Fred sit behind a big evergreen growing a few yards back from where the stone emerged from the mountainside. He squatted in front of them and pitched his voice just above a whisper. "Keep Fred quiet. No matter what you hear, don't move until I come back."

"You said your gun could kill a bear." Her voice wavered.

"At close range, maybe. But I don't want to kill him. I want him to go after Killingsworth and company. They're closing in as we speak. I'll rile him up from way up here. When the bad guys appear he'll charge them. That's when we'll give 'em the slip."

He cupped her face in his hands. Fear vibrated up his arms. "We're going to do this, Meli. We're going to make it. You have to believe."

After a second, her head bounced up and down in a shaky nod. "What are you waiting for?"

Something big huffed in the distance. She flinched. Freddy growled deep in his chest.

"Keep him quiet," he said.

Meli nodded. "Please be careful."

His gaze dropped to her mouth. Recklessly, he leaned in and kissed her. She opened to him and energy as heady as champagne poured into his mouth. He broke the kiss and waited for his body to absorb the power. His senses sharpened. Pain faded. For one dangerous moment, he felt invincible. He stood and strode toward the edge of the cliff. He scooped up boulders the size of soccer balls as if they weighed nothing.

Luckily, the energy rush passed as quickly as it had manifested. The world around him shifted into normal focus. Gravity latched onto the boulders in his hands, forcing him to drop them. But he breathed with ease, feeling alert and rested and ready for battle.

Choosing a solid-looking spot, he got down onto his belly and army-crawled to the edge of the cliff. A rustling drew his eyes down the hillside. A minute passed. Then a huge cinnamon bear with a telltale hump lumbered uphill between the trees. A wide grin stretched his cheeks. Against all odds, a grizzly roamed Mount Astor.

Instincts one, logic zero.

The creature paused, sucking in air through its keen shovel nose. Two small, round ears pricked forward and the big animal headed toward the base of the bluff. Taking advantage of the little time he had left, Hector quietly added to his meager pile of big rocks.

He stopped when he heard the bear shuffling along the bottom of the cliff. The light breeze carried the animal's musk to him.Sweating from nerves as well as effort, Hector hefted his biggest boulder in one hand like a shot put and prayed he wouldn't miss. Then he heaved the heavy stone at the animal's exposed back.

11

THE CREATURE MUST HAVE sensed movement because his enormous head angled upward and little pig-like eyes squinted in Hector's direction. The boulder bounced off the bear's massive hump with an audible thud.

Shaking his massive head, the grizzly roared and gouged great chunks of earth from the ground with monstrous claws. Next he reared up on hind legs like tree trunks and attacked the cliff face.

Hector ducked out of sight. His heart thundered. He'd underestimated ferocity of the creature's reaction to his attack.

Needing to deflect the animal's attention, he grabbed a couple of egg-sized stones and scuttled further back from the edge. Keeping out of sight, he pitched the missiles one at a time against an alder a few yards behind the enraged bear.

With unbelievable grace and speed, the monster spun around and dropped to all fours in one sleek motion. He charged the tree, pulling to a stop inches from the trunk. He huffed his unease and growled his frustration.

Hector fisted his talisman, closed his eyes and dowsed for the search dogs. Two-hundred yards and closing fast. He grinned and opened his eyes. Killingsworth must have heard the bear and ordered his men to attack. The Hound wanted Meli alive.

The animal's golden-haloed head swung around on mammoth shoulders until his snout pointed down their back trail. Cavernous nostrils flared. Grunting, he lumbered a few steps down the trail and lifted his nose to test the air again.

Grabbing a second, smaller boulder, Hector rubbed the rock in his sweaty armpit to mark it with human scent. He pitched the heavy stone over the bear and watched the small boulder roll down their back trail, back toward their pursuers.

The angry creature charged the moving object. Discovering a rock that smelled like fresh human, he swatted the stone into the side of an ancient evergreen with one huge paw. The boulder exploded like a snowball hitting a brick wall.

Hector swallowed. That was some bear.

SARAH RAPLEE

As if sensing his human gaze, the beastie looked over his shoulder. He could have sworn the grizzly smiled.

A hound bayed. With a snort, the bear made a beeline toward the sound and disappeared into the forest.

Trusting the first stage of his plan had been successful, Hector scrambled back to where Meli waited with Fred in a stranglehold. The dog's brown eyes implored Hector to free him.

"Mission accomplished." He peeled her arms from around Fred's neck.

A wave of tenderness squeezed his heart. He couldn't begin to imagine how hard it had been for her to stay put and keep Fred quiet while listening to his encounter with the bear.

She latched onto him like a human octopus and buried her face against his shoulder. Shudders wracked her slender frame. Her silence bothered him.

Wishing he could take the time to comfort her, he managed to get her to her feet. "Take slow, deep breaths. You'll feel better in a minute."

Shouldering the backpack, he hooked her arm in his and weathered the bite of her nails digging into his flesh through the fabric of his shirt. Tags jingled as Freddy glued himself to Meli's side.

Hector half-dragged her upward through old growth forest. He didn't know how much time the bear would buy them. Soon he had to pause to let her catch her breath. She was gasping like she'd run a marathon. He was still on an energy high. She hadn't had time to adjust to the altitude.

"We have to climb to the tree line," he said. "Then we double back and run like hell."

She nodded.

After her respiration slowed they scrambled further up the mountainside. His ribs began to ache with the effort. Hounds bayed a couple of times, but the bear stalked his prey in eerie silence.

Hector called a halt at the edge of the forest. They'd reached an altitude where trees did not grow. Meli's lungs pumped like a bellows. He scanned the sky for Mendoza's helicopter, letting her catch her breath. The only sign of an aircraft was the wispy white contrail of a passenger jet, a bizarre reminder the everyday, normal world still existed.

He let his gaze drop to the broken top of Mount Saint Helens silhouetted against ominous gray clouds to the west. There would be unseasonal storms again later.

Mist rose off the snowfields decorating the rim of Mount Astor's caldera. Rivulets of snowmelt sparkled like distant ribbons of silver. Nothing moved on the talus slopes above them.

Meli's dog woofed a warning.

Somewhere below all hell broke loose. Men shouted and dogs howled like crazy.

They ran. His head began to pound. God willing, neither of them would turn an ankle on the loose rock.

A scream lifted the hair on the back of his neck— whether human or canine, he couldn't tell. Shots rang out in the distance, followed by the bear's roar.

The thin air made his heart hammer so hard he was afraid it would burst. Dark spots at the edges of his vision forced him to slow to an unsteady trot. Fred took the lead.

An agonized cry rose above the pandemonium below. His skin puckered. Definitely human. Meli stumbled and retched, covering her mouth with her free hand.

Once they'd put a little distance between them and the sounds of the fight, he led her back into the trees for cover. She dragged him to a stop and retched again. He held her hair out of the way while she vomited her scant breakfast onto the mossy ground.

Fred licked Meli's hand, then sniffed the small pile of half-digested food with interest. Hector blocked the dog with his foot and leg. "That's wrong in so many ways, Fred."

He scraped pine needles over the vomit with his boot and guided Meli to a seat on a fallen log. Then he dug his Lifestraw® out of the pack and handed it to her. "We'll rest here for a few minutes."

"Thanks," she said in a voice barely louder than a whisper. She flipped up the straw-like spout and sucked a mouthful of water through the filter, swished it around inside her mouth and spit onto the ground. Then she drank a few swallows of water. Fred sat by her feet and watched, probably hoping for a drink.

When Meli handed Hector the bottle he dug out Fred's collapsible bowl. Why should the old dog have to drink dirty water? Sucking mouthfuls of purified water through the Lifestraw®, he spat them into the bowl until there was enough for Fred to have a drink.

Meli flashed him a tired smile. "Thank you, Hector. It was kind of you to go to so much trouble to give Freddy clean water."

His face warmed. "Don't want him to get sick, either." He busied himself refilling the Lifestraw® from one of Meli's water bottles. After slaking his own thirst, he topped off the filter bottle and stashed it in her pack.

The sounds of battle had stopped. He reasoned Killingsworth had suffered losses but lived to fight another day. That the hound would end up as bear shit was too much to hope for, but he'd have to return to the compound with the wounded.

After resting for a few minutes they continued east toward the lava casts. Storm clouds moved in, darkening the sky. After a quarter-mile they descended the slope at an angle to bring them to the northern edge of the lava cast forest. His aches and pains increased as the effects of the energy rush wore off.

They'd come close to reaching their goal when thunder growled in the west. Meli's fingers tightened on his arm. Fred huffed and growled back, reminding

Hector of an old man who'd about reached the end of his rope.

He could relate. His knees begged for mercy. They must have ascended and descended half the mountain by now.

At the edge of the clearing, he stopped. Meli lurched against him.

"Honey, we're home. Just checking for prowlers." His crappy joke elicited the shadow of a smile that warmed his insides.

A quick scan of the area convinced him they were alone. He hoped the hound hadn't picked up Meli's energy signature during the fight with the bear. She would have had a hard time maintaining control through everything that had happened over the last hour.

Best to get her underground ASAP. "All clear."

They followed the raised edge of the rock ledge to their first, abandoned fire pit. Freddy whined. With a resigned sigh, the old dog jumped down beside the half-circle of blackened stones. Hector clambered down.

Turning, he placed his hands at Meli's waist to lift her down. She grabbed his shoulders to steady herself. Desire he could have sworn he was too spent to feel stirred inside him.

Even dirty, exhausted, and unkempt, she drew him like a flower in the desert. A rain-scented wind lifted tendrils of copper hair above her smoldering rhinestone glasses. He was afraid to move, afraid of what he might do, what he might feel.

Thunder grumbled, closer now, breaking the spell. He lifted her down and dropped his hands. "Let's see if we can beat this storm," he said, his voice sounding ragged.

They hurried to their underground refuge. Freddy scooted inside like a rabbit into his hole.

Hector needed to rebuild the wall. "Go inside. I'll be there in five minutes."

"Why not now?"

"Gotta cover our tracks."

She fisted a hand in his shirtfront and gave him a fierce little shake. His solar plexus buzzed a warning beneath his breastbone. "Be careful. We need you. Got it, Hector Protector?"

He swallowed. He was all she and Fred had. "Got it."

Releasing him, she turned and dropped to her hands and knees. He handed her the pack. Shoving the bag in front of her, she crawled into the cave.

A flash of lightning tore his gaze from Meli's backside. He squinted up at the threatening sky. Thunder boomed, closer now. Mother Nature had switched sides. Rain would hide their tracks and their scent.

The clouds spit rain while he collected the rocks he'd scattered in the morning. He piled them in front of the cave, burying the evidence of their fire.

When he'd finished, he dropped to all fours and peered into the dim interior of the small cavern. His gaze met Fred's. The dog's head lay on Meli's lap. Moving only eyes and eyebrows, Fred glanced up at Meli's shadowed face and heaved a sigh. She stroked his fur with hands that trembled.

Hector's heart tripped. He wished he could have spared her the horrors of the morning. She was a strong woman, but she'd been through the sort of battle that gives soldiers nightmares.

Rain came down harder on his back. "I'm coming in."

She scooted as close to Fred as she could.

He turned around and backed over the rock pile. Sharp edges bit into his palms. Pine twigs dug into his knees. His gun barrel dug into his left buttock. He reached back, pulled the weapon out of his waistband and laid it against the inside wall.

Reaching outside, he piled the big stones the way he had the day before. The wind howled through the clearing like a scared ghost. Thunder rumbled past. When he'd finished, he again plugged the hole at the top with the remains of his sleeping bag.

Then he negotiated an awkward turnabout inside the small space and sat on the pine boughs beside Meli.

She scooted away. "Hector, you've got some explaining to do."

12

THE SILENCE STRETCHED. Meli poked Hector in the shoulder with her index finger. She caught a whiff of his familiar scent. Was he going to keep his end of their bargain? "You promised to explain everything."

His clothes rustled. "So ask me something."

Meli bit back a growl of frustration. Why did he have to make everything between them into a game?

Freddy sat up and licked her cheek with his warm, wet tongue. She patted his head. It was time to beat Hector at his own game.

Taking her time, she crafted a precisely-worded question designed to catch him off-guard. "I'll start with something simple. Is Hector Guerrero the name you were born with?"

His hesitation told her she'd surprised him. Good.

"No."

Interesting. "Why do you use an assumed name?"

"Nope. It's my turn to ask you a question."

"But—"

He laid a wide finger across her lips. His breath warmed her throat. "Uh-uh. Turnabout's fair play."

She pressed her lips together to minimize contact with his skin and lifted a shoulder. Let him have his fun.

Inhaling deeply, he removed his finger. "What in the name of all that's holy were you doing at Mendoza's wedding?"

She stiffened. "I'm a wedding singer."

"You know what I mean. He's a notorious drug lord. You're a smart woman. I'm betting you at least suspected something was off before you accepted the job. Why work for him? Why take that risk?"

Her cheeks grew warm. She'd known the gig was a risky proposition, but they'd been desperate. Folding her arms across her chest, she scowled at him. "I don't work for him. I only agreed to do one gig. Freddy and I needed the money. I didn't know the groom was a drug lord."

"Where was your common sense? Your lives are worth a helluva lot more than whatever he paid you."

Meli bristled. "Nothing happened until you showed up."

He sighed. "Trust me, the hound—Killingsworth—already had you in his sights. Who do you think was behind the offer you couldn't refuse?"

She shook her head. "Why would Killingsworth be interested in me?"

"He sensed your psychic Talent. That's his ability—he sniffs out others with Talent the way he discovered you. And me, when you steamrolled my psychic shields with your kiss."

Meli's heartbeat quickened. She'd always believed she was the only freak around. She'd never been able to find someone else like her. "There are others like me? You're like me?"

"Yes and yes. Not exactly like you, but Talented."

"How many?"

"Don't know for sure. Around one in every quarter-million people has the potential to be a major Talent. That puts the number world-wide at around thirty thousand souls out of what? Seven-and-a-half billion?"

No wonder she'd thought she was alone. And Hector had Talent? Was that why he hadn't passed out when she'd kissed him?

"Why do you let a sleazebag like Mendoza use you and your Talent?" she said, digging back at him for his earlier remark. "You don't strike me as the happy-to-be-a-minion type."

Hector shifted his position and sighed.

"This is for your ears only, Melisenda. Extremely dangerous information."

She worried her lower lip and nodded.

"I work for a covert branch of the FBI made up of

agents with psychic Talents. I've been undercover in Mendoza's organization for over three years."

Her heart leapt. "I knew it! I knew you were one of the good guys."

"Then why did you blast me in the gazebo?"

"Sorry about that. I didn't really trust you yet. I needed to practice controlling my freak side. I figured if I knocked you out, it was okay because you were a drug lord's minion. Not my proudest moment." She found his cool hand and gave his fingers an apologetic squeeze. "Why did you try to save me from Killingsworth after I zapped you?"

"I was a little fuzzy at the time. Your energy penetrated my shields like lightning and stunned me with this incredibly sexy kiss—" He cleared his throat. "Anyway, my first coherent thought was you worked for Killingsworth, but I hadn't sensed that from your energy. When you tried to get away, I gave you the benefit of the doubt."

"So you weren't even sure I was on your side?" Yet he'd taken a beating to give her a chance to escape. And he'd called their kiss incredibly sexy.

"I was almost certain. Later I realized Killingsworth knew about you all along. He sensed your Talent, but didn't know what form it took, so he bided his time. He had a stroke of good luck when you kissed me and my shields went offline. He found the mole he's been looking for."

Meli's chest ached. She'd put Hector in danger, not

the other way around. "I'm so sorry. I had no idea—"

He laid a finger on her lips to shush her. "Just luck, remember? Good luck, because it brought us together and saved you from getting shanghaied. Killingsworth locates people with Talent, then assesses whether or not he can recruit them to work for Mendoza. Those he can't he kidnaps, imprisons and forces to work for the Cartel."

Meli shuddered. Without Hector, she'd have ended up a slave.

His warm, strong arm wrapped around her. "Enough about that. Is Melisenda Smith the name you were born with? 'Smith' sounds fishy to me. Not Irish enough."

Clearly he was trying to take her mind off her close encounter with a psychic Nazi.

"Smith is my stage name. For the sake of privacy, I don't advertise my real last name. Few performers do."

His sexy whisper scattered her thoughts. "If you tell me yours, I'll tell you mine."

Meli leaned away from Hector to clear her head.

What had he asked? Her real last name; that was it. "Sepulveda. My father was from Chile. His family came over as political refugees in the eighties."

"Huh. Are there many green-eyed, red-headed Chilenas?"

"No. Redheads are so rare, people pinch us for good luck. My paternal great-great-grandmother was a redheaded Spaniard. Mom was a redheaded Idaho cowgirl named Molly McKenna. My parents met in college at Portland State." She tapped his chest. "Now it's your turn."

He drew a deep breath. "Dominguez."

"I like Guerrero better. Warrior. I need a warrior."

He chuckled.

She wished he would laugh more often. "Change of subject. You have a Talent. Tell me what it is."

He hesitated. "I'm a Master Dowser. I can locate anything or anyone. That's how I knew where the bad guys were earlier, and that's how I found my gun so quickly. In fact, my Talent has guided me all along."

Meli turned the information over in her mind. "Why did the FBI send a dowser undercover?"

"The FBI plans to destroy the Mendoza Cartel. My assignments were to identify Mendoza's psychic hound and to locate the prison camp where he enslaves psychics in the Northwest. Obviously Killingsworth is the hound. I haven't found the camp, but I know it's in this area. A crazy-strong Shielder hides the place from psychic detection. We don't understand how they've hidden the location from satellites and infra-red detectors, but they have."

Fear skittered up Meli's spine. If not for her ill-conceived kiss, she would have disappeared—probably forever. For once she was glad she'd broken The Rules. In fact, she might have to consider burning her Rule Book.

Hector's arm tightened around her shoulders. "Don't

worry; I'll teach you how to strengthen your personal shields. When you spurt energy, Killingsworth may sense your unique energy signature. With that for a guide he can track your physical location."

What he said made sense to her. Sort of.

Hector continued. "Being underground blocks psychic energy, so this is a good place for you to practice your control. If you slip up, no one will know but me."

He could sense energy, too? "So you're a dowser and a hound?"

"Nope. At my level, dowsing is all about asking the right questions. Unless we're touching, I can only detect your energy spurts by continuously dowsing for psi within a certain distance."

She took another stab at it. "So a hound is kind of a cross between a dowser and a clairvoyant?"

He hesitated. "There's something akin to dowsing involved in that a hound senses directionality when he or she picks up an energy signature. But hounds sense psychic energy effortlessly within their sphere of influence. Their sixth sense works kind of the way the rest of us sense heat when we're close enough to the source, whether we're looking for it or not."

So some Talents were like the five normal senses, while others, like the shielder Talent Hector had described, were more active like hers. "How big is a hound's sphere of influence?"

"A weak hound might have to be within a few

hundred yards of the source in order to detect an energy signature. Killingsworth is a Master Hound. His sphere of influence has a diameter of at least ten miles."

"And mine is very small."

He nodded. "My Talent, dowsing, involves sensing or finding things, or predicting where or when they might be found. Since my psychic ability doesn't directly affect my environment, it's considered an afferent Talent. So is Killingsworth's hound Talent. Your expath Talent is what we call an efferent Talent, one that is directed outward and alters your environment. They typically have a small range."

He reached over and squeezed her hand. "I'll answer more questions later. We need to work on your control."

Meli stiffened. "News flash: I have no freakin' control. Every time I think I've got it down, things blow up in my face. I'm like an infant with a flame-thrower. You're the only man I ever kissed who didn't pass out."

"I watched you kiss Killingsworth. Your control was impeccable."

"The truth is, I gave up what little control I had and Killingsworth got clobbered by the blast."

Hector patted the hand he held. "Don't be so damned hard on yourself. You keep shields in place most of the time. As a rule, untrained people emit a constant stream of energy spurts. You'll master this in no time."

Fat chance. She was much more likely to get them killed. "What if I don't?"

"We'll be no worse off than we are now, right? But trust me, you will. Let's get started."

Meli sighed. Hector had told her the earth and basalt around the cave would shield them from detection when she failed. He understood the risk he was taking. She might as well try. "What should I do?"

"Relax. I'm going to talk you through a visualization exercise. You will achieve a deep state of relaxation to prepare to practice."

"Visualization and relaxation? That's what's going to keep you from getting hurt? You're out of your freakin' mind!"

It was Hector's turn to sigh. "Listen. When you dream, a self-protective mechanism kicks in to keep you from moving during those dreams. Something similar snaps your shields in place so you don't leak energy evoked by your dream emotions. Everyone with Talent battens down the hatches when they're asleep. All of us—including you—maintain strong shields for extended periods every single night. You can do this. You already do."

A tiny zing of hope pinged her heart. What Hector said sort of made sense. She shrugged. "It's your funeral, Hector Protector."

He snorted. "On that cheery note, we'll begin with positive self-talk. Repeat after me: I will learn to maintain my shields at all times because Hector is the most inspiring teacher I've ever known."

She couldn't help laughing. "Isn't this supposed to build my confidence, not yours?"

"Normally, yes, but you've undermined me at every turn," he said. "I could use some positive strokes."

She shook her head, still smiling. "I will learn to maintain my shields at all times."

"You forgot to say because Hector is the most inspiring teacher I've ever known. No editing allowed, Sparky."

"In your dreams."

Hector let out a long-suffering sigh. "We'll start over. Seriously." The playfulness had left his voice. "Concentrate on the meaning of my words."

Meli nodded.

"Remember times when you've exhibited these qualities." He spoke slowly and paused between sentences. "I am strong." His solemn tone raised the hair on her arms.

She felt strong on stage when she captivated an audience. And when she went rock climbing. "I am strong."

"I am invincible," he intoned.

When had she ever felt invincible? The closest she'd come was when she'd blasted Killingsworth with her rage. She tried to recapture the feeling. "I am invincible."

"I am woman," Hector said.

"Seriously? Lyrics from a sixties song? That's the

best you can do?" She smacked him in the chest.

"Quit complaining. I understand the general principles of shielding. I had to learn this way when I was a kid."

"You don't have a clue how to do this, do you?"

"So what if I don't remember the details? My mother insists those words filled a whole generation of women with confidence. Why should you be any different?"

"Ha." She chewed her lower lip. "Let's get to the relaxing part. You have a knack for making me tense."

Hector sighed. "You were born tense." She heard him swallow. "You managed to relax yesterday during the storm. Lean against me the way you did then."

He was right. She had actually relaxed during a thunderstorm. So why did she shy away from laying her head on his chest? They'd spent last night spooning on the same pile of branches, for heaven's sake.

Cheeks burning, she forced herself to do as he asked. A small disk pressed into her cheek through the fabric of his shirt. Curious, she reached up and located a metal chain around his neck. "May I?"

He sighed. "Why not?"

She pulled the disk out through the neck of his shirt. Exploring with her fingers, she discovered the disk was smooth on one side and engraved on the other—and warm with his body heat. She licked her lips. "Why do you wear this?"

He pulled the pendant out of her grasp. "My mother

gave it to me. It's a St. Jude medal."

The thought that Hector had a loving mother praying for his safe return was comforting. But wasn't St. Jude the Patron Saint of Lost Souls and Hopeless Causes?

"Why, out of all the saints, did she choose St. Jude?"

The muscles in the arm that encircled her bunched when he shrugged. "I never asked her. Let's get back to work."

She laid her head on his chest and concentrated on the steady beat of his heart.

"Take slow, deep breaths," he said, his voice raspy.

With each inhalation she smelled his familiar, no doubt testosterone-laced scent. Her heart skipped and fluttered like a butterfly in heat. She jerked upright. "It's no use. I can't control my breath, let alone my energy."

"Match your breaths to mine." He pulled her back against him. "Feel the anxiety flow out of your body with each exhalation. Inhale and exhale with me. You can do this."

Forcing her muscles to relax, she followed Hector's lead. They breathed deeply, in unison, half-a-dozen times. His heartbeat slowed toward a steady base rhythm. Hers would settle as well.

"You're doing great," he said. "Now soften your stomach. Relax. Feel air moving in and out of your lungs. Don't try to control your breath, just observe. When thoughts intrude, bring your attention back to your breath."

Meli did her best to follow his instructions. Freddy snored softly beside her. The thought that she did feel more relaxed intruded. In fact, she was calm. She turned her attention back to her breath. Hector's sturdy heartbeat soothed her.

This went on for so long she began to fall asleep.

Hector put his lips to her ear. "Feel better?"

Yawning, she nodded against his chest.

"Now, with each inhalation, say I control. When exhaling, say my energy."

She repeated the phrase for what seemed like hours, but it could have been minutes—or days. Chanting the words, she became aware of a place deep inside herself she'd never before noticed, a place between the words filled with amazing possibilities. Instinctively she sensed this was where her Talent came from.

Hector's faraway voice presented her with a new mantra: "I maintain—my shields."

She accepted his words, powerful words. She recited them in rhythm with her inhalations and exhalations.

After a while, Hector said, "Meli, it's time to return. Become aware of your body. When you feel ready, wiggle your fingers and toes. Then inhale deeply and exhale. Open your eyes."

Meli followed his instructions. The fresh scent of pine needles made her smile. She sat up.

He caught her chin and tilted her face toward him. "How do you feel?"

His fingers warmed her jaw. "Pretty good. Relaxed."

"You ready to practice?"

She lifted a shoulder. "As ready as I'll ever be." Doubt scurried up her spine like a six-legged insect.

Hector dropped his hand. "Everyone, even the non-Talented, has life-force energy, or qi, that gives us health and vitality. There are many kinds of qi. The qi that flows on the surface of the body, forming a protective sheath, is called wei-qi, or protective qi. Wei-qi is the anchor for a psychic's personal shield. The average personal shield is located adjacent to this outer wei-qi."

Meli nodded her understanding.

"When your energy rises, where do you feel it first?"

Meli frowned. "Seems like everywhere. But while I was relaxing, I sensed a place I'd never been consciously aware of before."

"We call that place the energy well. The Talented draw psychic energy from their wells. Efferent Talents draw much more energy than afferent Talents. We think the way a person's Talent manifests is determined by a combination of genetics and environment. The well is the path to the Source that drives Talent."

She nodded. "That makes sense, I think."

"A psychic shield is a constant flow of energy around a Talented person that deflects psychic energy kind of like the wind turns an arrow or a bullet, only stronger."

"Where does our energy come from? Is there a universal Source somewhere?"

"No one really understands the exact nature of the Source. One theory holds we draw power to us from another dimension. Many of us manipulate energy, but we don't know exactly where it originates."

She had a feeling he'd developed his own theory. "What do you think?"

"Maybe so; maybe not. It doesn't matter much in a practical sense. When you turn on your hair dryer, do you need to understand where electricity comes from in order to dry your hair?"

"Good point."

"Let's focus on your lesson. Visualize a well with a never-ending source of energy at the bottom. Try to send a tendril of your energy into that well to draw energy from it like a hose. When your energy rises, visualize constantly-flowing light sheathing you like a second skin."

Easy for him to say.

She visualized a flow of blue energy like the one she'd released into Killingsworth emerging from her well and encasing her body in a shimmering shield. A force as cold as ice water poured over her skin. Every muscle in her body contracted. She gasped and shivered.

Hector's hand warmed her cheek. *"¡Mierda!"* His

hand dropped away. "The good news is you guided energy into a shield. But I don't understand why you're frozen. Guide the energy back into the well."

The cold blue sheath coiled into a snake and slithered down her throat. She couldn't breathe. Then the force tunneled through her lungs and disappeared into nothingness. She coughed and coughed what felt like shards of glass. Tears ran down her cheeks as she gasped for air.

Hector pulled her onto his lap. He peeled off his baggy long-sleeved shirt and slipped it over her on top of her clothes. Meli shook against him while he cradled her as if she were a small child. She slipped her arms around his naked torso to draw on his incredible heat. Gradually her mind cleared and her body warmed.

She became aware of the sound of his heart pounding against her ear. The rhythm pulsed through her blood, heated all her private feminine places until she ached with need. She hungered for the taste of his skin, the scent of his hair, the touch of his hands exploring her body.

13

SITTING IN HIS LAP, she could hardly have missed the fact he wanted her. The knowledge made her feel powerful and desirable in a way she never had before. Maybe with Hector, she could finally make love.

She wiped her face on her sleeve.

He cleared his throat. "Let's try again," he said in a raspy voice. "This time, dig for warm energy." He swallowed. "Not hot—just a warm, velvety slide across your skin. When you let down your shield, pull the energy into the well through your skin. That won't hurt as much. You'll do fine."

She was thankful he finally stopped talking.

He wanted her. He swore he wasn't afraid of her. He might be the only man who could survive making love to her. She might never get another chance.

She turned her head and licked the skin of his bare chest, savored his unique flavor. Salty and musky.

He stilled.

She pressed her lips to his skin, delivering a tiny puff of fondness and sexual heat.

His arm tightened around her.

Her heart leapt. She'd kissed Hector without losing control. Granted, not on the lips, but this was a start.

She feathered kisses across the broad expanse of his chest. He trembled. Strong hands grasped her shoulders and pushed her back a few inches.

"Meli, don't." He peeled the shirt over her head and pulled it on like a protective shield.

Disappointment tore apart her control. Heat flared in an uncontrolled release. Hector swore and her damp clothes steamed.

Blinking back tears of hurt and anger, she scooted off his lap to sit with her back against the cold stone wall. Drawing her knees to her chest, she buried her hot face against her hot jeans.

He touched her shoulder gently. "Meli—"

She shrugged him off and scooted closer to Freddy. His wet, warm tongue caressed her cheek. She lifted her head and scowled at Hector. "Too bad you're not as good an actor as you are a liar. I know you can do this, Meli. You're doing great. That was bullshit and you know it. You're afraid of me."

His silence confirmed her fears. Not that she could blame him. She shook her head. "I thought..." God, she was pathetic. She should have resigned herself to being alone a long time ago.

"Never mind." She squared her shoulders. "I don't want your death on my conscience. I'm the one the hound can track. You have a better chance of making it to safety without me. Go on by yourself. Just leave me the gun and ammo in case the bear shows up. You can send someone back for me and Fred."

Hector gave a low whistle. "That was one hell of a speech. Are you finished?"

Biting her lower lip, she nodded.

"First of all, partners don't leave partners behind. We stay together. Understand?"

She lifted a shoulder. Partners were equals. In his eyes they were not even close.

Hector continued. "Second, I'm not much for introspection. I do what I do because that's who I am. But, for the record, I'm not afraid of you, Meli." He paused for a moment, as if choosing his words. "I'm afraid of hurting you."

Her breath caught. It was as if she'd heard a piccolo play a bass note. Inconceivable.

"Hell, Meli, I've wanted to make love to you from the moment we met. But I'm an undercover agent. That pretty much limits me to recreational sex. I don't do relationships."

Her heart skipped a beat. He wanted to make love to her. In spite of her freak side, he wanted to make love to her.

He kept throwing up excuses. "You're not a friends-with-benefits kind of girl. I don't want to ruin our friendship. When we get out of here, I'll be reassigned. I could be incommunicado for years. I'm not the kind of man you need."

Meli suppressed a smile. He did care about her. Caring made him vulnerable, and being vulnerable scared him. By the sounds of things, he hadn't let himself get involved with a woman for a long time. Could his fiancée's death have killed his ability to love?

She refused to accept that.

She let the corners of her mouth turn up. "So we can't make love because we're friends, and you're a player?"

After a couple of beats, he followed her lead. His tone lightened. "I prefer to think of myself as a connoisseur of the fair sex."

Meli cocked an eyebrow at him and shrugged. "Connoisseur, player, man-ho, whatever. Let's get back to shielding lessons. Don't worry. If you can't hang onto your self-control, I'll zap you."

"We're ready to roll," Hector announced an hour later. He watched Fred and Meli crawl out the cave entrance, confident Meli had developed enough control to maintain her shield. Killingsworth's hound Talent would not sense her energy. The three of them had to move on before their pursuers returned.

He crawled out of the cave after her. His stomach growled. "Maybe we'll get lucky and find some berries along the way."

She stood and shrugged into her backpack. "Where exactly are we going?"

"The village of Puma is located a quarter of the way around the mountain. Climbers get permits there to scale the eastern face of the caldera. Besides the campground, there's a restaurant of sorts and a little store. Not much else, but I'm betting the store has a land line or a wireless satellite phone setup."

"How long do you think it'll take us to get there?" Tiredness dulled her voice.

Concern for the toll this trek would take when she'd already endured so much weighed heavily on his shoulders. He framed his answer in the best possible light. "We should arrive by tomorrow night, or the next morning at the latest. I'll buy you lunch with the credit card I found. Puma's at a lower altitude, so the going will be easier than it was today."

She let out a long sigh. "Where will we sleep tonight?"

"The map I memorized indicates an abandoned logging camp a few miles from here. We can shelter there."

Straightening, she flashed him a tired smile. "Sounds like a plan, Hector Protector. Freddy, come. Time to go."

The dog left off sniffing around the entrance to

another lava tube and joined them.

At least Meli had stopped calling him a man-ho. He placed her hand in the crook of his arm. They headed east. After a quarter of a mile, Fred's ears perked up and he trotted ahead through the trees. Soon he was back in sight, tail wagging. He gave one short yip, turned around and took off eastward again.

"Freddy, come!" Meli called.

The yellow dog crested a hillock and disappeared.

"He ignored you," Hector told her. What had gotten into the animal? Fred rarely strayed more than ten feet from Meli.

The next time Meli's Guide appeared, his intelligent brown eyes caught and held Hector's gaze. "What is it, boy?"

Fred yipped and pranced before taking off back the way he'd come.

Frowning, Meli halted. "What's gotten into him? He always stays close to me. Does he seem upset? Scared?"

Fred had held his head high and wagged his tail. "He looks…excited, I guess."

"Maybe he wants us to follow him," Meli said. "He might have picked up a scent. Maybe a person's, or another dog's."

Hector dowsed for canines. Nothing. "Maybe, but why would he want to investigate? He's trained to ignore distractions, right?"

Meli nodded and worried her lower lip.

His unease grew with each passing second. The dog had alerted to some change in their environment, but dowsing didn't turn up any people or unusual animals in the area. Soon Fred reappeared. "There he is. Call him."

"Freddy, come!"

The big guy responded to Meli's command with an unhappy whine, then turned tail and disappeared again. "He ignored you and took off."

This time, he kept tabs on Fred with a psychic feeler. The Lab mix trotted steadily eastward.

"He wants us to follow him," Meli said firmly. "Guides are trained in Intelligent Disobedience. They act on information their human partners don't have in order to keep us safe—even if it means going against commands. I could tell you stories—"

He interrupted. "I'll take your word for it. You think we should hurry up and follow him?"

"Yes. He knows what he's doing. He's never let me down."

The tendril of energy tracking Freddy signaled the dog was headed back again. His behavior did seem eerily purposeful, but what that purpose might be was a mystery to Hector.

He didn't like mysteries. And he didn't like putting his life in the paws of an animal. But no way would Meli continue onward without Fred. She had complete faith in her Guide. What was it she had told him? Saying *Freddy is just a dog* is like saying *Ben Franklin was just an old bald guy.*

Hector's head began to throb. He sighed. "So we follow Fred."

Meli's Guide led them across the mountain's southern flank throughout the afternoon. The animal set a pace that soon had them sweating. Fred appeared to head straight for the old logging camp where Hector had planned to spend the night.

During one of his periodic dowsing forays, Hector spotted the hound's search party K 9s leaving the compound and heading back up the mountain. With luck, the bad guys wouldn't pick up their trail until morning. By then they'd already be close to Puma.

He called a halt beside an ice-cold stream. "Let's rest for five minutes and fill the water bottles."

Meli shrugged out of the pack. She unzipped the main pocket and handed him his blue Lifestraw®.

Kneeling, he removed the filter cap. He couldn't resist dumping a bottleful of cold stream water over his aching head. After the initial shock, he welcomed the frigid liquid dripping onto his shoulders.

After refilling the water bottle, he screwed on the filter and cap, then gently bumped Meli's hand with the Lifestraw®. She brought the tube to her lips and sucked hard. The filter made a squeaky slurping sound as water was pulled through and up the straw.

He climbed to his feet. "Didn't the Girl Scouts teach you to be quiet in the woods?"

Her rhinestones blazed in the dappled sunlight. She

paused to hand him a clear plastic bottle and flash him a mischievous smile. "You lumber through the woods like a drunken moose, *señor*."

His heart tripped over that smile. He frowned and filled the bottle with water from the stream.

A yip sounded ahead. Hector climbed to his feet and peered into the woods. The dog materialized. "Fred's back."

Waving his tail like a flag at a Fourth of July parade, Fred stared into Hector's eyes for a moment. Then he spun around and disappeared into the trees.

Crazy old dog.

He snagged Meli's pack. It was his turn to carry. Now that they'd eaten all the food, he barely noticed the weight.

Ten minutes later, Freddy put in a brief appearance at the top of the next ridge. He was still on course for the old logging camp.

When Hector and Meli reached the ridge top, he dowsed for their pursuers before he and Meli started their descent. He found them in the process of ascending the caldera's rim, probably in hopes of spotting their prey in the open bowl of the sleeping volcano. What would happen when Killingsworth learned the fugitives hadn't made for the caldera? Would he realize they'd doubled back toward Puma?

The hound might send for a dowser, but transporting the Talent to Mount Astor would take time. Unless, of course, Killingsworth had a dowser stashed in the prison camp somewhere in this wilderness.

Frustration burned in his gut. The closest he could get to finding the camp's location had been through map dowsing. His St. Jude's Medal acted as a pendulum which he held over a map of the Northwest. When he asked for the camp's location, the pendulum indicated a four-hundred square mile area, mostly wilderness, roughly centered on Mount Astor.

The Bureau had failed to locate the camp from the air. The place was invisible, although as far as they knew, no cloaking Talent existed.

Rumor had it the Chinese were close to developing a large-scale invisibility blanket device, but when Hector had dowsed for one on Mount Astor he'd come up empty. It might be that his Talent couldn't home in on the item since he'd never seen one, couldn't visualize one. And dowsing for natural shields never worked because they blocked psychic energy.

He'd managed to discover Killingsworth was Mendoza's hound and the commandant of his detention camp. But none of his efforts to locate the camp had succeeded.

Dowsing for anomalies, such as unnatural areas where no animals or people ever went had turned up nothing. He'd dowsed for the road to the camp. Nada.

He'd followed Killingsworth when the man left the compound, but he always went to Portland or Seattle for at least a day. And he never gave his employees more than one day off at a time. He was a cagey sonovabitch.

Today, as usual, Hector had hit a wall. His mood darkened, matching the false twilight of the cloudy afternoon in the shadowed understory of the ancient evergreen forest.

Meli worried Hector would develop a fever. She gave him the last of the painkiller for his headache and insisted he stop to drink often. He wouldn't let her share any more of her energy because they were out of food. He'd explained that using her Talent without sustenance was dangerous.

Freddy's unusual behavior persisted. Meli and Hector continued to follow her Guide.

Their path undulated across the ancient lava flows and ash falls that formed the mountain's flanks. After traversing ridge upon irregularly-spaced, tree-covered ridge, hunger gnawed Meli's stomach and every part of her body ached. She slogged onward, her admiration for Hector's strength of will increasing with each step. Injured, sick, and hungry as he was, she didn't understand how he kept moving—but he did.

It was late afternoon when Hector stopped dead in his tracks.

She halted, heart racing. "What is it?"

His tone was grim. "Fred's disappeared from my dowsing radar. One minute he was there, the next he was gone."

14

MELI'S HEART THUDDED. "What do you mean, *gone*?"

"I've been monitoring his energy with a psychic feeler. We're near the abandoned logging camp. Fred moved eastward beyond this ridge, angled downhill toward the camp and then poof. No more Fred."

Meli's heart dropped like a meteor. She dug her fingernails into Hector's arm. "Freddy isn't...He isn't dead, is he?"

Hector patted her hand. "No. Even sudden death is a process, a transition. His energy blinked out in an instant."

Her muscles went weak with relief. "What would—?"

"*¡Gracias a Dios¡*" Hector grabbed her shoulders and pressed warm lips to hers in an unexpected kiss.

The coil of dormant sexual energy in her belly sizzled to life. Shoring up her shield, she flattened her palms against Hector's chest and gave a desperate shove. A spark snapped between them, stinging her lips as they pulled apart. "Are you *crazy*?"

He grabbed her hands. "Freddy's found the Cartel's prison camp, the one nobody's been able to locate. That's why he disappeared."

Meli frowned. "What makes you think so?"

"They've got some kind of camouflaged shield hiding the camp. It's like an invisibility cloak. The thing fools the senses, both normal and paranormal. Everything seems identical to the surrounding area, but that's an illusion.

"Once Freddy passed through the shield, he disappeared to our senses, including psychic ones. That's why it happened so fast!"

Her stomach turned over. Freddy was in the clutches of monsters. "We have to get him out! How do we get him out?"

Hector laid a big hand on her shoulder. "If he doesn't show up in a few minutes, we'll figure something out. We can't go in blind."

Meli fisted her hands on her hips. "That's not a plan. That's a non-plan."

His hand dropped to snag her elbow in a no-nonsense grip. "We'll go to the exact spot where he disappeared and wait for him there. It's another hundred yards to the top of the ridge, but it's an easy climb. We're in old-growth forest, so the trees are spread out."

She let him guide her up the hillside under pine-scented boughs that creaked and sighed in the wind. Her ears strained unsuccessfully to pick up even the faintest yip or tinkle of tags.

"Fred started down the other side and then disappeared," Hector said in a low voice. "There's a rocky outcropping for cover up here. We'll watch from there."

Meli acknowledged him with a curt nod. Freddy would reappear soon. He had to. If not, Hector might not be able to go in blind, but she sure as hell could.

When they finally collapsed beside a pile of boulders, Hector touched her shoulder. "We'll give him five minutes to make an appearance."

"What if he doesn't?"

"Then I'll go in after him."

After a couple of minutes that seemed like hours, Freddy's tags jingled a few yards distant. He brushed through what sounded like clumps of ferns and padded up to them.

With tears burning her eyes, Meli dropped to one knee and grabbed his collar. "Sit!"

Freddy sat. Meli ran her hands over her Guide's body to reassure herself he was okay. He gave her cheek an apologetic lick.

"Well, I'll be damned." Hector said with awe in his tone.

"What is it?" she said, straightening.

"I was right. They've paired an Illusion to the camp's shield. They must have discovered an unknown Talent—an Illusionist. No wonder I couldn't find the place. The shield blocks psychic energy and the Illusion fools the other senses. The hillside in front of us looks, sounds, and smells identical to the one behind us."

Meli focused on her senses. A breeze whispered through the treetops ahead and toyed with her hair. She inhaled the sharp scent of pine sap and the sweet, heavy perfume of blooming bear grass. A couple of raucous jays squabbled nearby.

She furrowed her brow. "How do you know it's an illusion?"

"The air shimmered the way it does over hot asphalt in the summertime. First Fred's head poked through above the ground, as if he was coming up out of a pool of water, only sideways. The rest of him followed."

Meli tried to imagine what Hector had seen. She shoved her glasses up her nose. "Now what?"

"We could be walking straight into a trap," Hector said. "That's why we're not going in. Fred's safe now. As soon as I call the Bureau from Puma, they'll liberate the camp. The prisoners won't have long to wait."

Meli frowned. "What if Killingsworth suspects we've found the place? He'll move them, or worse. We can't just walk away. If not for you, I'd already be one of them. At Killingsworth's mercy." She shivered.

He set his jaw. "Getting caught or killed won't help them. We need back up. We have to go to Puma."

What Hector said made sense, but the idea of walking out on who-knew-how-many people trapped inside the camp felt wrong all the way down to the marrow of her bones. She didn't think she could do it.

Freddy lunged out of her grasp.

"Freddy, no! Stop!" Tags jingled and fronds swished back toward the shield. Following the sound, she shot downhill after him. If Freddy went through the shield, so would she. End of story.

"Meli, stop!" Hector's shout was the last thing she heard before she plunged through a moment of nothingness that must have been the shield. Her ears crackled and then she ran on the same cushioned, mossy ground as before. Fern fronds brushed her pant legs.

She pulled to a stop before she plowed into a tree. "Freddy, come," she called softly over the pounding of her heart.

A young male voice spoke directly in front of her. "Freddy's okay."

Meli gasped and jumped backward, flailing her arms to keep from falling. The stranger's voice came from above her head, which meant he stood more than a foot taller than her, but his voice had cracked. She placed him in his early teens.

He cleared his throat. "Sorry, I didn't mean to scare you. Jake's rubbing Freddy's belly. He's the one who called the dog."

Somewhere on her right, Freddy's tail thumped a confirmation. She resisted the urge to run to her Guide. Was she inside the prison camp?

As if sensing her question, the teen spoke again. "We're safe for now. You and me and Jake are the only people here."

A younger child spoke up. "Please don't be mad at Freddy. I begged him to bring you here. He only wanted to help us."

"Jake's an animal telepath," the older boy said. "He talks to them in his head."

An animal telepath. That explained Freddy's odd behavior. Meli dug up a smile. "Don't worry. I'm not mad, Jake. I'm just glad Freddy's okay."

She needed to feel her way carefully with these children. They must be some of the Cartel's prisoners. "I'm Meli Smith."

"We know," Jake said. "Freddy told me, and I told Denzel."

Meli blinked. Freddy really was a dog genius. She spoke to the older boy. "Why did Jake ask Freddy to lead us here?"

He answered in a tone that implied an accompanying eye-roll. "To help us escape."

Meli's heart twisted. No way on earth could she leave the boys behind. Either they took the kids with them, or Hector would have to go on to Puma without her.

She addressed the older boy. "What's your name?"

"Denzel Woods."

"Freddy wants to know where Hector is," Jake said.

Right on cue, heavy footfalls descending the slope behind her announced Hector's arrival. He grabbed her right shoulder to steady himself, nearly taking them both down.

"He has a gun, Denzel!" Jake's voice squeaked. Meli couldn't tell whether he was excited or scared.

Hector's weight shifted and his clothes rustled. He must have stowed his gun. His grip tightened until her shoulder hurt from the pressure. He gave her a tiny shake and spoke softly. "I ought to spank you."

Meli's heart began to pound. She'd never heard him sound so furious.

Jake responded before she could. "Please don't be mad, Hector. Nate said I had to get Freddy to bring you here. He said you were our only hope."

Hector gentled his tone, apparently taking the fact that the child knew his name in stride. "I'm not mad at you, buddy." He gave Meli another tiny, controlled shake. "She's the one who's in trouble."

Meli swallowed.

"Why?" Denzel's voice held a challenge.

The boy's question defused Hector's anger. He blew out a long sigh. His hand on her shoulder relaxed. "It's complicated."

What did he mean by that?

"Good job calling Fred, buddy," Hector said. "Did

you call the grizzly, too?"

Freddy's tags jingled at the sound of his name.

"Yeah." His voice was muffled, as if he'd hung his head. "Calling the bear was a mistake. I wanted to see one for myself, but Nate says they're too dangerous."

"Nate's right," Hector said. "But he helped the three of us escape from the bad guys, so I'm glad you called him. What's your name, son?"

"Jake. I named the bear *Grizz*. He hurt some men. One of them shot him. Grizz hurts real bad." The little boy's voice quavered. "When we escape we gotta find him a doctor, okay?"

Meli wanted to gather the child in her arms and tell him everything would be all right, but Hector gave her shoulder a warning squeeze.

"Sure," Hector said. "It's the least we can do for him."

"Exactly," Jake said.

Meli's throat tightened.

"Promise?" Jake asked Hector.

"We'll find him an animal doctor, I promise," Hector said.

"Hector always keeps his promises," Meli said.

Denzel spoke up. "We need to get moving. Nate told us to hide the two of you in the playhouse. The guards never go there. You'll be safe until lights out, when he'll meet with you to discuss our escape plan."

"Escape plan?" Hector's voice roughened with emotion Meli did not understand.

Impatience infused Denzel's answer. "Nate's had six years to prepare for this. Discuss it with him. We have to go."

"Wait a minute, son," Hector said. "We're on our way to Puma to call for help. One more day, two tops, and you'll be rescued."

Denzel's voice took on a steely quality Meli had never heard in someone so young. "Our Foreseer saw that future. No one is rescued." The boy swallowed. "Killingsworth catches the two of you, and none of us escapes. What happens is not pretty." Denzel's voice cracked on his last word.

Hector shifted his weight. "There's a foreseer among the prisoners?"

"Yeah. For six years, no matter what plan Nate came up with, Zinnia foresaw that we would die when we tried to escape. But the night of the drug lord's wedding, something changed. She saw a new future where you three found us. We all stayed together, and most of us survived."

"How many prisoners are there?" Meli said.

"Five adults and three kids. Sophie's expecting. The baby's due in two weeks."

Hector swore under his breath. "This just gets better and better."

Remembering his attempts to rescue her "baby" at the compound, Meli smiled into the tense silence. She was certain he would stay.

Hector cleared his throat. "Who's the baby's father?

Killingsworth?"

Meli shuddered.

"Mr. Killingsworth is old enough to be Sophie's father," Denzel said, sounding shocked. If only it were that simple.

"He told us her name is Sophie. She can't remember anything before waking up here. When she started throwing up a lot Mr. Killingsworth told her she was having a baby. He wouldn't tell her anything else."

Meli's heart went out to the young woman. Amnesia would be bad enough, but to not remember your baby's father, or to know if he is a monster…

"Okay, kid, we'll talk to Nate," Hector said, his voice rough. "Let's get a move on."

Clothes rustled and Freddy padded over to Meli. She bent down to stroke his head. "Good boy, Freddy."

Light steps approached. Jake. A trusting little hand slipped into hers. "I'll show you the way, Meli. Nate told us you can't see. Freddy says he helps you, but Hector broke his harness."

Forcing a smile for Jake, Meli nodded. "Freddy's my Guide. He sure likes you."

Hector brought up the rear of their little band with Meli's pack on his shoulder. The group had halted in front of a tall wire perimeter fence. A hollow large enough for a man to lie down in had been dug underneath. A cluster of prickly Oregon grape bushes hid the escape route from prying eyes on the inside.

Denzel ran a hand over his short, tightly-curled black hair. "Don't touch the wire. It'll knock you on your butt and alert the guards."

The kid sounded like he spoke from experience. Hector nodded.

The boy glanced sideways at Meli. When his brown eyes re-focused on Hector, a question lay in their clear depths.

Hector nodded. "Meli, we have to slide under an electric fence. Denzel's going first. He and I will help when it's your turn."

"Just tell me what to do," Meli said.

"I'll go first." Denzel folded his lanky frame and sat on the ground with his back to the fence. He stretched out and scooted into the hollow under the hot wire using his heels and elbows for leverage.

When he'd cleared the fence, he rose to his feet on the other side, taking care not to touch the bushes' sharp leaves. He brushed off the back of his jeans and gestured for Jake to follow.

"I'm next," the little guy told Meli. He let go of her hand and strode to the fence. After laying down on his back he extended his arms beneath the bottom wire. Denzel grabbed Jake's pale wrists and pulled him safely through.

Jake's gaze found Meli. "Don't worry. I'll tell Freddy how to go under without getting zapped. "C'mon, Freddy." He patted the ground.

"It's okay, Freddy," Meli said. She gestured toward Jake. "Go!"

The dog looked at Jake and whined. He trotted over to the hollow and belly-crawled under the fence.

Jake's eyes never left Freddy until the dog reached him. Then the little boy but his arm around the big dog's neck and smiled at Meli. "He's safe."

Meli was next. Hector helped her get situated on her back on the ground with her arms extended under the fence. He grasped her jean-covered legs below the knees so he could help the boy slide her under the bottom wire.

Denzel squatted and reached for her, but then pulled back and rested his forearms on his knees. His gaze locked with Hector's through the fences silvery strands. Uncertainty clouded the boy's eyes.

Hector's muscles tensed. "What is it?"

"I'm a Touch Telepath. When I touch someone, they see what I see. I can talk to them without speaking."

Jake piped up. "Yeah; it's really freaky."

Denzel frowned at the little boy.

Meli smiled. "Sounds awesome to me. We freaks need to stick together."

Denzel shrugged. "Mostly, it's not very useful."

Her smile widened. "Sure it is! I'll finally get to see Hector's ugly mug, and your handsome one." Meli pulled off her dark glasses and tucked them into her bra beneath her shirt. "Let's do this."

Hector's heart kicked into a gallop. His fingers

tightened on her calves. He was fourteen again, picking up his first date. He couldn't pull his gaze from her face.

The boy grasped Meli's wrists. She gasped and blinked several times. Then her eyes found Hector's. After a long moment her pink tongue darted out to lick her lips.

His pulse stuttered.

Denzel snorted. "Here we go."

He yanked her halfway under the fence before Hector remembered to lift and push on her legs. One more heave and she was through. Dropping her arms as if they were on fire, the boy shot to his feet and rubbed his hands on his jeans. He turned his back on them and appeared to scan the woods for threats.

A blush climbed Meli's cheeks, muting her freckles. She made no move to sit up. "Sorry, Denzel. I'm still learning to shield."

"That's okay," Denzel said. His voice cracked and he didn't turn around.

Hector pushed to his feet.

Meli fished out her rhinestone glasses and put them on. She propped herself up on her elbows and sent a crooked grin his way. "Looks like you've been eaten by a bear and pooped over a cliff."

"Not far from the truth," he said.

She shoved herself up onto her fanny and finger-combed leaves and twigs out of her bedraggled ponytail. "No worries. After you clean up, you will no longer disgust me or frighten small children."

Hector grinned. Liar, liar, panties on fire. He might look like hell, but her strong reaction to the sight of him had made poor Denzel extremely uncomfortable.

Meli adjusted her ponytail holder and gave her hair a last shake. Sunlight teased copper and gold sparks from the dusty strands. "I must look like something a bobcat hacked up."

She looked like a forest sprite, sweet and unspoiled by the dross of the world.

Little Jake manned up first. "You look like a princess. You're the fairest of them all, Meli."

Her rhinestones winked. "Spoken like a true gentleman, Jake. Thank you."

Grinning, Hector turned his back on them and lay down to negotiate the electric fence. He'd let a rug rat best him. Back on his feet on the other side, he grabbed Meli's hand and pulled her up to stand beside him. He leaned over to whisper in her ear and caught a whiff of dust and vanilla sunlight. "You take my breath away, Melisenda."

He watched her cheeks redden further. Feeling vindicated, he led her over to Jake and Freddy, who'd found a shady spot. "Jake, would you and Fred keep Meli company for a minute? I need to talk to Denzel."

"Sure." The little boy grinned.

Frowning at Hector, Meli sat on the mossy ground beside Jake and Fred. The dog shivered with the effort of not chasing a pair of ground squirrels that were chasing each other along a fallen tree trunk.

Hector turned to Denzel. The teenager stood ramrod straight with his arms crossed over his narrow chest and his back to his companions. Hector joined him, eyeing the laser sensor that seemed to have captured Denzel's undivided attention.

A quick glance at the bulging front of the kid's jeans confirmed his suspicion that Meli's raw sexual need had zapped the boy. Denzel was trying valiantly to hide his body's natural response to her energy.

Hector pretended not to notice. "How do we get past these?" he said. He gestured at the row of sensors and angled his body away from the boy.

"They don't work," Denzel said. "Nate took care of them a long time ago. The guards see what we want them to see."

Tampering with the high tech security system had taken intelligence, skill, and *huevos* the size of soccer balls. "I'm looking forward to meeting your friend Nate."

The fence and the lasers kept the prisoners inside, while the shield and the Illusion kept everyone else outside. New captives were no doubt drugged when the hound brought them here. Did they even know what country they were in?

He chafed at his current lack of information. "Has anyone ever escaped from this camp?"

Denzel turned his face toward Hector. Sweat gleamed on his brown skin. "Not successfully. One early prisoner tried. A hindseer. They caught him. They made an example of him to keep the other prisoners in line. Nate still has nightmares about his screams coming from the guardhouse."

The kid's Adam's apple bobbed in a swallow. "Nate says failed attempts would only make success less likely. We prepared until Zinnia foretold the possibility of success with few casualties. Our time has come."

The boy's certainty sent a chill skittering up Hector's spine. They'd thought the same about the raid on the camp in Sonora.

Denzel led them up a steep deer trail over a hill. On the far side, the ancient firs had been logged a hundred years before. The new forest was young at only a century, but already quite tall. Trees grew closer together than they had in the old growth. The land was littered with logs and other obstacles to their passing. Soon the downhill slope leveled into a little valley. The boy picked up the pace.

The scree of a Cooper's hawk hunting squirrels sounded nearby. Before long, Hector smelled wood smoke. The regular chunks of an ax splitting wood grew loud. A door slammed and a child's voice murmured.

His pulse picked up. They were approaching the heart of the prison, the old logging buildings. Someone revved a chainsaw. Were the inmates trying to hide the sounds of their little group's passage from the guards?

Denzel held up a hand for them to stop. He held a finger to his lips and pointed ahead.

Hector spotted the children's playhouse peeking through the trees like a fairytale cottage. The building was larger than he'd expected, but he was no expert.

Neatly-trimmed yews formed a waist-high hedge around the small house and yard. A woodchip path wove around Douglas firs from the direction of the camp and ended at the little red door. Red shutters on the windows and red gingerbread trim dressed up the miniature, white dwelling.

Hector's shoulders twitched. Would this be a safe refuge? Or a trap?

15

PRIDE INFUSED DENZEL'S whisper. "Nate chose this spot to build because it's over an old root cellar. Killingsworth doesn't know that. The secret cellar is part of our escape plan."

Hector shook off his fanciful misgivings and nodded. Impressive. He had to hand it to Nate, he had patience. His projects took years to pay off.

Jake pulled Meli down and spoke into her ear. Her smile froze, and Hector tensed. Freddy's tail drooped. She hugged the little boy and mouthed the words thank you, then smiled. Hector relaxed. His stomach growled. With luck, Jake had told her there would be food waiting for them.

He scanned what little he could see of the camp's

central clearing. With no one in his line of sight, he tapped Denzel's shoulder, pointed at the cottage door, and raised his eyebrows. The boy nodded. They all squatted behind the hedge and then scuttled around into the yard and up to the entrance.

One-by-one, they slipped inside with Hector bringing up the rear. He shut the door behind him without making a sound. The faint, clean scent of pine permeated the roughly ten by twelve room, somewhat wider than it was long. Light filtered through red gingham curtains covering windows on the front and back walls. A small basket of pinecones formed a centerpiece for the circular, child-sized wooden table-and-chair set that sat at center front on a round rag rug.

Hector noticed toys lining the back wall in unnaturally-precise order: a toy box, an assortment of doll-sized furniture and a block table beside a blue container of interlocking plastic blocks. Built-in bookshelves filled the side walls. An assortment of dog-eared storybooks, faded board games and not-so-gently-used cars, dolls and other toys were stacked on the wooden shelves with military precision. Worn, brightly-colored beanbag chairs had been placed on a couple of rectangular throw rugs to form a neat row in front of the toy shelves.

Remembering the chaos his three little sisters left behind in a room, Hector found himself frowning. "Looks like Killingsworth runs a tight ship."

"We always put things away," Denzel said. He moved toward the left wall and shoved aside red and green beanbags with his foot. Squatting on his heels, he reached under the edge of the woven throw rug and lifted. A hidden trapdoor opened silently on well-greased hinges.

The boy grinned at him. "An orderly room lulls the guards into a false sense of security."

Hector nodded. The kid was right. A neat, uncluttered space warranted only a cursory glance from a guard on patrol.

"Nate made a trapdoor to the secret cellar," Jake said to Meli. "You and Hector and Freddy can hide down there. Cool, huh?"

Freddy walked over to sniff the hole in the floor. Meli flashed Jake a small smile and nodded. "Very cool."

The feeling that he'd missed something important gnawed at Hector.

Denzel waved a hand at the opening. "You better get down there. Sorry it's not bigger. There's food, water and a flashlight under the crate."

Meli reached out and grasped Denzel's shoulder. She gave it a gentle squeeze. "This is amazing. Thank you."

The kid blushed. "Uh, you're welcome."

Hector dropped to the floor's edge and dangled his legs into the opening. Getting through would be a tight squeeze. The dirt floor was only four feet below.

Slipping Meli's pack off his shoulder, he braced a hand on the wooden floorboards and then dropped into the hole.

When he squatted down to inspect their hideaway, his shoulders brushed the sides of the opening. Thin strips of faded light filtered through the cracks between floorboards to reveal a lumpy pile of pine-boughs and blankets that filled half of the roughly eight-by-ten-foot room. An upside-down wooden crate waited beside the far wall.

The scents of earth and pine reminded him of holding Meli in the cave shelter last night. A lifetime ago. He craved the comfort of holding her again, but it was a bad idea. She was too tempting to resist. He needed to do the right thing by her.

He shoved the pack over to the crate, crawled back to the trap door opening and stood. Fred had moved back to Meli's side. "Come on down, you two," he said. "Dinner is served."

Hector lifted the old dog down and helped Meli into the cellar. He dropped to his hands and knees and crawled to the crate. Moving the makeshift table aside, he found bottles of water and sandwiches in clear plastic bags, just as the kid had promised. His mouth watered.

He glanced over his shoulder at Meli waiting under the trap door. "Come over and sit. Lunch is ready."

Meli ran her hand along the bottoms of the overhead floorboards and duck-walked toward his voice. He guided her to a seat beside him on the hard-packed earth. Next he unwrapped what smelled like a little piece of deli heaven.

Freddy head-bumped his arm. Hector sighed and handed the dog half the sandwich. Freddy wolfed down the food.

Denzel's head poked upside-down through the trapdoor opening. "Stay here. Wait for Nate. When he comes, don't shoot him."

Hector chafed at taking orders from a kid. "Tell Nate to knock three times before he opens the trapdoor. Otherwise he's a dead man, kid."

The whites of the boy's eyes flashed. Without a word, he disappeared. The trapdoor shut as silently as it had opened. The soft thump of the beanbags indicated the boys had put things back in order. Two sets of footsteps left the playhouse at a dead run.

Satisfied he'd made his point, Hector reached for another sandwich.

Meli frowned at Hector. Had he been serious about shooting Nate? Or was he teasing the boys? "Why did you scare them like that?"

"Builds character." He shoved a plastic-wrapped bundle into her hands. "Eat your sandwich."

Her stomach clenched so hard she couldn't speak. They'd run out of food hours ago. She opened the package, took a huge bite and moaned at the burst of meaty, salty and mustardy flavor. Who knew a simple lunchmeat sandwich could taste so amazing? Savoring each delicious morsel, she prayed there were more.

Hector pressed a cool bottle into her hand. "Drink."

She twisted off the cap, sniffed to confirm the container held water and drank.

"I gave Freddy a drink and half a sandwich," he said.

"Thanks." She capped the bottle and set it beside her on the dirt floor. "Is there more food?"

A smile lightened his tone. "More than enough." He handed her another sandwich and crunched into one of his own.

Meli forced herself to take a break between sandwiches. She didn't want to make herself sick. "How are you feeling? I'm going to ask the Great and Wonderful Nate if he has any antibiotics hidden away. An infection is the last thing you need." She took a small bite.

"You worry too much. I'm feeling a hundred per cent better." Hector chewed and swallowed. "Relax. Enjoy. What more could I need than a gourmet meal in a five-star hotel with a new friend?"

Her dreams crumbled. Friends. From what Jake had told her, they'd never have time to be anything but friends. Meli's sandwich turned to dust in her mouth. Her throat tightened on a dry swallow and she choked.

Hector shoved the water bottle back into her hand. "Drink."

The cool liquid cleared her windpipe. "Thanks."

He plucked the plastic bottle from her fingers. "Finish your food, but take your time. You're going to need your strength. The next twenty-four hours may prove even more interesting than the last."

A harsh laugh exploded from her lips. She clamped a hand over her mouth and swallowed back tears. Life was so unfair. She'd finally found a man she could have a romantic relationship with, and....She would not cry, dammit!

Her body had other ideas. Her eyes stung. She sniffled, then wiped her nose on her shirtsleeve.

The playfulness left Hector's voice. "What's wrong?"

How could she tell him what Jake had told her without sounding pathetic? Jake was a kid. Maybe he'd misunderstood what the adults had said. "Nothing's wrong. I'm exhausted, that's all."

"You lie like a Girl Scout, Melisenda."

Even now, he could make her smile. Her heart twisted. Who knew being in love would hurt so much? Because she was in love with him. He was noble and dangerous and unpredictable and beat-up and so beautiful that when Denzel let her see him she'd forgotten to breathe.

Hector cupped her chin and turned her face toward him. "Tell me, Meli. What's getting you down?"

She ached to tell him her heart was breaking because she loved him, and this was probably her last day on earth, so she'd never know if he might have been able to love her back. The words just wouldn't come. Instead, she shook her head and squeezed her eyes shut in a futile attempt to hold back the tears that insisted on slipping down her cheeks.

Hector brushed them away with the balls of his thumbs, then handed her a napkin and waited in silence until the flow of tears ended. She blew her nose and discovered that, while she felt stuffy and puffy-eyed, she also felt a little better.

"Tell me," Hector said.

She sighed. He wasn't going to let it go. She could save face by offering him an edited version of the truth. "Promise you'll hear me out before you say anything."

He enfolded her cold, shaky hands in his warm, steady ones. A burst of unstable emotional energy wormed its way toward her fingertips. It took a major effort to bolster her shield, but she managed to block most of the energy from escaping.

"I promise," he said. "Now tell me."

Finding strength in his touch, she straightened her spine. "Remember how Denzel told us the foreseer predicted most of us will survive if we work together?"

He squeezed her hands. "Yes."

"Jake told me he wished I was going to make it, too. He said Nate and I are too nice to die." She swallowed the lump that had formed in her throat before she trusted herself to finish. "He even offered to take care of Freddy for me."

Hector pulled her onto his lap and into his strong

arms. He kissed her hair and tucked her head under his chin. His arms tightened around her. "The future's not set in stone, *Chica*. I won't let you die. Come hell or high water, that's not going to happen."

Her heart lifted in the face of his fierce determination. He might not be in love with her, but he did care about her. "If anyone can find a way to cheat death, it's you, Hector Protector."

"Ah, Meli." He shook his head against her hair and hugged her as if he would never let go.

Her heart flip-flopped. His confident words had been for her benefit. Inside, he wasn't certain he could save her, and it was tearing him apart. If she died, he'd see her death as an unforgiveable failure—his failure. Not only would she never have the chance to earn his love, but Hector would blame himself for her fate. She couldn't let that happen.

A blue jay squawked outside, reminding Meli only a few hours of daylight remained. When darkness fell, Nate would come. Her time alone with Hector would be over.

Her heart knocked against her ribs. If she didn't make it, he might not be as hard on himself if he believed he'd satisfied her heart's desire. It wasn't fair to ask him for what she wanted most when he couldn't refuse, but she had to do it for his own good.

She leaned away from him and caressed his whiskered jaw, remembering how those whiskers had lent his face a sexy, bad-boy appeal when she'd seen him through Denzel's eyes. "I lied to you, Hector."

He stilled "When?"

"When Denzel let me see you. The truth is, even after all you'd been through, you looked every inch a hero. My hero."

Laying a hand over his heart, she tipped her face up. "I need you to do something for me. Something important."

She heard him swallow. "Anything, Melisenda."

She placed a kiss filled with yearning and tenderness in the hollow at the base of his throat. He trembled.

"Make love to me, Hector. We may not have forever, but we have this moment. I need you to hold me, to make the world go away for a little while. Please—"

Hector silenced her with a searing kiss.

Her heart sang while liquid fire pooled low in her belly. Her energy was tempered and restrained by the love she felt for him. The musty root cellar faded from her awareness. There was only the two of them, touching and tasting and exploring, giving and receiving pleasure and comfort and strength from one another until they were spent.

Hector's brain stirred in the afterglow of their lovemaking. Affection for the brave, beautiful, amazing woman in his arms washed over him. She sighed against his shoulder. He opened his eyes to a riot of curls dimmed by the poor lighting in the cellar.

She tipped her head back and reached up to trace the contours of his face with her fingertips. Soft as feathers, light as breath, they trailed coppery golden energy across his temples, his cheekbones, his jaw.

He pulled the blanket up to her chin. "We need to get some sleep while we can."

She smiled and closed her eyes. "Now I can die a happy woman."

Hector lost his breath. She'd brought him back to life. No way in hell was she going to die. Not on his watch.

A big, warm hand gently shook Meli's shoulder, waking her from a deep and dreamless sleep. With Hector's long, warm body spooned around her the last thing she wanted was to have to move. She moaned. "Five more minutes."

Freddy's tags jingled down by her feet. He echoed her moan.

Hector pulled the long hair off her shoulder and trailed kisses up to her earlobe, sending a shiver of anticipation dancing across her skin. She wanted to stay here with Hector and make love forever. Turning in his arms, she gave him a kiss that sizzled with promise.

With a groan, he pulled away. "Gotta take a rain

check. After dark is a non-specific timeframe. It's time to get dressed and eat something. Meeting the Great and Powerful Nate calls for clothes and a clear head."

Meli's heart quaked. "It can't be night already!" As if to contradict her, a cricket began to chirp like a sad metronome.

Hector's lips brushed hers in a fleeting kiss. He rolled onto his back with a sigh. "Yep. Pitch black."

She swallowed her disappointment as the cold hard truth hit her full force. Tomorrow could be her dying day. Shivering, she hitched the blanket higher.

Paper crackled as Hector fumbled with the food sack. After setting the bag between them, he rummaged inside and handed her a plastic-wrapped sandwich. She heard his stomach grumble. "Dinnertime. Peanut butter and jelly, I believe."

The thought of food had no appeal.

Freddy's tags tinkled at her feet and he whined. Poor baby must be hungry. She unwrapped her sandwich and held it out to her Guide.

"No you don't!" Hector grabbed her wrist. "Eat. You can't cheat death on an empty stomach. There's another sandwich for Fred."

He was right. She needed to remain strong. Hector said they could change the future, and she had to have faith he was right, or she'd undermine her chances of survival.

Plastic rustled, Hector unwrapping a sandwich. "Here you go, Fred." The branches under them shifted.

Freddy's tags clinked as he gulped his sandwich. Meli caught a whiff of peanut butter and salmonberry jelly and discovered she was hungry after all.

Staring death in the face should make a person appreciate each small pleasure in life. She wouldn't take anything for granted now. She'd enjoy the heck out of every second. Her new rule was live for the moment.

Meli bit into her sandwich and savored the creamy-sweet filling. The paper bag crackled again, Hector removing his food.

She chewed and swallowed. "Salmonberry jelly is one of my favorite things. Tastes as sweet as a sunny day, you know?"

Hector spoke around a mouthful. "You're right. This is amazing stuff. Wait till I show you what we can do with salmonberry jelly in bed."

Her breath hitched. He wanted to take her to bed again, wanted to be her lover. A future with Hector in it looked pretty damned good. She could cheat death for that any day. Couldn't she?

Hector chugged some water before pressing the bottle into her hand. Sparks snapped when their fingers touched. "Now cut that out."

Meli smiled. She finished her sandwich while Hector took care of Freddy. Water splashed into her Guide's dish. Hector laughed. "Whoa, Fred. Stand back or you'll get a shower."

Her heart warmed. Hector and Freddy were buddies

now. If she didn't make it out, at least they'd have each other. A lump tried to form in her throat.

"Where are my glasses?" She hoped Hector wouldn't catch the tightness in her voice.

"One second." He shifted and pressed the smooth plastic frames into her hand. "You okay?"

Meli nodded and slipped them on. By the time they finished eating she felt better. The future wasn't carved in granite. She could—no, she would—get out of this mess alive. The three of them would go berry picking and have a picnic lunch. She'd learn how to make jelly.

"We'd better get dressed," Hector said, interrupting her daydream. He pressed her bra and panties into her hands.

When they were decent Meli dug the hairbrush out of her pack and corralled her wild curls into a ponytail. "You can clean up with some of Freddy's wipes if you want." She planned to use one on her own face.

"No thanks. I'd rather smell like a manly man." He lifted her chin and kissed her lightly.

The moment he touched her she dropped the brush. Her hands found his shoulders and she pulled him into a deeper kiss. Her heart swelled with love for him. Wisps of the warm energy flowing through her veins flowed into his mouth.

Finally, they pulled apart. "What was that for?" he asked, sounding hoarse and sexy at the same time.

"I love you." She hadn't meant to tell him, hadn't intended to let the words sneak out. But he was her *media naranja*, her other half. Her soulmate.

He set her away from him. *"¡Mierda!"*

Heat rose in her face at his reaction, but she was glad she'd said the words. He was afraid to love again, afraid of being hurt. But she might only have a few hours left in this life. She deserved a chance to tell him.

"Don't be naïve, Meli. You're not in love with me. You haven't been with enough men to know anything about love."

His intense reaction did not surprise her. Still, his harsh words stung. "So how many men do I need to sleep with to be a love expert like you? A hundred? A thousand?"

His breath rasped in and out a few times. "This is what I was afraid would happen."

She threw up her hands. "At last, some honesty! When it comes to your emotions, you're a coward. You're afraid to love."

"Don't be silly. We had sex, but that doesn't mean we're in love. Hell, Hector isn't even my real name."

She blinked. He'd offered up his last name in the cave, but he'd let her assume Hector was his given name. She shook her head. Irrelevant. "I'm not in love with your name. You—"

Heavy footsteps chunked onto the step outside the front door.

Meli froze.

Freddy growled deep in his chest.

16

HECTOR'S INDRAWN BREATH sounded loud in the sudden silence. Metal scraped on wood. He must have grabbed his gun off the crate.

The front door latch clicked open.

Heart pounding, Meli crawled over to keep Freddy quiet. She stroked his big head and tried to calm her breath. Floorboards creaked with each step as someone crossed the front room. The door to the back room creaked open above them.

Meli shivered. If this was Nate, he'd better remember to knock.

Three muted taps sounded on the rug-covered trapdoor. Her breath hissed out. Freddy huffed.

A low-pitched, muffled said, "Don't shoot! It's me, Nate. Nate Brickman." The trapdoor lifted on a whoosh of air. "Come on up. I brought coffee."

Freddy's tail swished, always a good sign. The rich scent of strong coffee made her mouth water.

Hector's gun scraped into his waistband. "Hell, the bad guys never bring coffee." Meli heard him fumble with something on the floor and put the item in his pocket.

Freddy whined for help from under the trapdoor.

She moved to crawl over, but Hector stopped her with a firm hand on her shoulder. "I'll go first."

His protective gesture convinced her she'd been winning the argument when Nate arrived. Hiding her smile, she followed on Hector's heels and waited while he hoisted Freddy up. Doggy nails clicked on the wooden floor overhead.

A chuckle rumbled above her. Nate kept his voice just above a whisper. "Hey, Freddy. I've heard a lot about you. Who's a good boy?"

Freddy let out a *someone-is-scratching-behind-my-ears* sigh of ecstasy.

Grunting, Hector hitched himself up to sit on the floorboards. He helped Meli up and they both scrambled to their feet. Hector tucked her hand into the crook of his arm and placed his body between her and the hole in the floor. She thought of asking him to close the trap, but leaving the bolt hole open would save time if they had to hide.

Orienting on Freddy's excited panting, Meli aimed a smile Nate's way. Rule Number Twenty was always be polite. Good manners are good defenses. "Hi. I'm Meli."

"A pleasure to meet you," he said from well over her head. He must be even taller than Hector. "I hope the root cellar isn't too uncomfortable."

Memories of making love to Hector heated her face. "It's been—lovely. You've thought of everything."

"I only built the playhouse. Lorelei outfitted the cellar."

Hector's arm stiffened. What was wrong? Who was Lorelei?

Nate continued in a matter-of-fact tone. "There's no easy way to break this news, man. Lori and your boy are alive."

It took Meli a few seconds to make sense of what Nate had said. She stumbled back a step, tried to keep her balance as her reality shifted. *Hector has a family.*

"Alive?" Hector's voice cracked. "They can't be alive. Lori's twin telepath, Leah—"

Nate shook his head and held up a hand, palm out. "I know what she told you. Leah lied." Nate sighed. "I know this is lot to digest, but we don't have much time to talk. Leah lied for good reason. Lori will explain it all to you."

"They're—they're here?" Hector sounded as stunned as Meli felt.

"They're here," Nate said. "Lori's a wonderful mother and he's a great kid. You're a lucky man. She named him Rafael, after you. We call him R.D."

Her pulse pounded in her ears. Hector was a figment of her imagination, a man who belonged only to her. There was no Hector, only a stranger named Rafael who belonged with his son and Lori.

Meli's breath came out in a sob. Whether she lived or died didn't matter. Either way, she would never be with Hector.

Warm hands cupped her face. "I thought they were dead," Hector said, his voice pleading for understanding. "I would have told you about them."

Meli pulled away. "Tell me now." She wiped her wet cheeks with fingers that shook. When had she started to cry?

He didn't touch her again. "Lori—Lorelei Dawson— was an FBI Special Psychic Agent. Like me, only different. A twin telepath. She could communicate telepathically with her twin sister, Leah. Lori and I hooked up once when we were both coming out of deep cover. Pure recreational stress release with no strings attached—or so we thought."

His laugh was bitter. "A couple weeks later she discovered she was pregnant. We tried to build a relationship for the baby's sake. Lori and Leah, grew up in foster care. We both wanted our son to have a stable home with two parents. The Cartel kidnapped Lori two months before the baby was due."

Memories of her time in Mendoza's torture chamber flooded Meli's mind—all those horrible tools and sharp blades. *"¡Dios mío!"* she whispered, feeling sick.

"She wasn't tortured," Nate said, as if he'd read Meli's mind. "They couldn't risk harming the child. He was too valuable. Killingsworth sensed he was highly Talented."

Hector's voice snapped like a whip. "Why did Leah tell me they were murdered?"

The grief and dawning anger that sharpened his tongue made Meli's heart ache for him. She couldn't imagine what it was like to experience his dead family's sudden resurrection. To learn that people he implicitly trusted had betrayed him.

"I'll leave it to Lori to explain the rest," Nate said.

Hector—No, Rafael remained silent for a couple of heartbeats. "I want to see them. Now."

Freddy growled at the anger in his tone.

"Now, here's the thing, Rafe," Nate began, steel underlying his easygoing drawl.

"Call me Hector. Rafe died a long time ago."

Warm fingers briefly touched her hand. Meli shivered. She fought the urge to grab his like a lifeline, instead wrapping her arms around herself.

"Hector," Nate said. "Whatever you call yourself, you must be chomping at the bit. I know I would be if I were in your shoes. But the meeting will go down the way Lori wants it to go down."

The big man sounded like a Hollywood sheriff telling the bad guy to get out of Dodge. He might seem laid back, but he wouldn't hesitate to put his life on the line to protect Lori.

Hector's response was surprisingly mild. "How is that?"

"Lori says a family reunion's no place to talk business," Nate said evenly. "She told me to fill you in on the situation we're up against beforehand."

Inexplicably, Hector laughed. "Then fill me in."

"Over coffee," Nate said. "Meli's cold. Cream or sugar, kid?" Liquid streamed into a cup.

A mug of hot coffee would give her something warm and solid to hold on to. "Cream, thanks."

"I hear you take yours black," Nate said to Hector.

Meli's throat ached. She hadn't known how he took his coffee. Lori must have told Nate. After all, the woman had lived with Hector, had been engaged to him, had given birth to his baby. Whereas Meli had only known him for two days.

She's Thanksgiving Dinner and I'm trail mix.

Not that it mattered. Lori and R.D. were Hector's family. No way was Meli a home-wrecker. She couldn't stand between a child and his father. Not after losing her own parents.

A spoon clinked on stoneware. Nate stirring her coffee?

"Hand this to Meli, please," he said.

Hector guided her fingers to the handle of a mug as if he'd done it a thousand times before. She blinked back more tears. He watched out for her, stood by her, accepted and respected her. How could she give him up?

Heat seeped through the ceramic mug into her hands. I am strong. She took a sip of the hot, creamy liquid. If I have to, I can do anything.

She loved Hector, heart and soul. But she and Freddy were doing just fine before the drug lord's wedding. Before Hector. Well, maybe not exactly fine, but they managed. She could give him up, if that's what she had to do to make him happy.

Remembering the four achingly lonely years since her uncle's death, she discovered a lump the size of Mount Saint Helens lodged in her throat. During the last couple of days, terrible as they'd been in so many ways, Hector had filled a gaping hole in her heart. They'd become friends. Partners. Lovers.

Nate's gravelly rumble broke the silence. Meli forced herself to drink her coffee and focus on his words.

"First, you need to understand that one of us, Zinnia Washington, is a foreseer. She gets glimpses of the most likely future. Our lives are not entirely predestined, you understand. We have free will. Think of life as a river flowing within high banks. Diverting or even blocking the flow is possible, but those things take a lot of energy and effort to accomplish. A group of people working together over months or even years might change the river's course."

A floorboard creaked beside her. "What does this have to do with us?" Hector said.

"When Zinnia and her father arrived a few months

after me, she foresaw our most likely future. There would be no escape for us. For nearly six years we've worked to alter that future. We've accomplished a hundred little changes in preparation for an escape attempt, altered our plans over and over in hopes our efforts would add up to a big change in our future. After a couple of years, Hector showed up in one of Zinnia's visions, but still no one escaped. Other than Hector's appearance, only the details of our future changed. Despite all our efforts, the end result was always the same. We failed. We died. Hector died."

Meli turned cold. She couldn't let Hector die. Somehow, she had to protect him.

Nate continued. "The night of Mendoza's wedding, something finally shifted. That night, Zinnia got a flash, a brief glimpse, of Lori and R.D. and Hector somewhere in the future. From Zinnia's description of the room and the older Hispanic woman who held R.D. on her lap, Lori recognized Hector's mother. R.D. blew out four candles on a birthday cake. He turns four in a few months. The three of them will make it out alive."

Meli's heart lightened. At least Hector and his son would escape—and Lori.

Hector's warm, familiar hand enfolded hers. "What about Meli? The rest?"

"I'm sorry. We don't know. Zinnia believes the fact that the glimpse of the future she got was so brief indicates things are still in flux. She's seen nothing specific to indicate the rest don't make it. If we work together, I believe all of us will escape."

Hector was no doubt sure he could dowse a way out for them. But Meli knew the truth. Nate didn't believe the rest of them would survive. Little Jake had told her so right after they'd arrived at the camp.

An unexpected calm settled over her like a warm, heavy blanket. She and Freddy were the key, the new elements in the equation. She had to figure out what they must do to save Hector and his family. This was her destiny. Protecting them would give her life—and her death—meaning.

Nate cleared his throat. "Will and Zinnia monitored Mendoza's wedding and reception as part of the security detail. Will is Zinnia's father, and a farseer. Their job was to watch for an attack from outside the camp. When Zinnia secretly told her father the probable future had shifted, he immediately scanned Mendoza's compound and the surrounding forest. He spotted you in the gazebo, kissing Meli. He's followed you as much as possible ever since."

Meli's lips curved into a small smile. Their kiss had changed the probable future.

Hector swallowed a mouthful of bitter coffee and scrutinized Nate in the dim starlight that filtered through the curtains. Six-and-a-half feet of solid muscle, a thirty-ish white male with light eyes and close-cropped brown hair whose agenda might not be what he claimed.

Learning Lori and the boy were alive had released a

storm of emotions that were hard for the agent to keep in check. His initial moments of shock and joy were followed by darker feelings. Pain. Anger. Betrayal. But Meli's anguish had gutted his own reaction. He needed to focus on protecting her. Wearing his Hector suit helped him to compartmentalize.

The question at hand was whether or not Nate was telling the truth.

Having experienced the power of Meli's kiss firsthand, the man's claim that what had happened in the gazebo had changed the probable future seemed plausible. Certainly, that kiss had changed everything for him—and for her, too. Combined with their decisions to help one another escape, the kiss had set them on the path leading to this moment.

He frowned. The fact that Zinnia didn't see Meli in her glimpse of the future that mirrored his dream from the cave didn't mean she wouldn't be there. No way in hell would he leave without Meli. In both the dream and Zinnia's vision, he made it out. In his dream, Meli had lost her way—whatever the hell that meant. His shoulders twitched.

He touched the familiar comforting shape of his St. Jude medal through the fabric of his shirt. Thank God R.D. and Lori would survive. God willing, he would find the right path for them all.

Hector refocused on Nate. Clearly the prisoners' leader was in love with Lori. The man had nothing but good things to say about her, he let her tell him what to do and he insisted that she ramrod their little family reunion.

Huh. Why aren't I jealous?

No time to ponder that now. He needed more information. "What are the prisoners' Talents?"

"You already know about Lori, Zinnia and Will," Nate said.

Hector nodded in the darkness. "And Jake and Denzel."

"Right. Sophie has no Talent of her own, but she's expecting a Talented child. We think that's why Killingsworth targeted her. Unfortunately, that's all we know. She has no memory of her life before she arrived eight months ago. She didn't even know she was pregnant."

Nate paused. "We're not sure about R.D., although he's really good at puzzles. He may take after you."

Hector's throat tightened. My son. The son he thought he'd lost forever. A finger tapped his chest. He blinked down at Meli, who seemed to have regained her composure.

"If R.D. is lucky, he's a regular Mini You, Hector Protector. A hero." She took his hand and turned to Nate. "What about you? What's your Talent?"

Hector gave her hand a little squeeze.

Nate lifted a shoulder in response to her question. "I'm just the handyman. I keep the camp running. I don't have a Talent."

Hector scowled. The non-Talented didn't attract a

hound's attention.

"I know how it sounds, but it's true," Nate continued. "Killingsworth kidnapped me a couple of months before they completed making over this camp. I was working my way through Oregon Tech as an apartment maintenance man. One night on my way home from the TriMet station, I heard a woman scream. Two guys were forcing her into a van down the street. I ran toward them, yelling at the top of my lungs, hoping to scare them off."

Nate crossed his arms over his chest. "Turned out the tall one had a gun. It was Killingsworth. I ended up in the van, bound and gagged, along with the woman. Then they drugged us."

The big man stared into his coffee mug for a moment. When he spoke, his tone was bleak. "I woke up here. I wish I knew what they did with the woman. I never even got a good look at her."

Hector found himself repeating the words his boss had said to him after Lori disappeared. "Whatever happened to her wasn't your fault."

Nate was quiet for a moment. "Anyhow, once he convinced himself I wasn't a cop, just a handyman, he decided to let me live. He needed a jack-of-all-trades, and he didn't have to pay me."

Nate paused for a swallow of coffee. "I didn't understand Mendoza's plans for this place until Zinnia and Will arrived a couple of months later. Up till then, I thought psychic Talent was a figment of society's collective imagination."

If what Nate said was true, his reality had been hit with a wrecking ball. The fact he'd made the transition without coming unglued said something for his strength of character. "How long have you been here?"

"Six years." Nate shook his head. "Six crazy years."

Meli spoke up. "And nobody suspects you've been working on an escape? How is that possible?"

Nate's tone lightened. "Luck and complacency. They have a shielder working for them, someone strong enough to shield the entire camp from detection. They keep the shielder in the guardhouse. We figured it out because that's the one place that's completely off-limits. Prisoners are allowed into the infirmary, but that's it. And the shield blocks Talent from both sides. That's why Jake had to be outside the camp shield to communicate with Meli's dog."

Hector held up a hand to halt the info dump. "Give me a minute to process."

He added that last bit of intel to his mental Must Tell Doc folder. A shielder with a huge sphere of influence was something they'd never encountered before. When the Cartel had work for one of the prisoners, the hound took him or her outside the shield because the energetic barrier limited their effective range to 'inside the camp.' Mendoza's Talented thugs wouldn't be able to observe what happened inside the shield from outside for the same reason.

"So the guards depend on technology to keep track

of the prisoners and to monitor the perimeter fence?" he asked.

Nate chuckled. "Did I mention I was an electronics engineering major?"

Meli tilted her head to the side. "Don't they have a farseer or a hound among the camp guards?"

Hector knew the answer to that one. "Only a handful of the Talented are on the Cartel's payroll. Mendoza needs them for unsupervised assignments, stuff he doesn't trust to his captives. With a shield around the camp, he doesn't need to waste loyal Talents on guard duty. Instead he invests in high-tech fencing, laser sensors and security cameras."

He drained his last drop of coffee and handed the stoneware cup back to Nate. "Denzel told us you tinkered with the laser sensors and security cameras. I'm impressed. That alone gives us a leg up."

Meli pressed her empty mug into Hector's hand. "So you'll stay?"

Wishing he could see the expression in Nate's eyes, Hector handed over Meli's mug. "We'll stay. But Nate and I have to agree on a final plan." Just in case he's lying.

The big man nodded. "I wouldn't want it any other way."

Freddy climbed to his feet and trotted to the door, tail swishing, as if he sensed someone's approach. Hector fought to keep his heartbeat steady. Meli's hand slipped from his grasp.

"Guess it's time for that family reunion," Nate said. "Give us a minute." He strode to the door, opened it and stepped outside before closing the door behind him.

17

MELI'S WHISPER CARRIED a note of urgency. "Lead me to the trapdoor, Hector. The three of you don't need an audience."

He wanted her to stay by his side, but she was right. This first meeting should be between him and Lori and R.D. He cupped her lovely face in his hands. She pressed her cheek against his palm.

His heart tripped. "Meli—"

She lay a gentle finger across his lips. "Shh. I know. It's okay. They love you. You're R.D.'s father, his hero. He needs you." She pressed her lips to his palm. Soothing warmth flowed up to calm his heart. "He's a lucky little boy."

Nate's rumble carried through the door, followed by a soft murmur.

Hector helped Meli hop down into the shadowy cellar. She disappeared into the darkness and his throat ached. Freddy sent him a reproachful look. He jumped down and helped the old dog into the cellar. Then he climbed out and eased the trapdoor shut. Air escaped in a sad sigh.

Sweat beaded his forehead, though cool night air chilled his skin. The prospect of facing Lori alone filled him with unease. He straightened and glanced around the shadow-shrouded playroom. The events of the last few hours felt surreal, a dream. Had he really made love to Meli, taken her virginity? Were Lori and his son truly alive? What the hell was he supposed to say to them?

The door opened and a woman called softly. "Rafe?"

Recognizing Lori's soft contralto, he squared his shoulders. "Come in."

A slight female figure silently slipped inside and shut the door. Her ghost-pale face bobbed down and back up in a nod. "Rafe. Or should I call you Hector?"

His heart hitched. Who was this sinewy wraith, returned from the grave? Lorelei had been curvy and strong-willed. Four years of slavery had stripped away her softness, but not her steely core. She stood, feet apart and her knees slightly bent, braced for battle.

He raised his chin. "Call me dumbfounded."

A tight ponytail held back her straight dark hair. He remembered her eyes were a clear blue that could frost up in an instant. He'd forgotten living with her sometimes felt like walking through a minefield. She was always waiting for him to screw up, to prove he wasn't dependable so she could leave the relationship.

Were her eyes frosted now? Why would they be? Hadn't he proven he was the most reliable man on planet Earth?

She drew a deep breath. "Nate will bring R.D. in a few minutes. Before you see him, you and I need to talk."

Hector's jaw clenched. When they were together, those words had been a red flag that Lori wanted to argue—and that she planned to win. Damned if he'd let her lead him around like a fool.

"Leah told the Bureau you were dead. Not that I'm unhappy that was a goddamned lie—" he said, choking on the last word.

Lori flinched.

He stepped closer, pressing his advantage and forcing her to tip her head back to look up at him. "I put up headstones for you and the baby at the cemetery in Albuquerque. All I had were the stones, since we didn't..." He forced the words past the sandpaper lining his throat. "We didn't have your bodies. Sometimes Mom and Leah and I would run into each other there. We cried together, for Christ's sake. How could she lie to me? How could you?"

Lori spread her hands, palm up. "We had to protect the baby. Please try to understand!"

Have patience, mi hijo, his mother whispered in his head. *Hear her out.*

He shook his head and turned away from Lori. The last thing he wanted to do was have patience. He wanted to rant and rage at her. But what good would come of it? As usual, Mom was right.

Hands on hips, he inhaled a slow, deep breath and then exhaled just as slowly. Then he spun on his heel. "Okay," he said to Lori. "Explain."

She answered quickly with a question. "Do you know why I was kidnapped?"

He blinked at the unexpected change of subject. "Because you're an agent."

"No," Lori said. "That's what I thought at first. But I wasn't their target. The baby's energy spurts sometimes broke through my shield. Mendoza's hound sensed R.D. was a Level Ten Talent while he was still in the womb."

Hector's head began to hurt. "They didn't know you were an agent?"

"They knew—but that wasn't their motivation for kidnapping me. They needed another powerful child to mold into a weapon. They knew the chances were slim they'd get a chance to kidnap the baby once Doc got wind of his potential. I was just their incubator. As a trained agent, I would be a liability among the camp inmates. They'd torture me for what I could tell them about the Bureau's operations, then kill me."

She began to pace. "I couldn't let that happen. I had

to protect our baby. I had to offer Mendoza something he couldn't refuse in exchange for my life."

Hector braced himself for what was coming.

"I told him Leah and I would spy for the Cartel."

His lungs compressed. His father had died under torture without betraying the Bureau. But Lori had volunteered to spy for Mendoza. He clenched his teeth to keep from saying something he might regret.

Lori's speech quickened. "Please try to understand. Nate was already working on an escape plan. I believed we only needed a few months. No mother in her right mind would abandon her child to Killingsworth."

Hector forced his muscles to unknot. His father had sacrificed himself to protect innocent lives. Lori had made her choices to protect her innocent baby from monsters. Her only bargaining chip had been her link to her twin and the information they could obtain for the Cartel. The sisters' had committed treason to save his son.

Lori resumed pacing. "Without consulting me, Leah went to Director Grayson with everything and proposed we'd act as double agents. She knew I'd never agree to risk a double-cross. If the betrayal came to light, Mendoza would have slit my throat. By the time I found out, it was too late."

She reached out as if to touch his cheek, but let her hand fall to her side. "I thought I'd never forgive her. But eventually I realized Leah and Doc had given us a way out. If we ever escaped or were rescued, we wouldn't be considered criminals. We hadn't betrayed the Bureau. We fed the Cartel what Doc wanted them to believe, along with just enough truth to convince them all the information was true." She heaved a heavy sigh.

"Try to understand. When Mendoza took me outside the shield to communicate with Leah, she told me how you searched for us, how you almost found us twice, how you wouldn't give up. If the Bureau attempted a rescue the guards would have killed all the prisoners. They still have orders to kill us, even the children. We had to protect R.D."

He shook his head, remembering the small bodies they'd found at the Sonoran camp. He hated that she was right.

A humorless laugh escaped her. She began to pace. "After we faked mine and R.D.'s deaths, Leah told me how you brought flowers to the cemetery whenever you were in town. How, even though you thought we were dead, you devoted your life to finding all the camps. I knew then I'd been wrong about you. I was terrified you would find us."

"I would have protected you," Hector said.

Lori stopped in front of him. "You would have tried, but Zinnia—our foreseer—told me you would have failed. We would have died."

Intellectually, he knew what she'd told him was the truth. Emotionally, it was going to take a while for him to accept it all.

Lori touched his hand. "We betrayed you. I thought about the pain I caused you every single day. I hope someday you'll find it in your heart to forgive me. Leah and Doc, too. I'm truly sorry I couldn't find another way to protect our son."

A wave of sorrow for what she'd had to endure washed over him. She'd lived on a razor's edge for four years, but she'd kept their son alive and well. She took responsibility for what she had put him through.

"I'm pissed, but I'll get over it," he told her. "You're not to blame. Mendoza and Killingsworth will pay for their crimes. We'll destroy the Cartel. I swear it."

Lori's posture softened. "You're a good man. Your son knows that. R.D. is going to be over the moon with excitement when I tell him you're here."

Something in the way Lori said it told him Nate's affections for her were mutual. It was as if she'd said, "You're a good man, Hector, but…"

"So R.D.'s over the moon, but your feet are planted firmly on the ground," he said gently. "Am I right?"

She backed away. "Things were never going to work out for us. We wanted everything to be perfect for R.D., but a loveless marriage between two hard-headed loners would have been a nightmare for him."

He'd always been so sure they could work things out. But the more he'd insisted, the more she'd pulled away from him. She'd been afraid to love because she'd been abandoned as a child.

The way you are afraid to love Melisenda, mi hijo? his mother whispered in his head.

He stiffened. He wasn't afraid of loving Meli. Was he? His mother's presence faded.

"We're old enough to know better now, aren't we?" Lori said.

Hector focused on the woman in front of him. The dream of the three of them happy together had kept him going until Lori and R.D. supposedly died. But the truth was his and Lori's life together hadn't been easy. Not like his own parents' relationship.

Lori cupped his jaw with one hand. "You can't lose R.D. He worships you. No one can replace you in his heart. And you can't lose me. I'm your son's mother. We're tied together for life. Family."

He hugged her to his chest before setting her free. He'd lost her and mourned her years ago. And he knew now that he and Lori had never really been in love.

She tipped her head back. "You okay with this?"

At peace for the first time in a long time, he smiled. "I'm good."

She laid a hand on the door handle and paused. "I'll warn you, R.D.'s been asleep. It's way past his bedtime. Don't expect too much from him tonight."

Hector's stomach flipped. He was finally going to meet his son. Not an infant, but a small boy. R.D. waited on the other side of the door. His pulse quickened. "I only want to see him, Lori. To touch him.

I don't want to scare him."

She nodded and opened the door. Nate stepped into the shadowy room with a blanket-wrapped child in his arms. The little boy's dark head rested on the big man's chest beneath his chin. His arms clung to Nate's neck the way a drowning man clings to a log.

Hector's eyes stung. His arms itched to hold the miracle that was his son, but he held back. Lori shut the door behind Nate. The boy whimpered in his sleep. His mother reached for him.

Nate nodded to Hector before relinquishing the child to Lori. "He had another nightmare. Be careful when you wake him up."

"Do you know what the dream was about?" She settled the toddler on her shoulder with practiced ease.

Nate shook his head. "No, honey. I wish I did."

Hector watched R.D. transfer his death grip to Lori without awakening. He studied the little boy in the dim light of a full moon. Dark hair like his and Lori's. Were his son's eyes nearly black like his own? Would he grow up to be a dowser?

R.D. stirred in his sleep. Nate reached out a hand to rub circles on the boy's back while he spoke to Lori. "When I reached the bunkhouse, Zinnia had him in the rocking chair, trying to comfort him." R.D. quieted under Nate's soothing touch. "He grabbed onto my neck so tight I could hardly breathe."

On one level, Hector listened to the conversation. On another level, one closer to his heart, he observed the three of them together. A bitter taste filled his mouth. For all intents and purposes, they were a family. Nate had stepped in as Lori and R.D.'s protector. The man clearly loved them.

Forcing his muscles to relax, he focused on what Nate was telling Lori.

"A few minutes ago, his teeth finally stopped chattering and he went back to sleep." Nate turned to Hector. "R.D. started having terrifying dreams a few days ago."

Nate turned to Lori. "He hasn't been alone with Killingsworth or one of the guards, has he?"

"Over my dead body." Hearing the frost in her tone, Hector winced.

Nate touched Lori's shoulder. "Sorry. Stupid question." He moved toward the door.

"Wait," Lori said. "You have better luck waking him up than I do when he's like this. Stay. Please. I want meeting his father to be a happy experience."

Nate shook his head. "I don't want to intrude."

R.D. sucked in a sobbing breath, then sighed. Hector ignored the jealous ache in his heart. The important thing was to see that his son's needs were met.

"Lori's right. The boy needs you. Night terrors are a sign his Talent is awakening. He's frightened and confused. He needs to stay grounded, to feel safe. Security is something you can give him.

"We all know I can't. Not yet."

18

NATE FOLDED HIS ARMS across his chest and watched Lori. She nodded for Hector to go on.

"At first, Talents involved in sensing rather than projecting energy manifest during sleep. Night terrors indicate R.D.'s Talent is afferent, like mine. He's receiving information in his sleep. He's like a newborn baby, bombarded with strange and often frightening input. When he's overwhelmed by the flood, he shuts down. That's why he sleeps so deeply after a nightmare."

"I don't remember having nightmares like his," Lori said. "But Leah and I often had bad dreams when we were kids, especially when we moved to a new foster home."

"Your dreams wouldn't have reached the intensity of

R.D.'s. You two only receive information from someone you know almost as well as you know yourself—each other. You love and trust one another."

R.D. moaned in Lori's arms. "Right," she said softly. She rocked back and forth on her feet to try to quiet him.

Hector lowered his voice. "The good news is his Talent will mature and the dreams will subside. His personal shield will kick in during sleep."

R.D. shifted his head to rest on Lori's other shoulder.

"He's waking up," Hector and Nate said in unison. *¡Mierda!* If the boy wasn't awake before, he would be now.

"Mommy?" R.D.'s sweet, childish voice arrowed straight through Hector's heart.

Lori's tone was soothing. "Are you awake, sweetie? You had a bad dream, but it's over now. Don't be scared. Mommy and Uncle Nate are here."

R.D.'s head jerked up and he twisted in his mother's arms. He caught sight of Hector and froze like a rabbit that had spotted a coyote.

"Everything's okay, R.D.," Lori said. "This man is your daddy. We always knew he would find us, didn't we? He never stopped looking, and here he is. We call him Hector."

R.D. began to shake. "No!" He hid his face against his mother's breasts. "Make him go away," he sobbed. "He—He's a bad guy."

The little boy's words were a punch in the chest. What the hell was going on?

Nate covered the child's back with one big hand and murmured something into his ear. Lori kissed the little boy's tousled hair. She spoke in a firm, calm voice. "Sweetie, your daddy is a very good man. Tell me why you're afraid of him."

R.D. shook his head violently. Nate returned to rubbing the little guy's hunched shoulders. "No one's going to hurt you, Tiger. Tell us what's wrong."

Hector had to strain to catch the boy's muffled words. "He has a gun. I saw him, Uncle Nate. He has a g-gun."

Nate clicked on his penlight and shone the beam on Hector's face.

Hector gave a slight nod, his thoughts skittering like raindrops on hot asphalt.

How did R.D. know he was armed? Obviously the weapon would scare the little boy. The only men with guns in the camp were the guards. Lori would have instilled a healthy respect for them in their son. But why had the child dreamed about Hector and the Glock tonight of all nights? Was R.D. a farseer?

Nate spoke softly. "That's all right, Tiger. He brought his gun to protect us from the bad guys because they have guns. Your Daddy is definitely one of the good guys."

R.D. shook his head again. "He shot you, Uncle Nate. He's bad."

Hector flinched. Had seeing Hector's gun while farseeing triggered an ordinary bad dream? Or had R.D. seen the probable future?

And if so, why would Hector shoot Nate?

The big man spoke calmly. "You had a bad dream, Tiger. I'm fine. Nobody shot me. We're glad your daddy is here to help us. And I'm very glad he brought his gun to help us get away from the bad guys."

R.D. turned his head and peeked at Nate. "But you b-bleeded and b-bleeded and—and—"

Lori made shushing noises and hugged the child tightly. "It was only a bad dream, sweetie. Nate's not bleeding. He's fine."

R.D. lifted his head to look. Nate passed the beam of light over his body from top to bottom. "See? Just a bad dream. I'm right as rain. And you know what? Your daddy and I are partners. He's going to help us escape. Ask your mom."

R.D. faced his mother. "It's true, sweetie."

The boy squirmed around in Lori's arms and frowned at Hector. Addressing his father for the first time, R.D.'s voice wavered with uncertainty. "Partners don't shoot partners. Partners have each other's backs."

Hector's heart lifted. The little guy was talking to him. Not the first words he'd hoped to hear from his son, but he'd take them. They would be hard to forget.

He nodded solemnly. "That's the number one rule for partners—or if it's not, it should be. Partners don't hurt each other. Did Nate and your mommy teach you about partners?"

R.D. gave him a tentative nod.

"I'm sure lucky your mom and Nate were here to teach you important stuff like that until I could find you."

R.D. studied him. "Promise. Promise you won't shoot Nate, no matter what."

Pride swelled his chest. The kid played hardball. Nothing on earth could make him shoot Nate and break R.D.'s heart. He'd do anything for his son. "I promise. I won't let you down, son."

R.D. seemed to be taking his measure. Finally, the boy nodded.

Tears of relief stung the backs of Hector's eyes. He blinked them away and smiled, not sure that R.D. could make out his expression in the dim light. "I hope you'll let me teach you a thing or two someday—after we get to know each other."

The little boy's thumb crept up to his mouth. "Okay," he said, and popped it in.

Hector's smile stretched into a grin. They'd get along fine. Luckily he'd had a crash course in partnerships from Meli.

"R.D. needs to get some sleep," Lori said softly.

He suppressed a twinge of disappointment. She was right. The kid was tough, but he'd been through enough for one day. "We all need to get some sleep."

"See you tomorrow, Tiger," Nate said. He nuzzled the child's neck and kissed him with a loud smack.

R.D. giggled and removed his thumb. "G'night, Unca Nate."

"Good night, son," Hector said. He longed for the easy camaraderie Nate and R.D. shared.

"G'night." R.D. lay his cheek on his mother's shoulder. "See you tomorrow, Daddy?" His thumb returned to his mouth.

A part of Hector's soul that he'd held back for years, rigid and unyielding, broke free. A warm tear slid down his cheek. "See you tomorrow."

Thank God the boy couldn't see him cry. R.D. was already confused. He wouldn't understand they were tears of joy.

Hector wiped his eyes on his shirtsleeve and offered Nate his hand. "I meant what I said. We're partners. Meli's taught me the value of teamwork."

Nate clasped Hector's outstretched hand and they shook. "We're gonna make one helluva team," the big man said, releasing Hector. "Get a couple hours' sleep. That's all the time we have. We leave at first light."

After Lori and Nate left to take R.D. back to bed. Hector paced the playhouse floor in the dark. The fact that Nate was alive and well implied R.D. had seen the probable future, a future Hector had to change if he was to win the boy's trust. But first he and Meli had to figure out why he would shoot Nate in the first place.

He swallowed. Meli.

His emotions were all over the map, but mostly he felt like a heel. Hurting Meli had been the last thing he'd wanted. He should have told her what had happened to his family before he'd made love to her. To be honest, at the time he'd thought of nothing but Meli.

He owed her an apology. She was right. He was an emotional coward.

Before they became lovers, he knew her well enough to trust her with his life. Hell, they were partners. She'd had his back from the beginning, and he'd tried to have hers. They liked and respected one another. Then, when he learned Meli was afraid she wouldn't survive, he'd felt...Hell, he didn't know what he'd felt. Overwhelming tenderness, maybe. He'd wanted, needed, to comfort her. When she'd asked him to make love to her, he couldn't refuse. Didn't even want to, although he was afraid he might hurt or disappoint her. He'd never been with a virgin before.

But making love with Meli had been the most incredible, most pleasurable, most memorable experience of his life. Was Mom right? Was he falling for Meli?

Meli heard the whoosh of the trapdoor opening followed by the thud of Hector's descent into the cellar. She'd spread a blanket on the dirt floor in front of the crate. She listened to him crawl over to sit beside her on the blanket. She'd only caught bits and pieces of his meeting with Lori and the little boy. Not enough to know how it went.

His big, calloused hand engulfed hers. "I thought they'd been dead for nearly four years. But I should have told you what happened to them before we made love."

His concern for her made Meli's soul ache for what might have been. What could never be.

He pressed the back of Meli's hand to his warm lips. "I'm sorry, Meli. I never meant to hurt you."

In some crazy way, Hector blamed himself for what had happened to his family. And now he blamed himself for making love to her when he'd thought Lori was dead. She had to make him see the truth.

"What happened to Lori and R.D. wasn't your fault. Neither was what happened between us. You're a dowser, not a foreseer. And if I die, at least I'll die happy. I mean, happier. Much happier. Because of you."

Way to cheer him up, Meli. Thoughts of imminent death.

She changed the subject. "Tell me about your son."

Hector cleared his throat. "R.D. has dark hair like me. And he's smart. He may be a foreseer. His awakening Talent causes night terrors—glimpses of the probable future that can be frightening to a small child. He had a vision of me shooting Nate." He drew a ragged breath. "He was terrified—of me. His father."

She touched his arm. "I'm so sorry."

"I swore to him I'd never hurt Nate. I said partners don't hurt partners, and Nate and I are partners. He started to warm up to me."

He shook his head. "At the time, I meant what I said."

His bitter tone send a cold finger trailing up her spine. "You're afraid you might have to shoot Nate in spite of that promise. Why?"

"The only reason I can think of for shooting him is that he works for Mendoza."

Meli's jaw dropped. "Nate? Nope. It's obvious he loves Lori and R.D."

Hector snorted. "The two are not mutually exclusive. If he's a traitor, chances are I'll have to take him out. R.D. will hate me."

Meli weighed her words. "If you're right about Nate, which I doubt, we'll find another way to put him out of commission."

"Don't count on it," he said. "Haven't you learned by now? Life isn't fair."

She could tell that trying to convince him they could change the future a second time wouldn't do any good. His emotions were too raw.

Instead she peeled back the blankets from their makeshift bed and climbed onto the fragrant, lumpy mattress. She patted the spot beside her. "C'mon. Time to sleep. Life will still be unfair when we wake up. You can rail against the universe then."

He grunted. Pine boughs cracked and shifted as he joined her. When he rolled her onto her side and spooned around her, they both pretended to ignore his erection. The warm weight of his hand didn't wander from her waist.

After what seemed like forever, he began to snore softly. For a long time after that, until she finally drifted off, Meli worked on her plan to save Hector from himself.

19

A REPEATING PATTERN of three soft taps awakened Hector. He rolled off the pine bough mattress onto the dirt floor and stilled, listening. Fred's tags jingled and his ears flopped as he shook himself awake.

"Must be Nate," Meli said in a low voice. "Freddy's not upset."

He glanced at Fred, who had lifted his head. The dog's tail gave a couple of lazy wags, telling Hector Meli's Guide knew and liked whoever was upstairs.

The trapdoor muffled Nate's deep voice. "Things have gone south. We need to talk."

Hector's gut clenched. Had Killingsworth already tracked them to the camp?

The trapdoor opened to the pale light of early dawn. Nate's shadowed figure leaned above Hector. Before he'd fallen asleep, he'd dowsed for anyone who meant the prisoners harm. Nate had come up clean. Hector wanted to believe the prisoners' leader was on their side, but he wished to God he knew for sure.

"Fill me in," he said, standing. He hoisted himself onto the edge of the floor, his breath fogging the cold air.

"A second crew of guards arrived a few minutes ago," Nate said "More are due in an hour. Guess the hound has decided you two are headed this way. It's only a matter of time before he'll search the camp. We leave in fifteen minutes."

"I'll create a diversion to keep Killingsworth busy in the camp," Hector said. "You take the others and run like hell."

"No!" Meli popped up through the hole in the floor. She grabbed his pant leg with both hands. "Don't you see? Right now, the guards' attention is focused outward. We should take over the camp, take out the shielder—take a stand. You told me the Bureau monitors the mountain with satellites and Talents. When the shield falls your boss will pinpoint our location and send help. All we have to do is hold our position until they arrive."

"Whoa, Meli. Slow down." He bent down and lifted her onto the edge of the floor beside him. She scrambled to her feet.

What she said made sense, but once they committed to defending the camp, there was no way out. They'd be surrounded. If the Bureau's response was too slow, or if they failed in their attempt to take over the guardhouse, many would die—just as Zinnia had foreseen.

"We'd be trapped," Nate said. "I don't like it. We've spent years preparing for an escape."

Hector agreed. "He's right, Meli. We can't risk it."

An owl hooted outside the window.

"That's Will's signal," Nate said, scowling. "Now what?"

Hector's pulse ratcheted up a notch. "Could be a trick," he said softly.

Nate nodded.

Pulling the Glock from the back of his waistband, Hector aimed the barrel at the ceiling and kept his finger on the trigger. With his free hand, he guided Meli over to Nate. "Stay with him."

Meli nodded once, her rhinestones glittering in the dim light.

Catching Nate's eye, Hector pointed to the corner of the room behind the door. Nate ushered Meli to the sheltered spot.

Fred snuffled the crack under the door.

Nate pointed at Fred's wagging tail.

Hector dipped his chin. He crouched in hopes any possible bad guys would aim their weapons high.

Someone rapped softly on the door twice. Nate shoved Meli behind him and reached for the handle. On Hector's nod, he jerked the door open.

One lanky, gray-haired black man stared down into the unfriendly end of Hector's Glock. The man raised his hands. He appeared unarmed.

"Nice to meet you, Hector," he said. His even white teeth showed in a smile. "I'm Will. Will Washington."

"The farseer," Hector said. "You were in Mendoza's mansion during the wedding reception."

Will nodded. "Killingsworth brought me outside the camp's shield to watch for a possible enemy attack. My Talent can't penetrate the shield." He lifted his chin, indicating Hector's weapon. "I'd feel a lot better if you'd put away your gun. I'm alone, unarmed, and on your side."

Rising to his feet, Hector shoved his weapon into his waistband and winced when the barrel scraped the sore spot it had scraped on his ass.

The floor behind the door creaked and Nate appeared. Will's expression turned grave. "Sophie's water broke. She's in labor."

Nate swore under his breath.

"You can't expect a woman in labor to run like hell through the woods," Meli said. "And you can't leave her behind. We need to stay here, take over the camp and wait for the cavalry to arrive."

Despite Hector's uneasiness about being trapped inside the camp, the idea of leaving the pregnant girl behind did not set well. He raised his brows at Nate.

"She's right," Nate said. "Sophie can't run. We leave no one behind."

Meli responded before Hector could. "Are there things you've put in place for an escape that could be repurposed to help us take over the camp? What can we use to defend ourselves?"

"Any weapons?" Hector added.

Nate frowned. "Nothing more than garden tools. But I can hide our movements by sending dummy videos to the security monitors. We can hide the kids with Will here in the playhouse cellar. He'll keep them calm and quiet."

"With guidance, Jake may be able to bring animal attacks into the equation," Will said.

Hector hadn't thought of that. What else could the children do?

"Denzel is old enough to take care of R.D. for you," Meli said.

"Yes, he is."

Nate scratched his head. "The infirmary is in the Guard House. Sophie's the key for getting Lori inside. They'll expect her to want a woman with her while she's in labor, at least until the doctor arrives. Lori and Sophie can fake a medical emergency to get the guards to open the door leading into the main building."

He nodded thoughtfully. "Lori's a trained agent. She'll handle them and take out the shielder. After that we circle the wagons until help arrives." He cocked an eyebrow at Hector. "See any holes in the plan?"

"You mean any big enough to drive a truck

through?" Hector said.

Meli scowled at him. Her rhinestones sparked. "You think get outside and run like hell is a better plan?"

"It will be easier to defend ourselves from inside physical structures," Will pointed out.

True, assuming Nate was on their side. Jake's Talent would be a wild card, but if nothing else he could use insects to create a distraction. As a farseer, Will could monitor the effects of Jake's efforts inside the shield and shift the boy's focus whenever necessary. And none of the children would be in the line of fire.

Hector gave a firm nod. "I'm in."

Meli smiled. "I guarantee Denzel and I together can bring down at least one of the guards."

His heart stuttered. He shook his head. "You two have to get up close and personal to be effective. Too risky. We'll take out the guards from a distance. Will could use help with the kids."

Meli's rhinestones flashed and she set her jaw. She was angry at being relegated to nursery duty, but that was too damned bad. He couldn't let anything happen to her.

Nate began to pace the playhouse floor. Boards creaked with each step he took. "When the kids are hidden and Sophie and Lori are in the infirmary, I'll switch from the dummy video to the live feed. The guards will see that we're missing and realize they've been tricked. Most of them will head out to search for us."

He stopped and spread his hands, palms up. "When they hear the commotion, Lori and Sophie can fake the medical emergency. Lori will only have to handle a couple of guards and the shielder. When the shield falls she'll report our status to the Bureau through Leah. She'll hole up with Sophie until help arrives. Hell, she'll even have access to medical supplies."

He paused in front of Hector. "You and I will barricade ourselves inside the bunkhouse. We'll wait for Lori's all-clear before we start to pick off the bad guys from a third floor window, you with your gun and me with canned food."

The big man grinned. "You with me?"

Half an hour later from his vantage point behind a fallen log, Hector watched Will and the children slip through mist-shrouded trees down the path to the playhouse. Meli and Fred had remained in the playhouse to wait for them.

R.D., in brown footy pajamas with a red rocket on the back, was sound asleep in the old man's arms. The long night had worn the little guy out. Hector couldn't tear his gaze off his son until he disappeared inside the little cottage.

Despite the cool morning air, sweat beaded Hector's forehead and upper lip. Before all hell broke loose or he lost his courage, he needed to talk to Meli.

She'd been right to call him a coward. He'd been afraid of his feelings for her, afraid he couldn't survive another loss. He'd loved her from the moment their first crazy kiss had blasted through his shields and given him a taste of the sweetness at her core. He'd wanted more than sex, he'd wanted her, and that had scared him shitless. Now, faced with the possibility of losing her, he could no longer deny the truth.

His heart knotted. She deserved to hear him say the words I love you.

So far their plan had gone off without a hitch, but hiding the kids with Will and Meli was only the first step. Even now, Sophie and Lori were talking their way into the infirmary. Time was running out.

He pulled out his St. Jude medal and brought it to his lips for luck. Crouching low, he made for the playhouse. His hand was on the doorknob when an alarm bell went off in his head. He froze.

He'd been tracking Sophie and Lori's progress with a psychic feeler. They'd separated, which meant something had gone wrong. The girl in labor had entered the infirmary, but Lori was moving toward the bunkhouse.

What the hell had happened?

Without Lori inside the infirmary, their plan would fail. Hector turned on his heel and hurried to meet her.

By the time Meli heard footsteps outside the

playhouse, she'd made the bed and stowed her pack and the bag of trash at the foot of the bed. Both she and Freddy had eaten a granola bar and drunk some water. Not knowing exactly what was to come, she'd taken the precaution of donning her knit gloves.

Although her control was vastly improved, she felt ready to explode. The last thing she wanted to do was to frighten one of the children with an energy spurt.

Will would monitor Lori and Sophie's attempt to take over the guardhouse. He'd send important information to Hector, Nate and Zinnia in the bunkhouse by way of Denzel.

The big central building was key to their defensive efforts. Hector could take shots in any direction from the third-floor windows. Nate and Zinnia planned to MacGyver additional weapons out of kitchen tools and supplies.

The front door opened. Heavy footsteps creaked across the floor overhead, followed by lighter ones. The soft thump of Freddy's tail assured her they were friends.

Three muffled knocks sounded on the trapdoor before it whooshed open. "It's us," Will murmured. "Look, boys. Freddy's come to say hello. Go on down, Denzel. Help the younger boys. You're next, Jake."

The rustle of clothing was followed by a thud and the jingle of dog tags. "Hiya, Fred," Denzel whispered.

Meli suppressed a smile. Only Hector called her Guide Fred. "Any problems?"

"Nope." The boy's voice vibrated with excitement. "Lori and Sophie are on their way to the infirmary. Nate, Zinnia and Hector have the bunkhouse locked down."

Her heart tripped. Hector wasn't coming back. She wouldn't get the chance to say goodbye.

"C'mon Jake," Denzel said.

"Hi, Meli." Jake's childish voice wavered.

The little boy must be terrified. Tucking away her grief, she smiled and patted the ground beside her. "Come sit with me, Jake."

He barreled into her lap. She cradled his trembling, sturdy little form in her arms and kissed the top of his head. His silky hair smelled of baby shampoo.

Freddy padded over and sat down beside them. The slurp of his tongue told her he was working his magic on the frightened little boy.

"Denzel, take R.D.," Will said. "I can't bend over and carry him with my arthritis acting up."

"Yes, sir."

Fabric rustled, followed by Will's deep chuckle. "Poor little guy is worn out. Probably for the best if he sleeps through what's coming."

Meli found Will's grandfatherly presence comforting. "Lay him on the bed," she told Denzel.

The shuffle of feet was followed by the creaking of pine boughs. Their uplifting scent seemed to make the air lighter. Denzel dropped to a seat beside her. "Hey, Fred."

Freddy's tail thumped against her thigh.

Will's grunting descent was followed by a whoosh of air from the trap door shutting. Aging tendons popped in the stillness as he found a seat. The old man sighed. "Now that's better."

"What do we do now?" Denzel said.

"We wait. Waiting's the hard part. You all need to keep quiet. I'll take a peek at Lori and Sophie. When the guards let them inside the infirmary, Nate will change the video feed. They'll realize the bunkhouse is empty. Most of the guards will leave the building to— well, to search for us."

Meli was glad Will chose his words with care so as not to frighten the children.

"I h-hate to wait." Jake muttered.

"Then you'll be glad to have a job to do right away. While I'm Farseeing, put out a telepathic feeler to locate any animals inside the shield. Squirrels, birds, bugs, anything. We may need their help."

Jake nodded his head against Meli's shoulder. His trembling stopped.

Only their breathing inside the cellar and the breeze whispering outside broke the silence. She tried not to think, not to feel, but responsibility blanketed her shoulders. What if they followed her plan and things went wrong? What if the Bureau wasn't prepared to strike? No way could they hold off their attackers for more than a couple of hours. Even that might take a miracle.

She worried her bottom lip. What if the future changed so Hector's family didn't survive? He'd insisted on positioning himself inside the woods behind the toolshed, ready to divert the guards' attention from the kids if something went wrong on their way to the playhouse cellar. Tears pricked her eyelids. Hector Protector.

She drew a deep breath to steady herself, inhaling the fragrances of earth and pine and baby shampoo. How had her forlorn, safe, rule-bound life blossomed into a heroic life-and-death adventure?

In less than a week, she'd found Hector and fallen in love. With his help she'd learned to control her Talent and laid to rest the fear she'd never be able to make love to a man. Together they'd escaped from kidnappers and bears. And she'd discovered a tribe of people who made her feel she belonged. She wasn't a freak, she was a Talent.

And today was probably the day she would die. Her eyes stung. At least her death would have meaning. And she would be mourned.

Jake stirred in her arms and spoke in a stage whisper. "Freddy says to tell you the future is not a set of rocks. What does that mean?"

Meli sniffed and gave Freddy and Jake one-armed hugs. Freddy's tail thumped. She managed a smile. "It means we're not giving up without a fight. Freddy heard Hector tell me our future's not set in stone. Our choices, the things we do, can change what happens."

Even if she couldn't be with the man she loved, she had Freddy. And she'd found her strength and her people. The needy, desperately lonely freak she'd been was gone forever. As long as Hector was happy, she could bear to let him go. Her heart throbbed in protest, but she'd do whatever it took to ensure his happiness. She loved him.

Will spoke, his voice thrumming with tension. "Sophie's inside the infirmary, but Lori was turned away. That's not part of the plan."

Meli stiffened. Lori's presence in the infirmary was key.

"Something's wrong," Denzel whispered.

Meli's galloping heart agreed.

20

JAKE SQUIRMED IN her arms. "Too tight!"

"Sorry." She loosened her hold and he settled.

Freddy heaved a long sigh.

"I found a big garter snake," Jake said out of left field. "I think he's in Zinnia's vegetable garden."

Meli gave him a little hug. "Good job."

"I wish I could talk to Grizz," the little boy said, sounding like he'd lost his best friend. "I hope he's okay."

"Don't worry. Bears are tough. And Hector always keeps his promises. We'll take care of him."

Before Jake could reply, Will gave them an update. "Lori told Nate what happened. The head guard insisted Zinnia be the one to help Sophie. He knows Lori is a greater risk."

He laughed softly. "People tend to underestimate my daughter. Zinnia's as strong as her mother was, and that's saying something."

Denzel's biceps bunched against Meli's arm. "Zinnia's a lover, not a fighter," he said.

"Love and strength go hand-in-hand, son," Will said. "We aren't all blood relations, but we're a family of the heart. Zinnia will do whatever the Good Lord requires to protect her family."

Down to the marrow of her bones, Meli believed him. After less than a day bonding with them, she'd give her life to protect these kids in a heartbeat.

Denzel reached across Freddy and clasped Meli's gloved hand. She gave his a squeeze. It was easy to forget the boy was only fourteen.

"There's a yellow jacket nest in the shed wall," Jake said.

"You rock, little bro," Denzel answered. "High five!"

Hands slapped together. Meli smiled.

"Sophie's a trooper," Will said. "After each contraction, she gives me a secret thumbs-up."

Meli swallowed. She couldn't imagine having to fight for her life while in labor. Yet she was the one who'd come up with this plan to turn a perceived weakness into a strength. She prayed all Sophie would have to do was fake a seizure.

"Now Zinnia's in the infirmary," Will continued. "Nate's switching the video feed."

"How long will it take the guards to notice we're

gone?" Denzel said.

Meli worried her lip. Would all the guards but one or two exit the building? The two women didn't stand a chance if they were outnumbered.

"The guards scrambled," Will said. "Four outside the fence. Four inside. Two left in the guardhouse."

A single gunshot cracked. Meli flinched. Automatic rifle fire followed.

"Hector took out one of the bad guys who was headed for the bunkhouse," Will said. "We're down to three active inside the fence and two inside the guardhouse."

Blankets and branches rustled as R.D. moved on the bed. She heard the little boy yawn. "My dad shot a bad guy?"

"Yeah, squirt," Denzel said. "Come sit with me and Fred."

So much for euphemisms. Children were so much more aware than adults believed. Meli followed the sounds of the little boy crawling over to Denzel.

"Sophie's faking a seizure," Will said.

"What's a *seejer*?" R.D. asked.

"Quiet, squirt," Denzel said. "Will's working."

"But I have to pee!"

She remembered the empty water bottles in the trash bag. "Denzel, there's an empty bottle in the paper bag by the foot of the bed. Have him use that."

Two gunshots sounded from the direction of the bunkhouse. A rifle chattered. No one moved.

Will broke the silence. "The bad guys all missed." Meli remembered to breathe. "Hector's got them pinned down for the moment. He has to make every bullet count."

"That's my father," R.D. said with obvious pride.

She smiled.

"Bring me the sack, R.D.," Denzel said.

R.D. padded to the foot of the makeshift bed. Paper crinkled. He padded back.

A zipper whizzed. "Pee in the bottle," Denzel said, "and don't spill. You're big enough to do that, aren't you? Only big boys get to pee in a bottle."

"I'm big. I'm a big boy."

Apparently the prospect of peeing in the bottle had distracted R.D. from the gunfight. Meli listened to the rising sound of liquid streaming into a plastic bottle. She choked back a giggle. What was the matter with her?

The sound of R.D. peeing stopped. Plastic squeaked, Denzel screwing the cap on the bottle.

"Do I hafta wash my hands?" R.D. said.

"Not this time," Denzel told him. "Just wipe 'em on your PJs and sit down on my lap. Fred wants you to pet him."

After a moment of silence Will spoke. "We've got to get those guards moving! Zinnia may need help to subdue the guards, but Sophie's due for a contraction in a few minutes."

Jake stirred on Meli's lap. "There's a spider in the

corner of the 'firmary room on a black box on the wall. She's watching Sophie. That's why I know it's the 'firmary."

Meli blinked. Jake saw the room through the spider's faceted eyes. How did he recognize Sophie? Hector had told her his dowsing Talent sounded simple when it was actually very complex to use effectively. Jake's animal telepath Talent must be as well.

"Wonderful!" Will said. "He's on the video camera. Tell him to hurry up and build a web across the camera lens. That's the circle part on the front."

"Her. She's a girl," the little boy insisted. "She won't get hurt, will she?"

"I don't think so, Jake," Will said. "I certainly hope not." His tone was gentle but firm. "Let me know when the camera lens is covered. Then your spider friend can go hide."

Meli's admiration for Will went up another notch. The man was super smart. He'd immediately figured out how to take advantage of the spider to block the camera lens. A guard would be sent to investigate.

Jake sat up and turned in her lap until he could lean back against her chest. She circled her arms around him and her throat tightened. These children were so brave, so innocent and so vulnerable.

After a long minute punctuated by gunfire, Jake spoke. "She's there. I told her to cover the glass circle with her web."

"Good," Will said. "The guards haven't come despite

Sophie's fake seizure Zinnia's pounding on the hall door and calling for help, but they're ignoring her."

They waited in silence for several minutes.

Finally Will had something to report. "The captain's squinting at the camera monitor." A few seconds passed. "Yes! He sent his last man down the hall to check on the camera."

Meli's heart pounded. Could Zinnia subdue the guard?

"How's the spider doing?" Denzel said.

"She's done," Jake said. He yawned. "Can she go now?"

"Yes," Will told him with a smile in his voice. "Don't forget to thank her."

A few seconds of silence followed.

"Zinnia hit the guard over the head with a stool." Pride filled Will's voice. "He'll stay down for a good while. She shoved her shoe in the crack to hold the door open."

Meli smiled.

"Sophie's tying the guard's hands with his belt," Will continued. "They've got his gun."

The timbre of his voice deepened. "Now, things are going to happen real fast, kids. Please keep quiet so I can concentrate. I'll tell you all about it afterward."

The way the kids obeyed him impressed her. They kept silent through long minutes of waiting. When Will's breath sped up, the soft sounds of small bodies shifting was the only indication the kids noticed.

Meli said a silent prayer for the women's safety.

Freddy whimpered.

Meli stripped a glove off her sweating hand and grasped Denzel's, skin to skin. "Show me?" she whispered.

A shadowy image of an older Black man's handsome, angular face appeared in her mind's eye.

Will.

He'd knit his brows over closed eyes. A muscle ticked in his cheek. Meli's stomach began to burn as her energy rose. Watching his daughter put herself into deadly danger had to be torture.

The old man gasped and his body jerked. He shook his head, drew a deep breath and slowly let it out.

Denzel squeezed her hand tightly.

She worked at dampening energy roiling inside her and hugged Jake close with her free arm.

The lines in Will's face deepened and his lips moved as if in a whispered prayer. When he drew a deep breath and opened his eyes, his tormented gaze bore into Denzel/Meli's. She didn't need to be a Telepath to understand that someone he loved had died.

Meli's vision of the shadowy cellar rocked wildly as Denzel shook his head in denial. She withdrew her hand from the boy's desperate grip and bolstered her shield, automatically pulling on her glove. Tapping into his Talent now would be an invasion of privacy. Will didn't want the little ones to know tragedy had struck, but he couldn't hide the fact from the older boy.

Had they lost Zinnia, the gentle foreseer? The brave young pregnant girl? Or both?

"Our girls secured the guardhouse," Will rasped. He paused. "Sophie's having a contraction."

Zinnia, Will's daughter who was like a mother to the kids, must be dead. Murdered.

The energy vortex in her middle threatened to escape her shield. She tamped it down.

Denzel's sniff was followed by the slurp, slurp of Freddy's tongue as her Guide tried to comfort him.

"Where's Zinnia?" Jake said in a broken whisper.

Meli's heart broke for them all. She laid her cheek against his baby-soft hair.

Will didn't answer the little boy's question. "The shield and Illusion are intact. We guessed wrong. The guard captain wasn't the Talent. Killingsworth must be projecting the barriers from off site. But that's impossible. Shielders are always at the center of the shield. Always."

Meli lifted her head. If the shielder was outside the camp, all the prisoners were doomed. She refused to accept that fate. Think, Meli! Who else has always been here? One of the other guards? The captain would never have risked the shielder's safety by sending him into battle. Someone in hiding?

The answer smacked her like a low-hanging branch to the forehead. Nate.

Nate was the first prisoner at the camp. Hector had

worried Nate might work for Mendoza, but his dowser Talent told him Nate was an ally. And she was positive Nate had shared the truth about himself—or what he believed to be the truth. But what if Nate didn't know the whole truth about himself, just like she hadn't understood her Freak Side?

Hector had told her all Talented adults generate shields automatically in their sleep. What if Nate were a powerful shielder who projected a shield that was always on? One with a huge sphere of influence? He'd be unaware he projected a shield, because he wouldn't know how it felt not to project one.

All those years ago Killingsworth must have sensed Nate's shielder Talent when he'd tried to help the woman targeted for kidnapping. Once the hound was inside Nate's shield, he would have sensed the interfering young man was Talented. So he'd kidnapped Nate instead of killing him. After a couple weeks of torturing and drugging Nate, Killingsworth figured out Nate had no idea he was Talented. And then the hound discovered what that Talent was. To everyone else Nate's Talent would be invisible. Killingsworth had hidden his shielder in plain sight.

Meli lost her breath. No wonder R.D. foresaw his father shoot Nate. As long as Nate was alive—even asleep or unconscious—the shield around the camp would hold. Hector would sacrifice Nate so the rest of the captives could escape. R.D. would never forgive him, and Hector would never forgive himself.

She clenched her fists. There had to be another way. What if she explained things to Hector and asked him to dowse for an alternative way to lower the shield?

If they had plenty of time, that could work. But if Hector couldn't implement the new plan immediately, he'd still be compelled to kill Nate.

Unless someone else kills him first. Her blood turned to ice. Could she murder one innocent man to save many innocent lives? The children will have a chance to survive. Hector will have a chance at happiness.

Shivering, she rubbed the goosebumps roughening her arms. She had to try to save them. What choice did she have?She straightened her spine and squared her shoulders. People questioning her would only slow her down. She had to project unfailing confidence. "Will, I figured out how to disrupt the shield. I have to tell the others."

Gently, she slid Jake off her lap onto the dirt floor. "Jake, promise me you'll help Will take care of R.D. and Freddy while Denzel and I are gone."

The little boy gave her a quick hug. "Okay."

Denzel said, "Meli, I don't think it's—"

She cut him off with a firm shake of her head. "I don't have time to explain everything. Take me to the bunkhouse."

"She's right, son," Will said softly. "There's no time to waste. She must go with you. You two can do this."

Her whole body tensed. She didn't want to put the boy in danger, but she couldn't get to the bunkhouse safely on her own. Thank God Will believed in her!

"Come on," Denzel said.

21

MINUTES LATER THEY emerged from behind the row of bushes hiding most of the playhouse yard from the view of the guards and ran like hell. Meli clutched the teen's arm and concentrated on his subtle changes in posture that signaled changes in direction. A fall could be disastrous.

Wood and glass splintered somewhere ahead of them as a rifle chattered. They kept running.

Booted feet pounded on their left. "Stop or die, kid!" a man shouted, so close she heard the hiss of his indrawn breath.

Denzel angled them right and somehow they picked up speed. Her lungs burned with the effort. Instead of gunfire, Meli heard a heavy impact. What sounded like a body hit the ground. Sounds of pursuit ceased.

Denzel pulled her to a stop. "Don't trip over the step. We're at the back door."

She found the step with her foot and climbed onto the small concrete slab. Keys jingled. Denzel's arm brushed hers. A deadbolt scraped and he shoved her inside.

She spun around to face him. "What happened?"

"Nate pasted the guard with a can of vegetables. The sonofabitch is either knocked out or dead." The boy's triumphant tone sent a shiver crawling up Meli's spine.

"Wait here," Denzel said. The door snapped shut.

Meli flinched and then fisted her hands. The boy was too independent. With an effort she let go of her anger. Right now, the only thing that mattered was taking down the shielder. She shivered. Nate had just saved their lives. What if she was wrong about his Talent?

The door opened. "It's me," Denzel said breathlessly. The door slammed shut. "I doubled our number of guns. The guy Nate clocked had a rifle."

The pride in his voice whenever he spoke of his mentor shook her resolve. How could she kill Denzel's hero right in front of him? She swallowed hard. Who was she kidding? She hadn't even been able to kill the hound when she'd had the chance.

Lori yelled down to them from somewhere above. "We're up here!"

"On our way," Denzel called back. He grabbed

Meli's hand and pulled her forward.

Her chest tightened. She dug in her heels. "Wait!"

"What?" he said, his voice clipped with impatience.

"I need your help to destroy the shield, Denzel."

"But you said—"

Someone fired a shot upstairs. Meli clutched Denzel's shirt with both hands. "Listen to me. We don't have much time. Keep an open mind and hear me out." She gave him a little shake. "Can you do that?"

"I'm listening." Denzel radiated tension.

"What I didn't say before was that Nate is Mendoza's Shielder."

Denzel jerked out of her grasp. "Nate's no traitor!"

"No, of course not," she said quickly. "He doesn't know he's Talented. He's unaware of his shield the way other people are unaware of the heat they give off. It's just there."

A floorboard creaked as the boy shifted his weight. "You're saying the hound used Nate's Talent without him knowing?"

She hurried on. "Yes."

He took a moment to mull things over. "What's your plan?"

"We only need the shield to go down long enough for Lori to contact her twin telepathically. Hector told me his partner has an FBI SWAT Team on standby. They'll arrive within minutes."

Lori called down the stairs. "What's the holdup?"

"Coming!" Denzel answered. He lowered his voice.

"I don't want to believe you, but I do. Everything fits."

Thank God Denzel had a logical mind.

"What will you do to Nate?" he said, his voice cracking.

"I'll hit him with enough energy to drive him to the brink of death. I won't lie to you. This is dangerous. But his reflexes should kick in and draw on his shield's power to fight back. With his Talent weakened and fixated on me, Lori will get through to her twin. Then I'll let his shield bounce back."

She didn't tell him that whatever happened to her then would be bad. Probably extremely bad.

"What can I do to help?" Denzel said

Meli nearly kissed the boy. "I need you to run interference for me. Wait until I'm next to Nate. Tell everyone what happened to Sophie and Zinnia in the guardhouse." She was asking so much of him. Would he be strong enough? "I need for them to be off-balance and focused on you. I'll make my move while they're distracted."

"And afterward?" he said. She couldn't answer the question he was asking, so she pretended to misunderstand. "Tell them what's going on. Don't let anyone touch us while we're touching each other."

Approaching trucks grumbled a distant warning. Her mind blanked. A hand grabbed her arm and hauled her toward the stairs.

"Let's go," Denzel said. "We still have time."

They pounded upstairs to the second floor. She

heard what must be the rifle he carried thudding against his back.

"What happened?" Lori shouted. They shot past her.

Denzel didn't slow down. "Message from Will, and the hound is at the gates!"

They turned a corner and charged up the next flight of stairs. Lori's footsteps pounded after them.

On the top floor, Denzel guided Meli with a firm grip on her shoulder. They turned and her arm brushed a doorframe. Someone fired a gun a few feet in front of them.

She jumped. Hector?

"Get down!" Denzel said, pulling her to her belly on the carpeted floor. Air whooshed out of her lungs.

A rifle chattered outside and a string of bullets chunked into the wall behind them. Bits of drywall rained down. Coughing on acrid dust, she shielded her nose and mouth with her hand. Her ears rang.

"*¡Mierda!*" Hector said. "Why didn't you stay put like I told you?" A metallic click followed by the slide of metal on metal told her he was reloading his handgun.

Her heart contracted. She couldn't bring herself to lie to him.

Denzel answered. "Will sent us. Look what we brought for you." She heard him slide what must be the rifle across the carpet.

Hector slid a magazine home with a snap. "Where in hell did you get a rifle, kid?"

"Long story," Denzel said. "You can thank Nate. Take it."

A floorboard creaked in the hall behind Meli. "Why are you here, son?" Nate said.

Denzel barely hesitated. "Will sent us with an update."

"Are the children all right?" Lori said.

"They're all fine," Meli replied.

Hector fired twice. "All of you, clear out. Get into a back bedroom. Denzel, hand Lori the Glock."

Bits of fallen plaster dug into Meli's palms and knees as they crawled after Nate. They left the dust cloud behind and entered a room that smelled of lilacs. Her throat tightened. Was the perfume Zinnia's?

Denzel grasped her wrist above the edge of her glove. She got a blurred visual of a thin, pretty, pony-tailed woman with dark hair—Lori—sitting against the opposite wall. Lori turned toward a good-looking young man with close-cropped, light brown hair who sat on the floor beside the room's only window. The guy was big, but all muscle. Nate. Meli nodded to let Denzel know she'd had a peek at the room.

He let go of her wrist and pushed her ahead of him in Nate's direction. When she reached the outer wall she knelt and sat back on her heels. Her back brushed the bedclothes. Denzel plopped down beside her.

"Is everyone here okay?" Denzel said.

Good boy. Keep talking. Keep their attention on you.

Resolutely Meli concentrated on transforming her emotions into a mighty energy weapon. She pictured Killingsworth and Mendoza's many crimes. They'd kidnapped, tortured and used Nate, Will, Zinnia, Lori, Sophie, and the children for years. They'd crushed Hector's heart. Who knew how many more people they'd enslaved in the camps? How many additional lives they'd stolen or destroyed?

Anger and disgust roiled her stomach. She barely heard Nate reply to Denzel that everyone in the bunkhouse was safe.

Why had they committed these monstrous acts? For wealth. For power. And to satisfy their twisted cravings.

The heat of rage suffused her body. Drawing energy from deep in her well, she fed her fury until it formed a powerful, turbulent cloud deep in her chest.

Mendoza and Killingsworth had obviously ordered the guards to kill the prisoners rather than let them escape. They would destroy these people she cared about, people she belonged with, people she already loved, unless she stopped him.

A bolt of energy surged like lightning through her chest. Her heart shuddered.

I am strong. She gasped for air. The chaotic storm of energy within her ribcage organized into a tornado-like vortex. Summoning every speck of her control, she held the storm of energy in check.

I am invincible. The sounds of the gun battle faded

from her awareness. She focused on the conversation inside the bedroom, biding her time.

"What is Will's message?" Nate asked Denzel.

Meli shifted her weight, finding purchase with her toes. She homed in on the sound of his voice. Her muscles thrummed with tension. The energy vortex inside her pulsed like a living thing.

Denzel cleared his throat. "The plan went off almost without a hitch. Sophie's in the guardhouse. She needs help. Her contractions are coming faster."

Meli waited. She'd only get one chance to blast Nate. One chance to disrupt the energy flow to his shield. One chance to save them all.

"I haven't been able to get through to Leah," Lori said. "The shield is intact."

"That's because the shielder wasn't in the guardhouse like we thought," the boy told her.

Lori gasped. "Impossible! Shields manifest around their source. Always."

"Not this time," Denzel continued. "Will sent us to warn you. And to tell you about Zinnia."

"What about Zinnia?" Nate asked him.

Denzel faltered. "Zinnia's—Zinnia's—"

Meli's muscles bunched. This was the opportunity she'd been waiting for. Denzel had their undivided attention.

"She's dead," Denzel said, his voice cracking with emotion.

"What? How?" Lori cried.

Meli launched herself at Nate. Her arms circled his neck in a death grip. She kissed him like she'd kissed the hound, open-mouthed, giving the expanding energy vortex trapped inside her body a direction of release.

The power of her surprise attack drove his life force toward its Source. She followed her first stunning blow with massive pulses of turbulent power that tangled with his life force and pushed his energy ever inward, toward his core, toward the edge of the earthly plane of existence—a place from which she prayed his psychic reflexes would push back with the full force of his Talent, protecting Nate and collapsing his shield.

A bone-jarring shudder wracked Nate's body. Meli strengthened her personal shield in an attempt to protect herself. Even so, Nate's psychic power blasted through her in a scorching supernova of pain. Nate faded to nothing in her arms, her body faded to nothing.

And then—nothing.

Hector scanned the area below his third-story window, rifle at the ready. The additional long-range weapon bettered the odds of them holding off the hound's men until the cavalry arrived—assuming Zinnia and Sophie were successful in taking out the shielder. What was taking so damned long? And why the hell had Will sent Meli with Denzel to the bunkhouse?

Voices murmured across the hall behind him.

Movement at the clinic entrance caught his attention. Sophie fired a pistol through the slightly-open door. He grinned. The two women had overpowered at least one guard.

He picked off one of Killingsworth's men peeking around the corner of the guardhouse before the man could take aim at Sophie. She slammed the clinic door. Atta girl!

A surge of energy raised every hair on his body. What in hell was that?

He ducked away from the window and yelled, "What happened?"

"Hold on!" Denzel replied, his voice cracking.

Since when was the kid in charge?

Thirty seconds later Lori crawled through the doorway, her face pinched. "Killingsworth and his men have arrived. I got through to Leah. Help is on the way."

She closed her eyes for a second. When she opened them, their blue depths were dark with misery. "Zinnia's dead. Meli and Nate are hurt. Nate is the shielder. Meli figured it out."

Lori swallowed. "Meli blasted him to give me a chance to break through to Leah. Meli—she's in a bad way."

For one blessed moment, her words made no sense. Then his hands went slack on his weapon and he forgot how to breathe.

With the clarity of a Diviner, he knew what Meli had done. She had risked her life to derail the probable future in which R.D. saw him kill Nate.

Lori hurried over and took the rifle from his hands. "I got this." She pulled the Glock from her waistband and pressed the handgun into his hand. "Go!"

He moved into a crouch and sprinted for the back bedroom. There he found Denzel hunched over Meli's still form, clutching her hand to his chest and sobbing, all his bravado gone.

She lay face-up on the rose-colored carpet, as if someone had rolled her onto her back. Her skin was ashen. Yellow blisters bubbled on her soft, sweet lips, her cheeks, her eyelids.

The energetic blowback from Nate's shield would have been tremendous.

Glancing around the room, he located Nate slumped beside the window, apparently unconscious. What he could see of Nate's skin was reddened as if from a bad sunburn. No other obvious injuries.

Hector laid a steadying hand on the boy's bony shoulder. "Check on Nate. I'll take care of Meli."

Denzel nodded and gently lowered her hand to her side. He dried his face on his shirtsleeve and scrambled over to the injured man.

Hector dropped to his knees and laid his Glock on the rug. He touched her hand. Cold as the grave. His heart threatened to shatter. He held his fingers under her nose. Gentle puffs of warm air caressed his hand.

¡Gracias a Dios!

Denzel reappeared at his side. "Nate's unconscious. He has blisters on his lips, but he seems okay otherwise.

"Meli's alive," Hector told Denzel. "She's in shock. Put the pillows under her feet." While the boys followed his orders, Hector pulled the afghan off the bed and covered Meli to keep her warm.

"After Zinnia and Sophie cleared the guardhouse, Will told us the shield was still intact," Denzel said. "Meli knew the shielder had to stay inside the shield. The only person who'd been here all along with no obvious Talent was Nate. She figured he had a wild Talent Killingsworth used without Nate even knowing it existed."

The boy's fierce gaze speared Hector. "Nate would never help Killingsworth!"

Hector ignored him. "Meli attacked Nate to bring down the shield?"

Denzel nodded. "She figured his subconscious reflexes would protect him, but they would take most of his energy away from the shield. She was betting the shield would collapse long enough for me to tell Lori to contact her sister to send in the SWAT Team. That part worked."

Nate's shield slamming into place would have been equivalent to dropping a mirror in front of a laser beam. Besides getting slammed with Nate's power, she'd been hit with her own. There was no way to tell what damage had been done, no way to know if she would live or die. What the hell was he supposed to do now?

"You've got to hold off the bad guys until the SWAT Team arrives," Denzel said. "I'll take care of Nate and Meli. You have to go."

Hector swallowed. The boy was right. There was nothing he could do for Meli here. She had counted on him to lead the team, to keep everyone alive. He couldn't let her down.

He kissed her blistered cheek, wishing he had her Talent so she would feel his love. He'd never told her the truth. He loved her more than he'd ever thought it possible to love a woman.

Glancing at his watch, he noted only a few minutes had passed since Meli and the boy had arrived at the bunkhouse. Yet everything had changed.

Defending the camp fell to him, Lori and Will. And the kids. Meli would have told him not to discount the kids. Denzel's quick thinking had gotten them the rifle. When the shield was down, Will would have made strategic use of Jake's Talent to call on whatever Beasties lurked nearby for help.

Who knew what the little boy had recruited?

As if in answer to his question, a man screamed in the distance. "Get them off me! Get them off!"

Hector moved to the window to scan the grounds but saw no one. The terrified cries moved away through the woods in back not far from the playhouse. His grip on the Glock tightened. He couldn't see the little cottage from this angle.

He pointed to the open window. "Keep watch out there."

The boy nodded. "Yes, sir."

"If anything moves, yell." Hector strode into the hallway, pausing by the front bedroom doorway.

Lori turned, a frown darkening her face. "They're getting ready to ram the gate. What do we do?"

He dredged up Hector's cocky grin. "We kick their Cartel butts."

Denzel's, "Hell yeah!" and Lori's smile told him Hector had said what they needed to hear.

"You got any wine in the kitchen?" he asked.

Lori's smile became a grin. "Top cupboard to the right of the fridge." She turned back to peer out the window. "Don't miss!"

Glock in hand, Hector dashed down two floors and sprinted across the cafeteria-style dining room.

An engine roared outside followed by the sound of an enormous impact. The ramming had begun.

He darted through the open doorway, shot across the kitchen and wrenched open the pantry door. Two bottles of red wine lay side-by-side on a rack. He set the Glock on the kitchen counter and took the bottles out of the rack. Moving quickly, he set them beside his weapon.

Snatching a cotton dishtowel off a hook by the sink, he tore off two long strips of fabric. He rummaged through drawers until he found the corkscrew. After removing the first bottle's cork, he threaded his improvised wick down into the wine, leaving a few inches of fabric hanging out the bottle's neck.

"Need a light?" a friendly, familiar voice said from the kitchen doorway.

Hector froze. "Drew." Slowly, he turned. An unremarkable-looking man dressed in Bureau body armor stood in the doorway. "You're a little late to the party."

The man lifted his visor and grinned at Hector. "You're losing your edge, partner. I got the drop on you."

"I was about to kill you with my bare hands," Hector said mildly.

His friend reached into a pocket and tossed him a book of matches. "I dreamed you'd need these."

An engine roared outside again. Their gazes locked until they heard the crash of impact.

"Where are the prisoners?" Drew said.

Hector reached for the second bottle of merlot. "Four upstairs. Two of them need a healer. One adult and two kids in the playhouse cellar in the back woods. One in the guardhouse by the gate."

While his partner chinned his mic and reported everyone's positions to the agent in charge, Hector removed the cork from the bottle. They weren't home free yet, but the cavalry had arrived.

"SWAT will secure the playhouse," Drew said. He laughed and shook his head. "Never thought I'd say those words."

"Never thought I'd say these." Hector glanced into Drew's eyes. "You know how to deliver a baby?"

Drew blinked. "Theoretically yes, but—"

Hector grinned and began to assemble his second Molotov cocktail. "The prisoner in the guardhouse is a girl in labor named Sophie. No Talent, has amnesia, and her baby is a Level 10. A real spitfire, shooting at the bad guys between contractions. Watch out! She can't aim worth shit, but she might get lucky. She's not in a good mood. On top of everything else, she just watched a good friend die."

"She's having a baby in the middle of a battle," Drew said. "Well, shit."

Hector shoved the Glock into the back of his waistband and then carried his two incendiary devices past his partner into the dining room. "Good luck," he called over his shoulder. "Tell Sophie R.D. wants a girl. That way she'll know you're a friend.

Drew nodded and headed for the back door.

Hector took the stairs two at a time. Adrenaline got him to the third floor. He circled the stairwell and ran down the hall.

By the sounds of it, the third time the truck rammed the front gate the barricade gave way.

22

"THEY'RE IN!" Lori yelled.

He stopped in the doorway of the front room and spoke to her. "SWAT Team's on the ground. One of ours is leaving the bunkhouse for the guardhouse. Cover him!"

Her rifle chattered briefly.

A glance into Zinnia's room showed him Denzel on watch at the window. Nate sat propped in the corner, blinking owlishly and shaking his head. Meli remained on the carpet, laying still as death.

Hector forced himself to keep going to the last room on the right. He crept to the window and peered outside. Killingsworth's truck had stopped well inside the fence but not close to the bunkhouse. A few of the reinforcements used the vehicle for cover while a half-dozen fanned out toward the buildings, rifles ready.

He pulled back and swore. Killingsworth was being cautious.

Lori fired. He watched a wide circle of bullet spray follow the scurrying men back to the truck. One went down.

A small explosion sent a cloud of smoke into the air at the guardhouse clinic door. A lone figure in body armor pulled the door open and disappeared inside. Drew.

If anyone could keep Sophie safe and calm, it was Drew. Although she'd forget him by tomorrow, his partner would win the young woman's trust for today. Drew always had a plan, and he could charm the whiskers off a kitten. Too bad the girl would forget him almost as quickly as she would trust him.

"Hector?" Denzel shouted.

"Here!"

"There's movement near the playhouse," the kid called out, sounding uncertain.

Hector's heart faltered. He dashed into Zinnia's room and joined Denzel beside the window. Sneaking a peek into the woods, he spotted two men in FBI-issue protective gear. "Friendlies," he said, his gut relaxing. "Good job spotting them."

The boy flashed him a quick grin that faded when his gaze darted to Meli. "She's the same."

Hector kept his gaze on Denzel. He couldn't risk the sight of Meli shattering his focus at this crucial time.

"Hang in there. The SWAT Team includes a healer. They'll reach us in a few minutes"

If only he could be sure she would recover. He forced thoughts of Meli from his mind. "Keep watching the woods."

"Yes, sir." Denzel turned back to his vantage point.

Hector jogged to the front corner bedroom. He wiped his sweaty brow on his shirtsleeve, noting that Lori only fired one or two shots at a time now. She must be running low on ammo.

Setting the Molotov cocktails on the dresser, he pulled out the matchbook Drew had given him. The thought of burning men alive turned his stomach, but the guards would have orders to kill their prisoners and withdraw. Memories of the murdered children at the Sonoran camp hardened his resolve.

Hector peeked out the window and spotted four men in body armor running toward the corner of the building below. His Talent helped him identify Killingsworth as the tallest. Lori hit one of the others, who staggered but kept running. They disappeared down the side of the bunkhouse.

"¡Mierda!" He grabbed the bottle of merlot and the matches, dashed across the hall and set the bottle on the dresser. Then he opened the window and kicked out the screen. Dowsing for the right moment to light his improvised bomb, he tore a match out of the matchbook. After about fifteen seconds, he knew it was time. On the first strike, the match flared. Holding the flame to his improvised fuse, he watched the cotton ignite. Flames licked toward the bottle's mouth.

Holding the flaming incendiary device, Hector stuck his head out the window and watched one of Killingsworth's men poke his rifle barrel and helmet around the corner below.

"Up here!" Denzel yelled from the window past Hector's.

The guard's aim shifted upward and Hector threw the lit bottle at the man's helmet. The bottle shattered and flames erupted on impact, engulfing the guard and the grass around him. His screams were the stuff of nightmares. He staggered a few steps and collapsed, still clutching his rifle.

Denzel whooped in triumph.

Hector shook his head. When this was over, the kid would need therapy. Lots of therapy.

A large beast roared in the distance and a man screamed. Jake must have called Grizz.

Hector dashed across the hall to retrieve the second Molotov cocktail.

Lori fired once, twice. A small explosion shook the building. "They're inside!" she shouted. The sounds of heavy boots echoed in the stairwell. "Three of them."

No way could he start a fire in the stairwell. His team would be trapped on the third floor.

He placed the wine bottle on the floor by the dresser, pulled out his Glock and crossed to the doorway. Peering down the hall, he spotted Lori aiming her rifle at the stairwell from the next doorway on his side of the hall.

Denzel appeared in the doorway of Zinnia's room.

"Barricade the door," Lori told the boy.

His dark eyes flashed with rebellion. "But—

"Do it!" Hector snapped.

Frowning, Denzel shut the door.

Hector retreated into the room with Lori. The beat of a rotor grew loud, indicating the remainder of the SWAT Team was moving in. The playhouse had been secured. R.D. was safe.

A weight lifted from his shoulders. They only had to hold Killingsworth and company off for a few more minutes. A grinning Lori caught his gaze with hers and gave him a thumbs-up. She moved back into position in the doorway.

Seconds later she fired a short burst. A body bumped down the stairs. She withdrew into the room and lifted her rifle slightly. Then she held up a fist and extended her thumb and index finger, leaving only a small gap between them.

She was almost out of ammo. He nodded his understanding. Only the hound and one other man remained inside the building.

Hector got down on his belly and took a quick peek around the doorframe. The stairwell was vacant. He used his Talent to get a sense of the enemy's location—to the left of the hallway entrance.

Pulling back, he held up two fingers for Lori to see,

then pointed to give her their location.

She nodded.

He took aim around the base of the doorframe and waited for someone to try a shot around the corner. A few seconds later Hector's bullet spun Killingsworth's man around. He thudded to the floor out of sight.

Hector's ears rang in the moment of silence that followed. He checked his magazine. Two rounds left. Better than nothing.

"It would appear I need a hostage to ensure my getaway," Killingsworth called out to them. "Give me the boy and I'll leave."

"Go to hell, you sonofabitch!" Lori yelled.

The door across the hallway opened.

"Denzel, no!" Hector said. "He's lying. He'll kill us anyway."

"But he won't kill me," the boy said. "I'm sorry, but I don't want to die. We're outnumbered and outgunned."

He shuffled into the hall, his shoulders slumped, empty hands in the air.

Hector couldn't reconcile the earlier war whoop with this seemingly resigned kid. A hand on his shoulder made him look up. Lori shook her head.

"A wise decision, son," Killingsworth said.

"Denzel, please don't do this!" Lori called. She smiled and winked at Hector. "You're better than this!"

What the hell was going on?

"Signal when Denzel reaches the stairs," Lori whispered. "Be ready to shoot that sonofabitch." She positioned herself to the right of the doorway, rifle at the ready.

Hector squelched his need for an explanation. He had to trust his team. They had a plan. He peeked around the door frame.

"Move it!" Killingsworth yelled at the boy. The man backed toward the stairway. Denzel was blocking Hector's shot.

Hector could only wait and pray. Reaching the stairs, Killingsworth backed down them one step at a time. He was three stairs down when Denzel grasped the stair rail. Hector signaled Lori with a low whistle.

Lori stepped into the hallway, rifle raised.

Killingsworth's gaze snapped to her. His rifle barrel followed.

Denzel lashed out in a kick that knocked Killingsworth's gun barrel sideways. Shots sprayed the wall. Killingsworth fought for balance.

The boy threw himself to the floor, giving Hector a clear shot.

He hit the hound with both bullets. Killingsworth fell over the rail and landed twenty feet below with a sickening thud.

Lori ran down the hall. Hector climbed to his feet and jogged after her, watching her pull the boy up into a one-armed hug. She craned her neck to peer down the stairwell. "Clear."

Denzel lifted his head from her shoulder as if he'd caught sight of something to the left of the hallway entrance, out of Hector's line of sight. The boy's pupils widened.

Hector reacted, throwing himself around the corner to protect Lori and the kid. A bullet meant for them slammed into his chest. He stumbled back a step, then lunged at the wounded man who'd shot him and clobbered him with his empty Glock. The man slumped over sideways.

Lori set about handcuffing the unconscious *pendejo* with his own cuffs.

Next thing he knew, Denzel had pulled Hector's arm across his wiry teenaged shoulders. "You saved our lives." The kid sounded awestruck. "You took a bullet for us."

Hector drew a deep breath and then exhaled. He peered down at his blood-soaked chest and then wished he hadn't. "That's gonna hurt like hell when the adrenaline wears off."

Denzel pulled him toward the hallway. "C'mon! I need to stop the bleeding."

He let Denzel half-carry him back to Zinnia's room. The boy helped him lay down beside Meli's still form. He shoved the bloody shirt up to Hector's armpits, glanced at the wound and grabbed a folded hand towel to use as a compress. "Brace yourself, Hector. This is gonna hurt."

Denzel applied pressure to stop the bleeding and Hector passed out.

23

A WEEK AFTER the battle Hector paced the floor of a Mercy Hospital conference room in Olympia, Washington. Luckily for him, the bullet that hit him had missed his vital organs. He had a broken rib and damaged chest wall muscles but was healing well.

He'd been released from the hospital earlier in the afternoon, but he needed to remain close in case Meli woke up. So far, despite the doctors' and healers' efforts, she was still in a coma.

Doc Grayson had agreed to meet with him at the hospital. His boss had closed off one third-floor wing of the hospital and brought in Bureau medical staff to treat the injured.

Denzel and Jake had spent a night under observation before being released into Doc's custody.

Will insisted he remain with the boys, and Doc was happy to accommodate him. The other prisoners were the boys' only family. They needed to be together throughout what would be a difficult transition.

Kids from the camps needed long term help in making the adjustment to life on the outside. Some might never be able to rejoin surviving relatives.

Over the last ten years, Doc had managed to create an endowment to fund a non-profit private boarding school where Talented kids' needs would secretly be met. The school was scheduled to open in September.

Hector smiled. Kids from the camps and young Talents who had never been enslaved would attend the school together. Drew's father understood how hard it could be for Talented kids to grow up in a world where they must hide their abilities. Raising a Forgettable Kid hadn't been easy.

At the school the children would learn to control their gifts and to interact with Typicals—typical people—who knew of their Talents. They would learn how to fly under the radar in the wider world.

The students would study ethics and philosophy in addition to more traditional subjects, and hopefully avoid crossing over to the Dark Side.

Doc insisted Talented kids were more like other kids than they were different. Hector agreed, although sometimes those differences were doozies.

Jake was a case in point. Doc had a heck of a time finding a vet to work on Grizz. Then there'd been the problem of tracking the bear down and tranquilizing him. He was recovering from his injuries in a bear sanctuary in British Columbia.

The door opened and a wholesome-looking, unremarkable guy in jeans and a red polo shirt walked into the small conference room, followed by Doc Grayson.

"How's the baby?" Hector asked his partner as they shook hands. During the fight for control of the camp, Drew had won Sophie's trust and delivered her baby.

"Feisty," Drew said. "Sophie named her after Will's daughter, Zinnia. Both are doing fine."

Shaking hands with their boss, Drew's father, Hector noted Doc hadn't changed much in the last few years. His gray hair and beard were neatly trimmed, his suit as spotless as a nun's wimple and he'd maintained a runner's physique.

"It's good to see you, sir," Hector said.

Doc's blue eyes twinkled. "I swear that baby remembers Drew from day to day. She and her mama seem to have taken a shine to my son. Sophie told me she keeps a detailed daily journal as insurance against losing memories of Drew. She's flagged the day Zinnia was born and re-reads it daily because she wants to remember everything."

Hector raised an eyebrow at his friend. "How does it feel to have a woman find you unforgettable?"

Drew half-smiled and shrugged. "Still getting used to the idea."

Doc laid a hand on Hector's shoulder. "How are you doing? The healer said you were mending quickly."

Hector found himself pinned with one of his boss's famous piercing stares. He shrugged, then winced. "Getting shot sucks. But I'm well on the way to recovery. The surgeon and the healer both did an excellent job."

He motioned for the two men to sit at the room's small, round table. "How are Denzel and Jake doing with Will?" he said as he took his seat.

Doc smiled. "It's obvious the three love each other. They are doing better than I expected."

"What about Nate? Has he been cleared?" Nate had been kept under guard in the hospital for a day before being whisked away to be interrogated, evaluated and scrutinized by Doc's finest squints. Hector hoped to God the shielder passed muster.

While still in hospital Hector had signed an affidavit recounting his interactions with Lori's new man, including the fact his Talent had identified Nate as a friendly.

Drew nodded. "He's with Lori and R.D. now, in the waiting room. Said he wanted to thank you for your support."

Doc's expression turned serious. "Rafe—Er, Hector—I owe you an explanation. I hope you will understand why we let you believe Lori and the baby were killed."

"I hope so, too, Sir. Hector leaned back in his chair. Let the old man sweat a little.

Doc's brows pulled together. "Before Lori offered to spy for the Cartel, Zinnia foresaw her death under torture right after the baby's birth. What Lori did, making a bargain with the devil, was extreme. But she was desperate to change the probable future. You see?"

Hector nodded. He'd come to terms with that part of the story.

Doc continued. "As long as you knew Lori and R.D. were alive, Zinnia foresaw them both dying in an escape attempt before your son's first birthday. We tried implementing small changes in hopes of affecting the probable future. The end result was they would live a few months longer than before. Nothing we tried changed the future enough to save them. We failed."

Hector blinked. He had not seen that coming.

"When Lori convinced Leah to pretend they'd died, Leah told me the intel was false. But that was when the probable future changed. Zinnia foresaw all the prisoners' deaths in an escape attempt, but not for three years."

Doc shifted in his seat. "Your belief in Lori and R.D.'s deaths, your grief, bought them time. Time for us to narrow down the camp's location. Time for the prisoners to devise a better escape plan. Time for an unanticipated, seemingly random change in the future to occur."

The strained expression on his boss's face told Hector how much the decisions had weighed on him. "I knew you would keep searching for the camps on your own, so I put you and Drew undercover in Mexico in hopes you'd find the one we knew was hidden in desert. We knew from Lori's description of the terrain that she was not in Sonora. Each time you made a major discovery Zinnia saw changes in the probable future."

Hector turned to his partner. "Did you know the truth?" He didn't want to believe Drew knew, but he had to ask.

Drew shook his head and frowned. "No. I was in the dark, too."

"That is correct," Doc said. "Leah and I were the only ones at the Bureau who knew the truth."

Hector nodded his acceptance of the facts.

Doc continued. "Time was running out. I knew we were on the right track, but something was missing. We couldn't seem to prevent the slaughter at Lori's camp. Not until Mendoza brought you to Washington. At that point, Zinnia's visions indicated some of the prisoners would survive, but each vision differed in the details. The future was in flux."

Doc gazed directly into Hector's eyes. "When you kissed Melisenda, Zinnia felt the flux begin to slow. The options narrowed. Time was short. You two were the key."

Remembering that kiss, Hector smiled. Technically, Meli had kissed him.

"We had to do something," Doc said. "When Drew reported that you'd escaped onto the mountain with Melisenda, I got word to Lori through her sister. Lori and Nate took decisive action. They breached the camp's security systems and sent Jake out with Denzel to lure Meli's dog to the camp, knowing Meli would follow. Hoping the two of you would change the future."

Hector nodded. "And we did. You made the right calls."

Doc leaned back in his chair and his shoulders slumped. "Zinnia Washington died. That's on my conscience."

Hector knew in that moment he would not want Doc's job. The Director carried a heavy burden. What would Meli say in his place? "The rest of us lived, Doc. Zinnia knew what she was doing. Honor her sacrifice."

Doc swallowed. "You're right, of course. But I share the responsibility."

He straightened. "How is Melisenda? Any change?"

Goosebumps puckered Hector's skin. Doc was devious enough to have planned this conversation to prepare him for Meli's death. Had the probable future shifted? Had her passing been foreseen?

He set his jaw. It didn't matter. Like he'd told Meli, the future was a set of possibilities, not a one trick puppy. There was no way he would let Meli die. "She's resting comfortably. Which brings me to the main reason I requested this meeting, Doc. I want to settle down."

The director narrowed his eyes. "Settle down?"

Hector drew a deep breath. "I've applied for a job at the new school. So has Lori. In college I majored in English. I'm a master of personal shielding, dowsing and self-defense. Lori homeschooled the camp kids for years. She can teach non-traditional classes, too. Working at the school will allow us to share custody."

"Dad wants Nate to work at the school," Drew said. "His shield would help protect the students and faculty from discovery."

Hector cast his friend a grateful glance. "Melisenda can teach music. R.D. will have both sets of parents working at the school."

Meli would survive. Losing her was not an option.

The older man propped his elbows on the table and steepled his fingers. His gaze held Hector's. "Are you willing to do map and distance dowsing for the Bureau as a contracted consultant?"

The question told Hector Doc was giving his proposal serious consideration. He'd expected a few strings. Besides, keeping his hand in the law enforcement game was appealing. "Absolutely."

"Will you consider occasional special assignments?"

Hector grinned. "I'll consider them. No guarantees I'll accept them."

Doc folded his hands on the tabletop. "I won't lie to you. I've been thinking about this since spending time with the former captives. Having trusted adults on staff who have shared their experiences will ease the kids' transition. And you need time to bond with your son."

Doc glanced at Drew and smiled. "The father-son relationship is wonderful, but fraught with peril. Neglect it at your own risk."

"Having former agents on staff would bolster security," Drew pointed out.

Doc cocked an eyebrow at his son. "Good point."

He turned back to Hector, eyes dancing. "I believe we have an agreement."

They stood and shook hands. Doc took his leave.

Drew lingered for a moment, his expression earnest. "I hate to lose you, partner."

"Then you'll have to visit often so we don't forget you," Hector said. "You're my best friend."

Drew grinned. "You're pretty much my only friend. We make a good team."

Hector shook his hand, clapped him on the back and watched him walk away. Who knew what the future held in store?

24

YAWNING, HECTOR HEADED toward the waiting room to grab a cup of coffee.

The sounds of a cartoon playing on the television put a smile on Hector's face. He was crazy about his son. He peeked around the doorway and discovered Lori had fallen asleep in a chair with R.D. dozing in her lap.

Nate turned away from the coffee machine in the corner holding two steaming cups. His face looked gray from exhaustion. Catching sight of Lori and R.D., Nate smiled with such tenderness that a lump formed in Hector's throat. "They've missed you," he said.

Nate jerked and a little hot coffee squirted out the lids onto his fingers. He sucked air through his teeth and set the cups on the counter.

"Sorry, man," Hector said, crossing the room in a couple of strides. "I should have known you'd be a little jumpy. You look like hell."

The Bureau's interrogation teams and squints would have put Nate through the wringer. On top of that, the poor guy had been hit with the life-changing knowledge he was a Talent. He'd be wrestling a shitload of guilt over the way Killingsworth had used him to hide the prisoners.

Nate dried his hands on a napkin and tossed in into the recycling can. "It's been a helluva week."

Snagging the two coffees, Hector handed one to the big man and led the way to a corner occupied by a magazine-covered end table and two chairs.

"Sit," he said, doing so himself. "Doc told me you're in the clear. Very good news."

Nate fell into the other chair. Hector gestured at the sleeping pair in front of the television. "She loves you, Nate."

A slow smile eased the tension from Nate's face. "Don't I know it." He sipped his coffee. "Four years was a long time to wait."

Hector blinked. "Why the hell did you wait?"

Nate frowned. "At first, I didn't want to come between the two of you. She worried all the time about how you were this Super-Dowser who would come to rescue her and the baby. Even after she realized they had us shielded most of the time and well-hidden, she always insisted you'd come. When the sisters were exchanging information, Lori learned you didn't give up on finding the camp even after Leah convinced you Lori and the baby were dead."

Nate turned his cup in his hands. "I figured you were in love."

Hector shook his head. "We wanted to be in love. We tried for the sake of the baby, but we couldn't make the relationship work. We're too much alike."

Nate turned his cup in his big hands. "By the time I realized Lori didn't want to get back together with you, I knew I couldn't give Killingsworth any extra leverage. He'd already used threats against R.D. to make Lori and Leah spy for him. If Lori and I were lovers, he would have used our relationship to control us."

R.D. stirred and mumbled in his sleep. Hector couldn't help grinning. "He's really something, isn't he?"

"Yes. He's a credit to you both."

Hector shook his head. "Lori's done an amazing job. I owe you a debt of thanks for taking care of them when I couldn't."

Nate opened his mouth as if to speak, then hesitated.

"What?" Hector said.

"I'm going to marry her, Hector. I love her. I love them both."

Hector smiled. "You have my blessing, Nate. They couldn't do better."

Nate studied his face for a moment. "You couldn't

do better than Meli, either. I'll never forgive myself for not figuring out I was the shielder. I still have a hard time believing it." He shook his head. "Meli saved us all. I am so Goddamned sorry I hurt her—"

Nate was innocent in all this. The man carried a shitload of guilt for being duped, but he hadn't intentionally put Meli in a coma. "She knew what she was risking, man. What happened wasn't your fault. I don't blame you. I blame Mendoza, Killingsworth and the Cartel."

Nate held his gaze for a minute. "Thank you for that. It means a lot."

"I hope you take it to heart," Hector said. "You have nothing to feel guilty about. Forgive yourself or it will eat you alive. I speak from experience."

Nate slowly nodded. "I'll work on that. Thanks."

Hector swallowed some coffee. "Director Grayson wants you and Lori both to live and work at the school. Your shield will be a big plus in the security department. Not to mention your knowledge of high-tech security systems and how to hack them. You should apply."

Nate gave a thoughtful nod.

"Meli and I are joining the teaching staff," Hector added.

A slow grin spread across Nate's face. "Now that is good news. Meli will be a wonderful step-mom for R.D., right? After spending a couple hours with her, he's already bonded."

Hector's heart contracted. Meli was amazing. In one night, with one kiss, she'd blasted his dismal-excuse-of-a-life into a pile of rubble. By the end of that first day she'd convinced him the future was not as bleak as he'd believed. She'd awakened hope in him along with his long-dormant libido. She'd placed her trust in him, cared for his injuries and risked her life for him more than once. Meli clobbered him a few times when he deserved it and made him laugh when he didn't. She made him feel fully alive.

Hector's heavy heart lodged in his throat. He closed his eyes and shook his head. Meli lay down the hall in a coma. He might never get the chance to tell her the truth she deserved to hear.

He cleared his throat and stared at his coffee cup. "When she told me she loved me, I called her naïve. How could she love me when she'd never even kissed another man—more than once, anyway?" He plowed a hand through his hair. "The truth is I'm terrified. What if I can't be the man she needs?"

Nate pinned him with his gaze. "True love—the kind that lasts—changes a person. Makes us better. Stronger."

"Not me. Meli gave me her heart, and I treated her like a child."

"Lucky for you she loves you, mistakes and all. She'll forgive you." Nate flashed a grin. "No more excuses. Man up and apologize."

The truth in Nate's words soothed his battered soul

like healing energy had soothed his wounds. Hector's chest expanded. He'd gladly spend the rest of his life making up for the pain he'd caused Meli.

If she lived. No, when she lived. He couldn't let himself have doubts.

He rose to go to Meli's side. "Thanks for the advice."

"Anytime," Nate said.

Hector strode down the hall to Meli's room. The Bureau Healer had told him Meli had to want to wake up. His head ached with the knowledge of her reasons for remaining in the coma. She was tired and in pain and she'd lost all hope of ever achieving her happily-ever-after. She'd lost her will to live.

He set aside his guilt to focus on Meli. He had to convince her to fight her way back. Tell her how much he loved her and needed her in his life. Beg her for another chance. Ask her to be R.D.'s step-mom. Give her a reason to fight.

He shoved through the door into her dimly-lit room and let it whoosh shut behind him. The steady beep of Meli's heart monitor greeted him. He crossed to sit on the edge of her bed.

Her porcelain skin seemed paler than ever. Bright hair fanned across her pillow in a riot of coppery curls. The antiseptic odor of disinfectant made him ache for her scent of vanilla and baby powder. The taste of her skin. The spark of her energy snapping between them...

He put away his sorrow and focused on Meli. "Hello, Sparky. I'm here. I'm not going anywhere."

Lifting one of her small hands to his lips, he kissed the back of each finger. Turning her hand palm up, he kissed the lifeline crossing her palm. Gently, he lowered her hand to the blanket. "You were right. I am a coward. I've loved you from the moment I set eyes on you at the wedding reception, but I was terrified to admit it. I knew losing you would destroy me."

His eyes burned. He drew in a deep, steadying breath and let it out before continuing. "Melisenda, if I lose you, I'll die. God's truth, I'll die. I can barely breathe, knowing how lost and hurt and alone you must feel. Please come home to me. I need you. R.D. needs you. You'll be a wonderful second mother to him. And Fred, Fred won't eat."

Fred's tail thumped the floor on the other side of Meli's hospital bed.

"I can barely convince him to go outside to pee. We all love you and need you in our lives. Marry me, Meli. Please." He squeezed her fingers.

Meli lay like an ashen, peeling Sleeping Beauty cursed to sleep for a hundred years. He watched and waited for ten minutes, for twenty.

With a heartfelt sigh, he moved to sit in the chair beside her bed. He lay his hand over hers, resting his arm on the mattress beside her. Patience. Not his strong suit. But for Meli, he would wait as long as it took. For Meli, he would wait forever.

Please, God. Don't make me wait forever. Help me bring her back.

Hours later, a woman's gentle voice awakened him. "Excuse me, sir. The cafeteria will close in half an hour. You'd better get something to eat. You need your strength."

He lifted his head off his arm and blinked at the gray-haired nurse. "I'm not hungry."

She glanced at Meli's still form and sighed. "Tell you what. I'll have a tray sent up so you won't have to leave her."

"Thanks." He tried to muster a smile.

The nurse bustled out and Lori came into the room. Fred's tags jingled on the other side of the bed. Guilt twisted his gut. How could he have forgotten about Fred? Meli trusted him to take care of her Guide.

"Any change?" Lori asked, stopping in front of him.

He shook his head.

"You look like hell."

He shrugged.

"R.D. wants to take Freddy to our hotel for the night."

He nodded. That would solve one of his problems. When they'd arrived someone had found him a narrow pink dog lead suitable for a Chihuahua. He picked the leash up off the floor beneath his chair and attached it to the dog's collar.

Fred sniffed the thin pink leather strip. His tail drooped, brushing the floor. He whined uncertainly and gazed at the still figure on the bed.

Hector's throat constricted so he had to swallow before he spoke. He scratched behind the big dog's ears. "I'll stay with her, boy. I'm not going anywhere."

Fred turned his head and licked Hector's hand.

He resisted the urge to throw his arms around the lab's neck and bury his face in baby-powder scented fur for comfort. Fred needed reassurance

Forcing a smile, he tried to put excitement into his voice. "Remember R.D.? You like R.D., and he needs you tonight. Okay?"

The big dog's droopy tail lifted a couple of inches and swished back and forth like a disconsolate feather duster.

Hector gave Fred a final pat and handed Lori the leash. "Bring him back in the morning. He worries when he's away from Meli."

Her eyebrows lifted. "Will do."

Was there anything else Meli would want him to do for Fred? "He needs a manly leash. He's humiliated to be seen in public wearing a little pink ribbon."

Smiling, Lori nodded. "R.D. will enjoy picking one out."

The pad of Lori's soft footsteps and the tick, tick, of Fred's nails faded as the door swung shut behind them. Hector had never heard a lonelier sound.

When he came out of the private bathroom a few

minutes later after washing up, the scents of roasted chicken, mashed potatoes and coffee made his stomach growl. The nurse was right. He needed to take care of himself so he could take care of Meli. He forced himself to eat everything before he sat back in his chair to drink the coffee—and to wait.

After a few minutes, renewed energy made him restless. He had the nagging feeling watching and waiting weren't going to bring Meli back. She'd given no sign she was aware of anything he said or did.

He stood and began to pace. For all he knew, she could be slipping away while he did nothing. He needed to be proactive. He needed a new plan.

Hector had to make Meli understand how much he loved her, and that she had a future with him and R.D. and Fred. But she couldn't hear his words. He had to reach her another way. If only he could share his energy with her the way she could with him.

You can do this, mi hijo, whispered his mother's voice in his head. *¡Tener fe! Have faith.*

He halted. Mom's energy faded before he could ask questions. He was a dowser, not an expath. Was there a way to use his Talent to function like an expath?

Have faith. What did that mean, exactly?

He pulled his talisman on its chain out from under his shirt and studied the tiny face of the figure etched into the golden disk. St. Jude, the Patron Saint of Lost Souls and Hopeless Causes. When he'd believed Lori and the baby were dead, he'd lost faith. He'd thrown the St. Christopher's Medal his father had given him for his tenth birthday into the river and never set foot inside a church since.

His mother had become distraught and insisted he at least replace his talisman with one she gave him. He'd given in because doing so was easier than arguing with her. And the talisman helped him to focus his energy.

Meli had given him a new perspective. That she'd come into his life was a gift beyond anything he could have imagined. That together they'd found Lori and his son alive was a true miracle.

Holding the golden disk, he closed his eyes and thanked God for those undeserved gifts. He asked for forgiveness. A feeling of confidence and peace settled over him.

Then he drew on his Talent and asked, *How can I share my energy with Meli?*

Operating on instinct, he lifted the chain over his head. He kissed his talisman and then placed the warm, golden disk between her lips. He envisioned his love for her to be golden energy coursing through his veins like Meli's healing energy. He felt it pool in his chest, rising in a strong, sure tide in search of release. Then he kissed her on the mouth, pouring the surge of power through his Talisman into her body.

Come back to me!

His cheeks were damp when he raised his head.

Had the steady beep of the heart monitor picked up

a little speed?

Maybe he'd imagined the change in tempo.

He kissed her again with all the longing in his heart reaching out to her. *Together we are strong. Come back to me.*

When he sat back to study her face, Meli's complexion seemed to have more color. Her breaths came a little faster. He watched a tear form in the outer corner of her eye. The liquid sparked like one of her rhinestones and then slipped away.

He released the breath he hadn't realized he'd been holding, gathered her in his arms, and kissed her again. *I will always love you. Come back to me!*

Meli's eyelids fluttered. He settled her back against the pillow and took one of her hands in both of his.

Her gorgeous green eyes opened. Her brows knit together in a puzzled frown. She pushed the St. Jude Medal out of her mouth with the pink tip of her tongue.

Gently, Hector squeezed her hand. "I'm here."

She coughed and he gave her a sip of his coffee. "Better?"

"Much better," she whispered. She squeezed his hand. "Don't let go."

"Never."

She sighed. "I was lost, and so tired. Almost ready to give up. Then I heard you call me. Felt your energy build me up. You gave me the strength to find my way back."

Her words filled his heart like life-giving rain.

She reached up and skimmed his face with her

fingertips. "You cried over me," she said, as if he'd performed a miracle.

He drew a shaky breath. "I was dying inside. God's truth, Meli, I can't go on without you." He picked up his Talisman from her lap and slipped the gold chain over her head. St. Jude's image rested on her pale blue hospital gown between the mounds of her breasts.

Her fingers closed around the Talisman. "The others? Did they make it?"

"They're fine, Melisenda. Everyone made it, because of you. Freddy's with R.D., Lori and Nate. Nate told me he's going to propose to her." He was babbling, but he couldn't seem to stop. "Sophie had her baby. She named her after Zinnia. Denzel and Jake are with Will."

She relaxed against her pillow and closed her eyes.

Hector tucked a bright curl behind her ear. His fingers shook. "I love you, Meli. You were right about me being an emotional coward. You may be blind, but you saw right through me. I'm sorry for the things I said to you when you told me you loved me."

His throat tightened. "I was afraid I'd never get the chance to tell you the truth. Can you find it in your heart to forgive me?"

A smile toyed with Meli's lips. "I suppose I can let you make it up to me for the rest of our lives."

He kissed her deeply and thoroughly, leaving them both a little breathless. "Anything for you, *ángel mío*."

The End

Dear Reader,

Thank you for reading my book. I hope you enjoyed reading *BLINDSIGHT* as much as I enjoyed writing the story.

I would appreciate an honest review on GoodReads or any online bookseller site. Reviews give me feedback and help me find new readers.

(Generally you just go to the site, search for my book, click on the book cover and then scroll down the page until you find "Reader Reviews – leave a review.")

For the latest news about book releases or to sign up for my newsletter, please visit my website at **http://www.sarahraplee.com/**

Happy Reading,
Sarah Raplee

ABOUT THE AUTHOR

SARAH RAPLEE honed her love of adventure reading fairy tales and mysteries and exploring the tropical island where she grew up. Sarah's personal paranormal experiences gifted her with a love of the Unexplained that led her to write paranormal romance. Many of her heroes and heroines are underdogs, and dogs turn up in most of her stories in supporting roles.

When she's not writing, Sarah loves to explore new places, try new things or spend a quiet evening with a great book. She lives in the Pacific Northwestern US with her heroic husband, two adventurous dogs, a flock of free-range chickens and a cat who fetches silver bracelets.